# The Beginning of Magic

## Marat's Story

P.J. Schumacher

Kim & Arla
Your friendship and support is awesome!
Love you tons!

UpMesa Publishing



Cover by CK Cover Designs

ISBN 13: 979-8-476631-22-4

For Ursula K. Le Guin who told me research is worth it.
And always for Linda.

# Contents

# Acknowledgments

I owe much to the University of Pennsylvania Museum of Anthropology and Archaeology for the ePSD (electronic Pennsylvania Sumerian Dictionary). The ePSD was an invaluable source for finding cuneiform signs and determining concepts that existed in that age.

I visited the Princeton Theological Seminary (Special Collections, Cuneiform), NJ. Seeing actual samples of cuneiform was truly inspiring!

Special thanks to Caryn Mirriam Goldberg who helped me realize this was the right project at this time.

Beth Van Horn and her family were a great sounding board on the magic system.

My writing group, Lane Robins, John Laddusaw, and Heather Mockler, cheered, cajoled, and pushed me forward through writing, rewrites, and publishing. Thank you for helping me grow as a writer.

# Cuneiform

Cuneiform is the writing system created in Sumer (Mesopotamia) and used in other ancient civilizations. Characters were created using reeds pushed into clay.

A character represents an entire word or a syllable. For example, a scribe is "dubsar," written as:

# Map of Kiengir

# 0. Dubsaĝ [Before]

In the gloom under the Mountains of Sunset to the west of Kiengir where the dead drink from muddy puddles and eat dust, Ereshkigal, ruler of the underworld from which no man returns, harvested souls. She sulked. The Assembly of the Gods—the very ones sending men to their deaths through war, pestilence, and plague—thought she did not deserve a seat at their table. As if, she spat, power can only be evinced by the utterances of one's name in prayers or number of temples erected with gold and lapis lazuli likenesses.

Inanna, Goddess of love and war came to her older sister, Ereshkigal. Inanna to whom men build the tallest temples, for whom men fill granaries with devotions of the best grains, whose name men speak daily, descended through the seven gates to the underworld. Inanna left her scepter of power with the guards Neti and Nergal, and they let her pass.

Inanna, the more beautiful, the more loved, the more praised, came to Ereshkigal, the more striking, the more feared, the least named. As sisters, the goddesses spoke. Ereshkigal grew weary quickly of her sister's self-importance.

Inanna did not worry about justifying her seat at the table of the Assembly of the Gods; she wondered, rather, which to take? Ereshkigal would that such simple problems as her sister's were hers. And in that moment, the first green sprout of retribution pushed into Ereshkigal's grey heart.

An, the father of gods, listened from the sky. He, who ruled them all, despaired of their enmity. Enki, god of water, fertility and knowledge, counseled his father it was the way of their progeny to bicker over petty jealousies. Enlil, God of air and wind and storm, weary of bickering and rumination, proposed a diversion. The father, the sons agreed. And thus, magic came to men.

# 1. Marat [Marat]

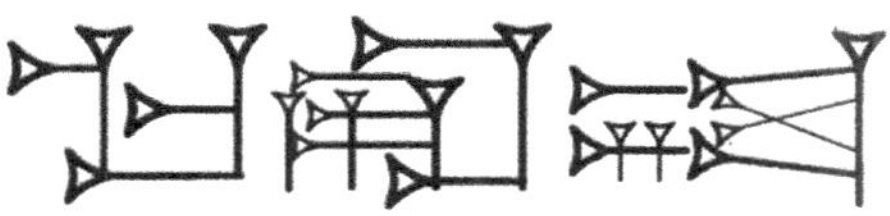

*Marat age 9.*

A breeze cooled the sweat on Marat's skin and tugged at her hair. She tucked a dark strand behind her ear as she looked across Adab's rooftops in their mosaic of shaded deep browns to evening sun-touched tans. Pride warmed her: Adab was the greatest city known in Kiengir, made strong against enemies by a thick wall and made prosperous by the Buranum River. Today the river flowed sluggishly, its deep dark blues and shallow light blues reflecting the sun in brilliant white flickers.

Canals took the water from the river, changing it to muddy brown on paths that fed dappled green date palm orchards, sprout-green broken rows of emerging chickpea and flax, slightly darker lentil bushes, and deep green mature sesame fields. Beyond the farms, sparse yellow-green scrub dotted the untouched plains. Marat's gaze came back to the city. The temples to the gods rose above all else, and Inanna's temple rose highest. Every person—from Lugal Daudu who ruled them to the priests, warriors, scribes, merchants, farmers, servants, and slaves—was devoted to Inanna, and the goddess smiled upon them. The lugal and his warriors never failed in battle, the priests held the demons and the pestilence they brought at bay, the scribes kept the order among men through well documented agreements and rigorously enforced laws, the farmers and slaves cleared the canals so the water from the floods brought bountiful crops instead of ruin, and the merchants traded their bounty for even greater riches. She felt blessed and offered thanks to Inanna, the strongest god.

The priests said she sat in the honored high seat at the assembly. The other gods were in awe of her powers.

Marat offered a quick prayer. "That I may better serve you, most powerful Inanna, may I have a husband who works hard and children devoted to you. That your people may better serve you, radiant Inanna, may we have fertile gardens, victory in war, and steady waters."

An imperious command rose through the house. Marat sighed. Her father's second wife would have her grinding barley to flour and fetching water the entire day. Marat slid away from the ladder and out of view.

Her thoughts wandered to her father, Melam. She much preferred the times she worked with him, cutting designs into the small kisib cylinders that served as the mark of a man on his contracts. She had even learned some writing, not through school, of course—that was no place girls—but from copying marks as part of the art of creating kisibs.

Her step mother's voice rose again and this time there was no ignoring her. Marat looked to the temple and offered herself to Inanna's will, which said children were to be respectful of their parents.

## 2. Pad [Find]

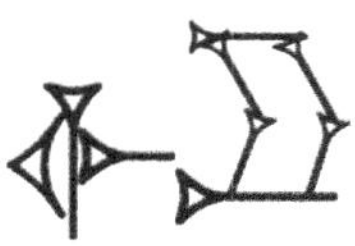

Marat hurried through the scorching streets to bring the morning meal—a pot of barley porridge resting in a reed basket on her back—to Melam's shop. She stayed to the right of the lane to keep in the shadows of the homes which was if not cooler, at least a little less bright. The warm sand was soft beneath her feet until she came to the market, where the lane opened and her feet slapped against hot brick paving. The smell of fresh rolls combined with fermenting beer, roasting duck, fresh fish, a dark incense, and manure. Merchants cajoled customers to buy their wares, farmers argued about the weather, and dogs barked as they ran through the market. Pigeons paced in their cages, cooing. Tied goats bleated complaints. A sculptor's hammer beat steadily against stone.

The sun beat down on them all. Though the morning shade was close to the goat merchants' tents, Marat moved into the sun and kept her pace to avoid being pulled into the merchants' banter and hands that were more apt to touch inappropriately. In her thoughts, she heard her father and stepmother lecturing her on the importance of maintaining her virtue and of the laws that would protect her. While she was too dark and stocky to be pretty, her stepmother said, she was serviceable, and a man might steal her away for her dowry. Marat shook her head; they were not dissimilar in looks as far as she could tell, yet her stepmother claimed to be beautiful and Marat just serviceable. Maybe if she braided her hair in the same fashion and learned to make bread without burning it, her stepmother would be kinder.

Ahead, in a small clearing in the crowd, a man with a lyre started to play and the woman with him clapped and started to dance. Several children emerged from the stalls and swayed before them. The woman encouraged them to join her. Marat paused. She would have liked to dance as well, but she was nine now, with work to do, and dancing might present an unseemly provocation to the men. As she turned to leave, a tunic caught her attention: blue linen, with nearly the same blue threads, but slightly darker and lighter than the background cloth, depicting a scene like the one on the palace walls. She stared.

"Good morning, child."

Marat's attention snapped to the man. He was tall and thin, with a large nose and long curled beard. He smelled of juniper. She had not realized she had approached so close to him; she stepped back.

"Do not be afraid." His voice was warm, unhurried. "I am Nam Eluti. What is your name, child?"

Marat bowed her head when she heard his title. "Marat, daughter of Melam the kisib maker, Nam Eluti." Her chin tilted, and she corrected him, "I am not a child, Nam. I am taking a meal to my father." She berated herself for her insolent response. Her eyes fell to the hem of his tunic. Gazelles were worked into the hem in a fine blue thread. They appeared to jump across a river to escape gold-tinged blue lions beneath a dark blue moon. The shekels it must have cost! She tugged her goatskin skirt down to her knees.

He said, "What do you see, small one?"

"Animals and rivers and stars," Marat mumbled in wonder.

He held a panel of his tunic to her. "Which color do you like most?"

She freed a hand from the basket straps and pointed to the lines, nearly the same blue as the fabric, which reminded her of the water in the middle of the river when the sky was clear and the water was high but not flooding.

"Any other?"

She touched a soft star.

"And?"

"Gazelles," she said. "The dark blue ones that move."

"You are quite a perceptive young woman." Nam Eluti smiled. "Inanna has blessed your father with observant offspring. Do you have brothers?"

Fear pricked Marat's skin. Young women did not talk to men who were not in their family. Men did not show young women their clothes or ask about their family. She turned away slightly. "Yes, Nam. Two. I am late to bring my father his meal."

"Hmm. I have delayed you. I will come along and explain so you are not punished." He gestured for her to lead.

"There is no need, Nam." If her father learned she had talked to a man, he would be angry.

"I insist, Marat. Take me to your father." His stern tone brooked no dissent.

Marat's breath caught. She had disobeyed her parents, but she could not refuse this wealthy man's order to take him to her father. Perhaps Nam Eluti would want to purchase a kisib, Marat thought. Her father would be pleased for the business. She turned and led the way.

# 3. Ĝalga [Forethought, planning]

In the heat of the late afternoon, Eluti sat in the shade of the garden palms pondering the day. His first wife's handmaid rubbed flax oil scented with juniper on his legs. Tension eased out of him with each stroke. He had thanked his gods when he found the child Marat who could distinguish the subtle colors of his tunic's embroidered design, but he had nearly cried when it became apparent no one else in her family had the gift. He scratched his jaw through his beard.

"Does Nam's beard irritate him?" the handmaid asked.

"Shh," He admonished her for interrupting his thoughts. She continued rubbing, but her fingers were tentative. He sighed and wished for a handmaid who wasn't so timid. "I would drink date wine," he said. She left him alone in the quiet of buzzing insects, and he mulled over his problem: how could he acquire the girl Marat?

Boys and men were easy—he could take them under the guise of training or work. But a girl often required marriage, and he already had three wives. His finger curled in his beard. No, not marriage. If she were his wife, she would have to do women's work and bear children. There would be no opportunity for her to work with the An-mašĝik. He wondered a moment if her sight would be impacted by childbirth. Perhaps it would be augmented? Would her children be blessed? His children weren't. Perhaps only a mother could give such a gift. But the odds of death in childbirth were great. No, he did not want to risk that: it took too much effort to find someone with the sight. He shook his head. She would not be allowed physical relationships. He would not acquire her through marriage, no.

A servant, then, he thought. Not for his wives, for again that would limit her time for his work—and it would put her at risk with household jealousies. He huffed. How they bickered at times! And over nothing of any import. His servant. Yes, that worked. He would, of course, have to explain to Aruru, and she could tell the other wives and servants. Aruru. A gift of some type would make this acceptable and prove her standing as his first wife. Again: the girl must never bear a child, or else his wives would not believe his intentions. They could take him to court over bastard children because they had proven their fertility by giving him sons and daughters, but they would not, he was sure: their lives were too comfortable to punish a man for noticing a beautiful girl. That Marat, with her darker complexion and undeveloped body, was only slightly pleasing would be helpful.

He thought a moment about her price. Melam's kisib business was mildly successful; there was no reason for him to sell rather than marry off his only daughter. But, there were sons that would eventually want to take wives and need bride prices. Perhaps a high offer would be too tempting to be refused. And if the offer was refused… there were other options—not as wholesome, but effective.

The handmaid returned, set a cup of wine by his hand, and resumed rubbing oil into his skin. Eluti sipped the wine. It was sweet in his mouth. The soft hands on his back stirred him. Perhaps he would visit Aruru tonight. Attention, a gift all wives desired, was easily given. It would be an opportunity to remind her of the importance of his secret work with An-mašĝik and how success would benefit his brother, Mundu, who was an ursag in command of 120 warriors for Lugal Daudu and the High Priestess Siduri, his spiritual counterpart. Mundu, who had given Eluti fields to plant and prosper from, deserved everything they could do to help him prosper in return.

# 4. Arad [Slave]

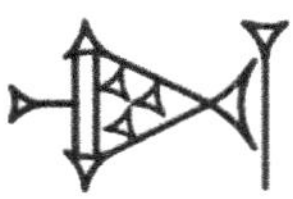

The sun beat down on Marat, yet she shivered. She stood still in the courtyard of her home, naked, as her father commanded, while a woman with a long face and linen tunic, Nin Aruru, gazed at her. They discussed Marat's attributes while the woman's two servants watched the proceedings disinterestedly. Nin's voice was steady, confident of the outcome, like the copper trader who had a line of hopeful buyers at his stall. Bile rose in Marat's throat. The scribe and female servant who had come with the woman stood by the brick wall where Marat's clothes hung on pegs, seeming to think nothing of the heat, the plain home, or Marat's nakedness.

Marat understood her father's business provided enough for the family's basic needs. Her father needed wheat for rent and tribute to the temple and lugal. He needed barley to pay debts. He would need silver and land for her brothers to acquire wives. Added to those burdens, an ašipu had recently determined that a demon was meddling in Melam's affairs, which meant he would need more cedar in his prayers and supplications to the Goddess Inanna. But Marat did not understand why he would trade her to acquire those things. She looked at him, willed him to meet her eyes, but he did not.

Nin Aruru was here on behalf of her husband, Nam Eluti, to purchase servants. Nam Eluti had discussed with Melam the need for conscientious young men and women to serve in larger households and the difficulty finding them. It was Melam, her own father, who had suggested his daughter.

Melam had explained the reasons for his actions to Marat without apology. If the demon was vanquished and he came into favor with the gods again, the shop would prosper and he would buy her back. In the meantime, her devotion to the Goddess Inanna would be through servitude. She had nodded. It was no use to disagree.

"She is intelligent, Nin," Melam asserted, hoping to drive up her value. "With a little training, Marat could bring wealth to your household. She has helped in my shop. She has a fine hand for detail—she was even able to etch the marks for names backwards and indented in quartz and hematite with no mistakes."

"Is she a virgin?" Nin Aruru asked. "Are you not selling her because she is with child out of marriage?"

Flies buzzed over the fish bones on the floor by the cook fire. Marat's cheeks burned.

"I avow she is a virgin and of good reputation, Nin."

Nin Aruru nodded. "Has her cycle begun?"

Warmth flooded Marat's neck and ears. A stranger was asking her father about that? Her stepmother came forward and declared she had not yet begun.

Nin Aruru told Marat to raise her arms and turn slowly in front of her. She instructed her handmaid to inspect the girl. Marat wanted to protest . . . or run away to the rooftop. She held her tongue behind clenched teeth and turned slowly for the woman's assessment. The woman prodded her belly, inspected her hands and feet, teeth and ears, and made her recite a simple prayer. The handmaid stepped back and reported the girl was of good health.

"But she is insolent," Nin Aruru said.

Marat nearly spoke out, but her father put his hand on her head and shook her gently like a child. "Her manner will temper as she learns her place, Nin." Melam bowed slightly. "Caning is often needed to improve the young."

Marat's eyes widened at her father's suggestion that Nam Eluti should beat her. She held herself completely still under the weight of her father's hand on her shoulder, barely even taking a breath. Her heart beat so loudly, surely the woman would notice and complain of that as well.

Nin Aruru turned and conferred with the male scribe who accompanied her. She turned back and offered: "Two silver minas."

Melam fell to his knee. "Two silver minas for Marat as you say, Nin Aruru."

Marat's mouth fell open. What was this? Her father always haggled, even over the price of barley. Was she a plainer value than that?

Her stepmother grabbed her arm tightly, pulled her clothes from the pegs, drug her to the back of the kitchen, and thrust Marat's goatskin skirt and shawl into her hands, "You will go with this Nin Aruru," she whispered fiercely. "You will do everything she says without quarrel." She gave her a shake. "Whatever she asks, you do. Do not ever make her regret her purchase."

Marat did not answer. Her mouth felt dry and sour. Her eyes darted to the back door and the front. She knew she could reach it and be out in the street before they caught her. But then what? Run to the temple and beg to be accepted as an acolyte? Run to the market and be taken by men who would defile her? Run … where?

"You will not bring shame on your father by disobeying your owners. They have paid a high price for you—enough for three strong slaves! A price too high for a girl your age," her stepmother continued. "I know your father has said he will try to buy you back some day, but I tell you now: we will never have enough to buy you if wealthy men desire you."

Tears came to Marat's eyes. A slave her entire life! Her breath came harsh.

Her stepmother straightened the shawl on Marat's shoulder and tucked the hair behind her ears. "You might marry a free man and he will buy you from your master." She sighed. "If Adab is defeated, we will all become slaves." Tears welled in her eyes and she wiped them away. She gave Marat a quick, tight hug and took her back to where the scribe was marking two palm sized tablets with the terms of the agreement.

The handmaid asked for water, made Marat kneel before her, wet and soaped her head, and shaved it with an obsidian blade. Tears pooled in Marat's eyes and slipped over her cheeks as her long shiny dark locks fell to the floor. When the handmaid turned away from her, she surreptitiously touched her bare scalp and found a single shank of hair left. Everyone who looked upon her now would know she was a slave.

The scribe finished his work. Her father rolled his dull orange carnelian kisib onto the clay tablets. Nin Aruru rolled her polished black obsidian kisib and gave him two rings of silver. Each kept a clay tablet.

"I ask Nin Aruru to allow you to keep this memory of us." Her father held a charcoal black hematite kisib on a thin strip of hide up to Nin Aruru to inspect the simple inscription "Marat, devotee of Inanna" with images of a sun over a river full of fish. She nodded, and he put it around Marat's neck and hugged her tightly. "I love you, daughter," he whispered and released her. Marat's tears continued to roll down her cheeks. Her father smoothed them away with his thumbs. "We were all made for service, my daughter. Perform your duties well, and Inanna will be pleased." He turned her from him, and Marat followed Nin Aruru out of her father's house.

# 5. Id [River]

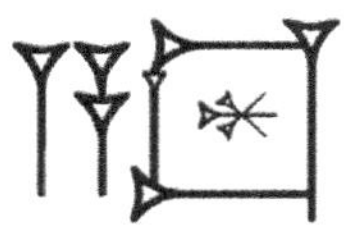

Marat silently followed her new mistress and entourage to the Buranum River where the rising water flowed swiftly like her tears. Nin Aruru paid a man to take them across in his coracle. Marat had never been in a boat. When she did not climb into the craft like the others, the ferryman lifted and placed her, much like a bushel of barley, in a spot that would not impede his ability to steer across the river. Water lapped close to the round rim and seeped through the reed bottom as the man pulled his oar through the water. The others sat calmly while Marat trembled. Maybe they knew how to swim; she did not. Water came over the rim—she jerked up. The ferryman barked at her to sit, and the scribe's hand compelled her to comply. Marat stared at the reeds beneath her: green, young, yellow newly cut, tan mature, brown weathered, and black rotted—all woven tightly together. The black pitch smeared on the outside showed through in patches. Water on the boat's floor sloshed with the ferryman's pull. It wet her hands and feet and penetrated her skirt so that it scrubbed her backside. When the coracle reached the far shore, the ferryman forced her hands to release their hold on the floor reeds and carried her to the bank.

When she did not move to follow Nin Aruru, the scribe pushed her along. They walked past barley fields turning golden and wheat fields still green and came to a walled estate where they were given entrance. The scribe bowed to Nin Aruru and left immediately. Several servant women came up to Nin Aruru. Before speaking to them, she turned and spoke to Marat for the first time.

"You are my husband's servant." Her voice was firm. "His work is holy. The gods watch our house closely. Your work is a reflection on our house. Do not anger my husband; do not anger the gods." Nin Aruru leaned in. A hint of fig perfume tickled Marat's nose. "You are not to have children. If a man touches you, come to me for cleansing." Nin Aruru directed one of the women to take Marat to Nam Eluti.

Marat frowned. She would not have children? What was cleansing? She wished to ask, but the woman tugged her along the wall away from the house and did not speak. They passed barns with goats, herb and vegetable gardens, and came to a small temple painted white, green, and blue. A tall man with a long beard and fine pale brown tunic came out of the shadows of the door. Nam Eluti. Her owner. Marat's body shook. She tried to remember what she had been told to do upon greeting him. The servant at her side slapped the back of her head: "Bow to Nam Eluti—do not gape at him!"

"N-Nam Eluti," Marat stuttered as she bowed and remembered the rules, "I am your humble servant."

# 6. Zeh [Piglet]

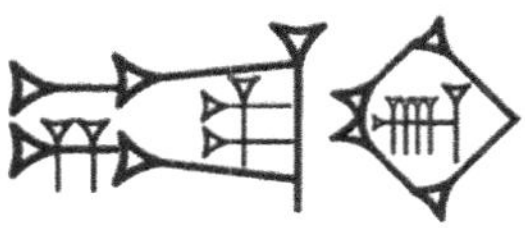

Eluti dismissed the house servant. He bade Marat to stand up. He smiled. It had not been easy to convince Aruru, and here, now, the girl was his. "I am full of joy to have you at last, Marat." He ruffled his tunic. "Tell me, how many colors do you see in this fabric?"

Marat's gaze darted up, then back to the dirt. "There is brown, Nam."

"And?" he prompted.

"Brown, Nam."

He frowned. "Are there variations of brown?"

Her head remained bowed as she answered, "There is only the brown, Nam."

Anger entered Eluti's heart. The child was withholding! His hand clenched as he took a step towards her. Words came harshly through clenched jaw, "Untruthful, unruly, ungrateful servants are beaten. They are given food that is for the pigs. They are locked in a pen. They are animals." Eluti had not realized his voice had elevated. He turned away. He had spent too much effort to get her and not have any results. As if to mock him, a wisp of An-mašĝik drifted through the courtyard… a shadow unattached to a form. He watched it float through the wall.

"N-nam, please… p-please forgive me. I-I do n-not w-want to be a p-pig, Nam." The girl's voice quavered. She must be crying. He remained facing away from her. He remembered she had only become a servant today—and she was young. His finger twisted a curl at the end of his beard. It had been some time since he had a newly impressed servant. They required a certain harshness, he recalled.

"Nam, I have looked again." Her voice was steadier. "It has four different browns, Nam."

He grinned. She saw the four browns with no dietary enhancement! He turned and looked down at her kneeling form. She was beautiful. He could not help but admire her. "Maybe you are not an animal." But she would require training. He remembered her resentment at being called a child when they had met in the market. "Until you behave as you should, you will be called Zeh: little pig." He marveled at his name choice, for she was rare, somewhat wild, and dirty. Reaching down, he took the kisib from around her neck. "All that you have, all that you do, and everything that you make is mine, Zeh. Remove your clothing."

Her shoulders trembled and a whimper escaped her lips, but she did as he requested.

"Zeh?"

"Y-yes, N-nam?"

Humility was a good lesson. "I will take you to the others. We will begin your training."

## 7. Bara [Color]

Zeh. Marat hated the name. She hated Nam Eluti for shaming her. She hated this place that was not home. Her head had been shaved, she'd nearly been killed crossing the water, no one offered her drink for her thirst, everything had been taken from her.

Nam Eluti had said her training with others would begin. "What training?" she wondered. The temple stood behind him.

"Whatever I wish."

Images of Naked bodies held in the roar of the crowds assailed her. The spring equinox Sacred Marriage rites. The high priestess represented the Goddess Inanna, the earth and fields. The lugal represented Inanna's lover, the farmer sowing the fields. Their consummation honored the goddess and ensured fertile fields and abundant harvests for her devoted worshipers in Adab.

Inanna's oiled body was draped in dark blue cloth and her arms and neck and ears were decorated with sacred, deep-blue lapis lazuli jewelry. The farmer laid his gifts at her feet: bushels of freshly winnowed barley and wheat, thick silver shekel rings and thin gold mina rings crowded on a leather braid long enough to be a necklace, and bronze swords that shimmered dully in the midday sun.

They shared a jeweled cup of date wine. As the crowd chanted the sacred marriage prayer, the acolytes removed the farmer's long goatskin skirt and Inanna's sacred robes. The man moved against the goddess until they both cried out—and the crowd broke into a cacophony of shouts and whistles, clapping and stomping. The feast began. Female attendants stood bare-chested along the temple wall, offering physical pleasures for a donation in the name of Inanna.

A goat bleated. Marat held her hands crossed over her body. Never had she been outside her house without her skirt. She felt dizzy. A hand grasped her shoulder—Nam Eluti's—and she flinched. He said "come" and turned from her.

She bent to retrieve her clothes.

"Leave them!" He commanded.

She followed him past the small temple. Blue was Inanna's color—which god took white? Green? Could it be for demons and not gods? No, Inanna would not abide demons in her city. Still, cold crept up her spine, demons sometimes did unspeakable acts on people to mete out the justice of the gods. "N-nam Eluti, w-which gods do you pray t-to in this temple?"

"An, Enlil, and Enki." He paused and gave thanks to An.

"Do you have a temple f-for Inanna?" she asked.

"No."

"H-how…" she could not find the words and just looked at him. Inanna was the greatest of the gods—if you didn't give her devotions…

"In my house, you will give your devotions to An, Enlil, and Enki." He turned and walked away. She hurried after him.

They came to a reed hut. Nam Eluti called out, "Dakum!" An old man with grey stubble on his head and chin and a light-skinned young man cleanshaven with a long shank of brown hair came out. Eluti introduced them as Dakum and Gibil and her as Zeh. Dakum looked like the man who brought wood scraps and reeds to her father's workshop for the fires needed to bake the clay kisibs. Gibil—with that light skin and hair, flatter nose, and stocky body—could not be from Kiengir, where everyone had hair black like pitch and skin brown like wet sand.

Gibil snickered when he heard Zeh's name. He openly looked at her naked body. Marat immediately decided she hated Gibil.

Nam Eluti barked at Gibil to give Zeh one of his skirts. He retrieved one from the hut. It wrapped almost twice around her body and covered her from chest to knees.

Eluti asked Dakum to bring them unumun tea and moved to sit at a table beneath a nearby date palm. Gibil followed. Marat followed them. Dakum brought four cups and a pot of hot water.

"We drink this each day before we begin our work," Eluti said. He poured tea into the cups, put one in front of each person, and drank. Dakum and Gibil drank. Marat sniffed the gold liquid; it smelled like wheat. She took a sip. Her mouth puckered and she nearly spat its bitterness out.

"Drink it all, Zeh," Eluti instructed her.

She thought of throwing the tea to the ground but remembered her service to this man for Inanna. She sipped again, and again the bitterness attacked her mouth. She forced it down in one gulp. She hated this unumun tea.

Eluti led them in prayers to An, the most supreme god; Enlil, the god of sky and earth who cared for mankind; and Enki, the god of water, wisdom, and crafts. They did not pray to Inanna.

Eluti had them sit in the shade of the tree, and the naming of colors began. He pointed and Dakum and Gibil named the colors they saw. They used descriptions Marat had not heard. Blue. Clear sky blue. Water blue. Lapis lazuli blue. Shadow blue. Brown. Dirt brown. Tree bark brown. Dead tree leaf brown. Brick dark brown. Plaster light brown. Marat's skin tingled. They were naming the variations of color as they changed from one to another—as nobody she had ever known saw them. As she saw them.

"Zeh, do you understand?" Eluti asked.

"Yes, Nam." She rocked her head in acknowledgement, forgetting to be angry at her new name. "They name all the colors."

"You can see all colors, but you do not know their names. Dakum and Gibil will teach you." He hesitated, then said to them, "If the zeh sees a new color, she will tell us. Our sight is a gift from the exalted gods An, Enlil, and Enki. Each new color shows them how well we see the world they have brought us to. Even a zeh can help us with this work."

Marat's teeth clenched. He demeaned her to these men. She could not look up. She could not bear to see the laughter in their faces at her disgrace. She hated Nam Eluti, she hated all of them. An, Enlil, and Enki were not her gods—Inanna was. She prayed silently to Inanna: "May I serve you well, Inanna. You are the strongest of gods. May every person come to worship you. May the other gods fear you."

Eluti was also praying. Aloud, he asked the gods for help in using their gifts of sight and instructed Dakum and Gibil to look about for An-mašĝik.

Dakum pointed at the reed hut. "There, Nam." Marat looked and saw only a hut. The three men watched the nothingness. Eluti nodded.

Gibil pointed at the garden. "There, Nam." Marat followed their gazes across the barley fields. where there was a shimmer of heat. Dakum's eyes darted to Eluti.

Eluti nodded. They continued to look about until dusk. Slaves coming from the fields passed by them, the scent of sweat and dirt trailing behind them. Crickets and frogs began their noisy evening calls. Marat could not feel her legs. Her back ached. She had seen nothing. Eluti led them in prayers, oversaw their evening meal, told the men it was forbidden to touch Zeh, and left.

Marat looked from Dakum to Gibil in the airless hut lit by a small clay lamp. Would they perform unspeakable acts on her now that Eluti was gone? Would Gibil take back his skirt and leave her naked again? Where would she sleep—if she could sleep? Cold spread through her tired limbs. A tear rolled down her cheek.

Dakum spoke. His voice was so soft it did not reach the door. "Zeh will be our little sister. We will help her learn her place in Nam Eluti's household and help her earn back her name."

Gibil agreed. "Yes, Dakum. You are the elder of our household. I will do as you say."

Marat remained silent. Her father had two sons by his second wife, her brothers. She had watched after them, made skirts for them, helped cook their meals. Was this what Dakum and Gibil were offering—to be brothers and not… not husbands?

In the dark, the two men quietly told her their experiences with other owners compared to the ease of their life with Nam Eluti. Dakum had sowed, weeded, and harvested fields in the burning sun from first light to last. He had pulled clay from the riverbank, formed it into bricks, and laid them out in the sun to bake until his bent back ached and his skin blistered and peeled. He had been beaten and caned when his work was slow or imperfect. For sustenance, he was given sour beer and rancid barley and foraged in the harvested fields for food. Within the slave quarters, the best food was given to the master of the slaves and his family. There were beatings and fights as punishment and to establish dominance, and there was work there, too: grinding barley, carrying water, patching holes in their huts, and making garments from the goat skin scraps they were given.

The old man's stories made Marat's skin prickle with cold. She had helped in the cooking at home, but she had never been made to work past her body's endurance, or been beaten or starved.

Gibil had much the same experience as Dakum, but he had also dredged canals, waist deep in mud, handing out basket after basket of muck every day until the damage of the floods was repaired. The water softened his skin and the reed baskets rubbed and tore it. Gibil worked hard to avoid beatings but was often selected to be punished for having been in the party of mountain men who had attacked the farms years ago.

Dakum described their life with Nam Eluti. They kept a garden from which they gave half the produce to Eluti, a quarter to the master slave to keep peace with him, and the rest they kept for themselves. During harvest they worked in the morning with the other slaves to get the crops in, bricks made, and canals repaired. They received beer and barley provisions from the main house. Every day they drank unumun tea, named colors, and looked for An-mašĝik. They lived, just the two of them, in this hut. It was a good life for a servant or slave. Gibil agreed.

Marat sat silent. She had worked in a garden, but not a field. Never had she made bricks or repaired canals or buildings. Would she be asked to do this? The naming of colors was enjoyable but watching for the thing An-mašĝik was strange. She wanted to go back to her home in the city. She hadn't liked her stepmother, but the chores were not so bad, maybe, as she had thought, and there she had a place to sleep and her own clothes, and her father.

Dakum and Gibil pleaded with her to understand how her actions had an effect on them. If she did not acquiesce, they would all suffer. They confessed they did not understand why they named colors and looked for An-mašĝik—only that they understood it was important to Nam Eluti and when they did well, he treated them well. In the dim light they had her look upon their backs and touch their scars. Gibil cried. He did not think a young girl, yesterday laughing and walking about as she pleased, could understand this new world she lived in. They would all suffer.

"It is true one often must suffer to gain understanding," Dakum said somberly. "We can hope that if our suffering is too great, we will go to the underworld."

Marat's stomach clenched. It could be so bad that Dakum would rather die? He would rather be in that cold, grey underworld where Inanna's cruel sister Ereshkigal ruled? And this would be Marat's fate as well for all the days with no end? "I will try," she told them. Her father had said her devotions to Inanna would be through service. He and her stepmother needed the silver shekels. One tear and then another ran down her cheek. She wiped them away.

"We will help you." Dakum clasped her hand. He reached out and took Gibil's. Zeh reached out for Gibil's other hand and he took hers. "We are a family. We will help each other."

# 8. An Mašĝik [Sky, god] [Vision]

As the river rose and the days warmed, the barley matured, and the fields changed from a sea of gold to one of stubble with stacks of sheaves as the field slaves cut and left it in the fields to dry. The male date palms sprouted their bright white-yellow spathes, and the field slaves began climbing in the orchard daily, pollinating the female flowers with spathes cut from the male trees.

The herders took the goats out onto the plains to graze. Eluti purchased several aurochs and a man who knew how to keep them. Their lowing soon became part of the everyday farm noises of slaves singing, goats bleating, and insects buzzing. Their manure stank as much as any other animal's and was just as good for the crops.

In the mornings, Dakum, Gibil, and Zeh worked in the garden and did chores for their small household. Eluti sometimes took Gibil to help with the harvest. In the afternoon they drank the bitter unumun tea, named colors, and searched for An-mašĝik. Almost a full cycle of the moon passed in this way.

Zeh began to see more colors—all the ones the others saw and some they did not. One day when Dakum pointed at the sky above the main house, there was a shimmer like a false lake in the desert—maybe it could be described as a dusty shadow as Eluti said; she did not know for it appeared as nothing she had ever seen in her life. She nodded, as was the practice, to indicate she agreed with the sighting.

"Describe it to me, Zeh." Eluti sat across from her in their circle.

"It is long and thin, like a frizz of wool… It is not here, yet it is… It moves from the house to the wall…" Her voice trailed as she watched it float along as though there were a breeze. "Oh!" She cried as it went through the wall. She jumped up and ran towards the wall where there was no hole. "It went right through—there!" She pointed. "But Nam," she turned back to Eluti, "there is no hole! How has it done this?"

Eluti jumped to his feet. "Zeh sees An-mašĝik!" He cried out. "Zeh sees!" He pulled her into a dance, laughing with tears running down his face. "Join us," he motioned to Dakum and Gibil. "Rejoice!" They danced like warriors victorious in war, feasted like hunters who had slain a great beast, and drank like priests at a festival. Pride filled Zeh's heart. She did not understand what it was they were doing, but she was at least able to see An-mašĝik as the others did. She had brought joy—not suffering—to her new family.

Now she saw each An-mašĝik as the others did. Sometimes it could be seen from a distance, and sometimes they could not see it until it moved closer or turned to show a greater side of itself, like a barely visible flock of birds turning in flight to show their full dark wings.

Eluti began discussing the nature of An-mašĝik with them as they sat watching. It was a gift of the gods. What purpose did the An-mašĝik serve? It did not bring rain as the stronger clouds did. It did not rearrange the sands and clear bad spirits away as the wind did. Was it something the demons used? Could it be like fire, useful once understood and controlled?

Gibil suggested they net it, like a fish. An-maŝĝik slipped through the net. Spears sailed through it. Smoke did not choke it. Water thrown at it did not wet it. Dust did not settle on it. Wind did not change its movement. An-maŝĝik ignored their attempts to interact with it.

# 9. Adea [Flooding, flood season]

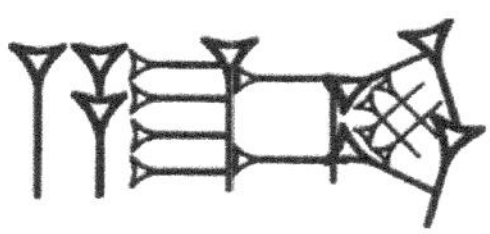

*Zeh age 10.*

Spring came with the floods. The Buranum River rose out of its banks and overwhelmed the canals to flood fields and topple homes and property walls, leaving a fine silt trail across fields and market squares. The river receded, and it was brick month. The servants and slaves went to the river to harvest clay and pitch, make bricks, and repair the damage.

Even here, in community work, Eluti kept Dakum, Gibil, and Zeh separate from the other servants. They worked upstream, away from the others who were cutting the red clay and mature yellow reeds from the riverbank, forming the clay into bricks and feeding the reeds to the fire that baked the bricks, cooling the bricks, hauling them to the cracked buildings and falling walls, and repairing them.

Eluti took their small family to a slow place off the river where there was a pond of the sticky black pitch used to bind and coat the bricks. Dakum and Gibil and Zeh scooped the rancid substance into woven reed baskets, loaded the baskets on tan and white onagers, and took them to the servants repairing the buildings and walls. They worked from the sun's rising to just after mid-day. After washing in the river, Eluti marched them back to their small hut where they drank their bitter tea, prayed, ate their meal, and looked for An-mašĝik.

They stumbled to the ground stiffly and sat as they had fallen—too sore to move. A house servant came by with an extra ration of beer, a reward for everyone's hard work. Gibil slurped his greedily through the straw as though he had not had anything to drink all day. Dakum drank steadily, spitting out hulls with each long draw. Zeh already felt a pleasant buzz from her first beer. The beer was not as dark and thick as her stepmother made, but it was sweeter and she enjoyed that. Her lingering thirst from the hot day encouraged her to drink more, and soon her cup was nearly empty. In a light daze, she watched for An-mašĝik. The servants sang as they worked. Insects droned.

Gibil belched and woke Zeh from dozing. She drew some deep breaths to waken her spirit. Her body felt rooted like a tree. She forced her eyes open. She didn't see any An-mašĝik. There was no shame in that: there were times they would go days without seeing any. Her gaze swept across the harvested barley and wheat fields where only a light stubble of their stalks remained. Sesame was sprouting in light green rows. The other fields were planted and would soon sprout lentils, chickpeas, and flax.

Dakum spoke, "There, Nam."

Zeh smiled. Dakum was the eldest and the first sighted one Eluti had acquired, and as such he claimed first sight of the An-mašĝik each day. Their household had agreed to this. She followed his pointing hand and watched the An-mašĝik glide across the field away from them. She imagined it coming to them, as a duck might come to see if they had grain to feed it.

"It has moved!" Dakum exclaimed.

Eluti, his eyes heavy, looked to Dakum and then to the An-mašĝik. "They always move. That is their way… to move through our lives with no acknowledgment."

Zeh's gaze went from Eluti back to the An-mašĝik. She thought again of the ducks. It was a memory of earlier times: her father had taken her mother and herself to the river for a small feast on a holy day. There had been ducks on the water that her mother had encouraged to come closer with breadcrumbs. "Here duck, duck, duck," she heard her mother's voice in her thoughts.

"It moves again!" Dakum and Gibil scrambled to their feet.

It had moved, Zeh realized. It had changed its path away from the fields and now came directly to her.

Eluti, Dakum, and Gibil watched as it approached them. Zeh, frozen in place by fatigue, wonder, and fear, watched it come to her. Even as she thought she should get out of its path, she remembered it had never interacted with anything. Fear moved her at last, but the An-mašĝik shifted course to intercept her. The others stared, open mouthed, as it approached. And then it was upon her, and through her, and gone. She gasped in air.

"You did that!" Eluti accused her.

"I do not know, Nam," she answered between deep breaths.

"What did you do?" He came to where she stood, bristling over her.

She kept her head bowed and her eyes lowered. She had seen him take his anger out on others: his voice would climb louder, his body crowd closer, and his fists and feet would lash out. She did not want to be beaten. "I did nothing, Nam," she tried to placate him.

"What were your thoughts?" His voice dropped a level.

She tried to remember. "My thoughts were that my body is tired, Nam." He grunted at her response. She added, "The beer makes my thoughts wander, Nam."

"Just that? Nothing else? Tired and drunk?" His words rose in pitch, making her flinch. "Where do your thoughts wander to?"

Zeh searched for something to give him and remembered. "Of ducks, Nam, as they come to a hand that might have bread for them."

He pondered over her reply, and asked, voice neutral, "Why did you move?"

A shudder ran up her back when she thought of the shifting nothingness moving to her. "Its path was coming through me. I feared it would hurt me, Nam," she explained.

Eluti stepped away. He turned back to her. "It moved again, and you did not."

"I was tired, Nam. When I saw it move again, I thought it was no use… it was coming for me."

He nodded. "It moved through you. What did you feel?"

"Nothing, Nam. I felt nothing." She looked to Dakum and Gibil. They looked at her strangely. Truly, she had not felt anything from the An-mašĝik. Did they want her to lie to Eluti to placate him? She could not lie, but she did remember to kneel in a gesture of submissiveness as they had told her.

Eluti's questions continued. Over and over he went about her tiredness, the ducks, how much she had drunk, what she had eaten, the sensations she had as it passed through her. He did not attack, but his badgering was tiring. When her eyes, heavy with sleep, closed, he pinched her. He asked still more questions. She had difficulty understanding him and forming answers. He made her stand. He threw cold water on her. She cried out at his cruelty in keeping her from sleep. She begged him to believe her limited explanations. Finally, his questions stopped, and he left them.

Dakum patted her gently, praising her discovery and endurance under Eluti's interrogation. Gibil drained the beer in her cup, carried her to the hut, and lowered her ungently to her cot. As she pulled the covers up, Zeh remembered the moment the An-mašĝik turned—twice she had made it turn! Warmth spread through her body and she slept.

# 10. Zu [Know, learn]

The second day of brick month, Eluti took them to the tar pond and demanded they do each task exactly as the day before. They hauled the same number of baskets of pitch, washed in the river, came back to their little hut, ate their evening meal of goat stew with bitter tea, drank the extra beer, and sat to watch for An-mašĝik. Eluti told them to relax, be comfortable as they sat, and call to the An-mašĝik not with their voices, but with their minds. Find a sweet memory, like Zeh's ducks, and call to the An-mašĝik.

Zeh was more tired than the evening before. She worried Eluti would be cruel and demanding, but he was not—he was gentle, concerned.

No matter what happened, Eluti told them, they should remain calm. Nothing bad would happen—the An-mašĝik had passed through Zeh without harming her. If it came to their calls, it would pass through them in the same manner.

Zeh believed his calm. She finished the beer, her body relaxed, and her thoughts softened. Music from the main house floated across the warm evening and mixed with the chirping of the crickets in the fields. A slight breeze played across her skin. Dakum sighted the first An-mašĝik.

They called out to it, "Here duck, duck!" Eluti laughed, for he had called out, too. He gave them more beer and reminded them, "Thinking, silently, not saying aloud."

They nodded, sipping. Soon the An-mašĝik began twitching this way and that. "Nam?" Dakum asked, "Could it be confused, with all of us calling?"

"Yes, of course," Eluti exclaimed. He bade them quiet their minds while he alone called. It moved to him.

Later, they would remember this as the day of wonders. The An-mašĝik came to each as they called. They found how two could call it equally and it would come exactly between them; but if one had more soft urgency, it would go more to that person. Working together, they got the An-mašĝik to circle within them, and through each of them. When they stopped calling, it eventually turned to its original path and glided away.

They drank and played and drank more—nearly passing out—before Eluti sent them staggering to their hut.

# 11. Akus [Toil, labor]

Dakum, Gibil, and Zeh were awakened the next day before sunrise and prodded down to the pond, cranky and sore.

In the river, bodies floated past. Zeh cried out, and Dakum calmed her. "Have you been to the river to watch the High Priestess ask the gods for judgement on a man?" he asked.

"Yes, once."

"These people," he pointed at the bodies almost out of view, "were guilty and the gods have drowned them. Their families will look for them; they will take them home and bury them."

Gibil whispered to her that his people, the Guti of the Zagros Mountains and their goddess, were not such barbarians.

Eluti ordered them to work. The pitch seemed heavier and more nauseating, the sun hotter, the insects thicker, the onager slower, the colors of the world starker than the previous days. Still, Eluti pushed them to gather as much as they had before. He plied them with beer after their meal. They moved An-mašĝir until it was too dark to see. Hard day followed drunken evening through the month until the moon waned and Zeh's fatigue turned into exhaustion.

Zeh's limbs felt as heavy as the pitch they gathered. When she could no longer shovel the pitch into the baskets, Dakum changed their work so she walked the onager to the house and back. Even that became difficult for her. There was no breeze. The stifling sun beat upon her head and arms and heated the sand beneath her feet. Her clothes chafed. She wanted to cry.

When Dakum found she had wandered in half sleep's confusion, he tied one of her hands to the onager's rope so it led her. When Eluti came to appraise their progress, he nodded his approval. Their household had maintained the process that had led them to move An-mašĝik.

One day on the path to the house, Zeh stumbled. The onager continued after she fell. Her weight in addition to the baskets of pitch was more than the onager could bear, so it stopped. In the animal's shadow, with respite from the sun's glare at least, Zeh fell asleep.

Eluti, coming from the house, found her in the garden, drug home by the onager, now contentedly chomping greens. He cut the rope that tied Zeh and carried her himself to the main house. He called his doctors—the azu and ašipu both—to examine her. Aruru and her handmaids cleaned the girl's body. Eluti sent for Dakum and Gibil and made them explain how Zeh came to be tied to the onager.

Dakum explained they were doing what they could to carry the same amount of pitch as nam ordered. The men's bodies had hardened to the work: their weak muscles had strengthened, their soft feet thickened, their skin darkened. Zeh's young female body struggled with the changes. Their household adjusted as best they could, giving the easier chores to Zeh, but instead of growing as strong as Dakum and Gibil had, she had grown weaker. Dakum begged Nam Eluti forgiveness for his ignorance: he cared for Zeh like a sister and did not mean her any ill.

***

Anger and impotence warred within Eluti. Did they not know how precious they were to him? They must not harm themselves! Yet, he tugged at his beard, they must exhaust their bodies to progress with the An-mašĝik. Yes, he must drive them, but they must not be driven to death! By the Gods, he thought, the time it took to find one with the sight—and to have such success with Zeh—then to lose her because of the work of brick month that any common slave could do? No, this could not happen. There must be another way. He must find this other way. He must pray to An, Enlil, and Enki.

Eluti sent Dakum and Gibil to their hut to rest. They were to go back to tending their garden. No longer were they to harvest pitch.

Eluti went to Zeh's side.

The old azu with long thin dark hair told him Zeh was too long in the sun with not enough to drink. She was young and would likely recover if she had rest in the shade with plenty of beer. In some cases, people of this malady regressed if they worked in the sun again.

The ašipu, younger and lighter skinned, told him a demon was at fault. This Zeh, he found, was not devoted to their gods. Other servants had heard her giving devotions to Inanna. Zeh must stop this worship and give her entire effort to An, Enlil, and Enki.

The doctors mixed and applied their potions and chanted their incantations. After they left, Eluti stayed at Zeh's side and prayed.

# 12. Ešgal [Underworld]

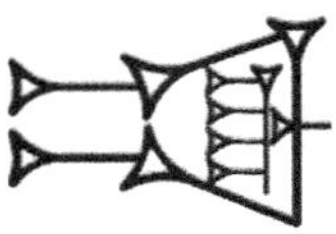

The hard ground left Zeh and she floated away from the heat and stink of the world to the underworld. As she passed the seven gates of Ereshkigal's domain with Inanna, the stones dulled their footsteps and diminished their light. Finally, they arrived. Zeh fell to the ground, like a stone herself, and the sister goddesses argued her fate.

Inanna spoke of her strong work and devotions. Ereshkigal exposed her weaknesses and traitorous prayers to An, Enlil, and Enki. Inanna defended: the young one had apologized for this, begging forgiveness and following every prayer to An, Enlil, and Enki with two for Inanna. Ereshkigal praised her sister for having such devoted followers; could she not spare one to her sister who had so few? Back and forth the warmth of life and cold of death argued. Zeh, at their feet not daring to look upon them, burned and froze with their words. Finally, darkness enveloped her and she heard and felt nothing.

Zeh imagined herself living in the grey underworld, seeing nothing, hearing nothing, feeling nothing, forever. She thought sometimes she heard the sister goddesses speaking. She prayed to Inanna to give her strength in her sister's cold home.

One greyness, the words came nearer. In the dark she saw a form, Eluti. He chanted quietly to his gods, An—of the sky and Inanna's domain—and Enlil—of the earth and Ereshkigal's domain—bringing them to visit their progeny.

* * *

Eluti kneeled in his temple at the alter crowded with a feast for An, Enlil, and Enki: carafes of the best grape wine, bowls of thick spicy baby goat stew, twelve kinds of cheese, and date cakes.

"Most ancient and revered Gods, I offer you the best of my household. Please come, partake of this humble meal that your most devoted servant offers." Eluti prayed, apologizing for treating their gift, Zeh, with so little reverence. He castigated himself for his shortcomings as a mere man trying to figure out the gifts they had given him—surely they could forgive him his mistakes and bring back Zeh? All his efforts were for their glory.

He told them he would bring more offerings to them. Surely, he had not been devoted enough. He would offer more to the temple, help them build another, larger one. He would make sure each of his wives, children, servants, and slaves added to his offerings. He apologized that Zeh and his first wife prayed to Inanna—a powerful, worthy goddess, true—but his house was devoted to An, Enlil, and Enki, Inanna's elders, and prayers to the elder gods surely benefited their offspring? If the gods released Zeh from the underworld, he was sure she would help Eluti bring the gods great glory.

* * *

In another time of unending greyness, Zeh heard Eluti telling An, Enlil, and Enki everything he knew of An-mašĝik and asking for more knowledge. The detail amazed Zeh. He categorized the colors and where they were found. Eluti thanked the gods for the gift of the unumun plant, which enhanced sight if one took it daily as tea for at least half a moon's phase. He listed the times to see An-mašĝik, how it looked at different times, and the state one's mind and body must be in to turn it—and how to get to that state—and how it reacts to more than one call.

Zeh listened as Eluti told the gods his knowledge was written on tablets and would be shared so more men would use it to praise them. The number of their devotees would grow. Eluti said he would find a way for the An-mašĝik to help them become a greater force in the world, and by being more prosperous they would be able to give even more sacrifices to the gods.

He praised their gift of Zeh, for her sight was exceptional and her simple understanding of the world had led to An-mašĝik responding to their calls. He protested that his progress was hampered because Zeh was a wild animal, needing to be domesticated before she could be of service to their cause. Eluti promised that if the gods returned Zeh, he would train her and find glory for them.

* * *

Zeh was at the goddesses' feet when Enlil opened the earth. An's brightness shown down, blinding Inanna and Ereshkigal. An breathed life back into Zeh. Eluti took her hand and silently led her up through the seven gates to life. The sky darkened and Enki poured down rain, wetting the earth into a great mud from which the goddesses could not free themselves to capture the fleeing girl.

## 13. Dubsar [Scribe]

Zeh woke with a gasp that brought Eluti to her side. He clasped her hand and said, "We must pray."

Her voice was rough with dust from the underworld. "Yes Nam," she croaked. She praised An, Enlil, and Enki for saving her and giving her this second life. Behind them stood the specter Inanna, cheated, shimmering anger. Zeh looked away in shame; she had forsaken the goddess. Zeh's voice rose as she prayed harder for the protection of the sky and earth gods, promising them every moment of her life.

Nam Eluti patted her. "You do well in your prayers Zeh. This is very good."

After her return from the underworld, Zeh was made to stay on a reed mat in Nam Eluti's rooms in the main house. As the days wore on, she drifted more to consciousness than sleep. House servants came and went constantly: sweeping the rooms of dirt and crickets, lighting sticks of cedar to ward off demons, bringing Nam Eluti wine and date sweets, or asking him to resolve a household issue. Even when the servants were not seen, the sounds of their shuffling feet in the passageway, voices singing for the family in the courtyard or practicing outside, or bickering quietly amongst themselves over scraps of food and clothing reached her ears. They did not speak directly to Zeh. The family members did not speak to her either. Only Nam Eluti did, and that was to remind her to pray or tell her to rest.

When she thanked the woman who swept the room, the woman ignored her. She asked the man who brought her meal if the sesame fields were flowering, and he responded that Nam Eluti wanted her to rest. On weak legs, she stumbled to the passageway and was promptly brought back to her mat. She wondered what Dakum and Gibil were doing. Working in the garden, pulling weeds, she thought, and fell asleep.

A scratching woke her: Nam Eluti was clearing clay tablets. He cursed, and she asked him what vexed him. He explained he wrote about An-mašĝik but had made an error in the clay that must be removed.

Zeh understood; she had removed designs and marks from unbaked kisibs for her father. The clay had to be rubbed smooth with no hidden gaps, otherwise when a new design was put to the clay and it was baked, the imperfections would weaken or crack the kisib. The loss of a completed kisib was the loss of many days' work. She told Nam Eluti of her experience and offered to help in this task to preserve what was known of An-mašĝik for the knowledge of men and betterment of gods. Nam Eluti accepted her help. She removed marks carefully and smoothed the surface so it could not be seen that there had been a correction. Nam Eluti was pleased with her work.

He had a room built off of his for her to work and sleep in. The smooth walls were washed white and the floor finished in dull brown baked bricks with a zigzag pattern. Her cot and a table with tools fit snugly. Pegs on the wall held her skirt and shawl.

In the mornings and evenings, she walked with Nam Eluti down to the hut where she ate with Dakum and Gibil, and they named colors and called An-mašĝik. The rest of the day, she worked with the clay tablets.

Family and servant mutterings about her special treatment reached her. She missed her father and Dakum and even Gibil. But she did as Nam Eluti asked. He had saved her and had given her a room of her own and work she had the skill to perform.

Zeh learned Nam Eluti's ways. They discussed what he wrote of An-mašĝik. She learned to read. When he taught her to write, he discovered how quick her mind was and how agile her hands for she mastered in two years what took most scribes six.

## 14. Gabašuĝar [Rival]

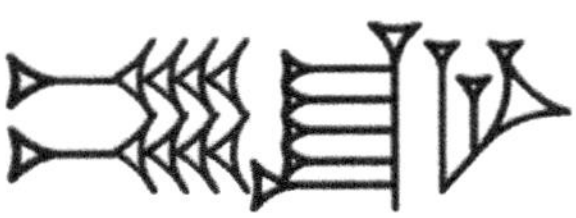

*Zeh age 12.*

Zeh pressed marks into the clay tablet, adding to the list of colors a burnished copper from a scrap Nam Eluti had brought from his brother's house. Heated copper produced several swirling colors, but if it was taken close to overheating, it acquired a new color. Ursag Mundu was displeased with this copper because it was brittle.

She ran her fingers lightly over the indentations documenting the long list of colors and their descriptions as well as where they were found. She looked at the tablet she had made to document the sighted: how each had come to Nam Eluti, how they came to see, and the differences in their sight.

She took up another tablet, the one only Nam Eluti wrote on, and removed the damp wool protecting his precise marks that explained how to tell if one had the gift of sight, and if they did, how it could be enhanced to see An-mašĝik, and how An-mašĝik could be moved. There were notes about the exhausted meditative state, and caution to not become too exhausted. Zeh thought back to the night of wonders, brick month, and her experience in the underworld. She smiled and gave a small prayer to the gods for her life. Covering the tablet, she said a prayer in thanks for a master who was dedicated to his pursuits.

A shadow fell across her. It was Meptum, the field slave whose skin was as light as barley hulls and who had lost several fingers and now worked in the house. He was foolish. He had lost his fingers, it was said, poking them in an onager's mouth. He had said he could see An-mašĝik when he could not; Nam Eluti beat him and marked him as a liar. Still, a slave had value—even a simple-minded one, Nam Eluti had said.

"Good day, Zeh," Meptum murmured. "I am to take the cot and clean it." He entered her room.

Zeh set the tablet down and moved out of Meptum's way.

He pulled the cot up and it slipped from his grasp. "Will you help me, Zeh?" He showed her his hand with only the two fingers.

She shook her head. "I have my own tasks." Since she had been brought to Nam Eluti's home, she had never been allowed to work with anyone except Dakum and Gibil. These were Nam Eluti's wishes, and she followed them.

Meptum's eyes narrowed and traveled up and down her body. "The Nam's little zeh has grown into a fine sow."

The sexual tone struck alarm in Zeh. Nam Eluti and Nin Aruru had instructed the slaves that Zeh was not to be touched, yet some still showed interest even though she did nothing to provoke them. She moved to the doorway. If she could get to the hallway there would be others, and she'd be safe—unless this encounter was purposeful to right a wrong in jealous minds.

Meptum grabbed her arm and pulled her towards him. He pushed her against the wall. "Such special slaves you three are." He pressed into her. "Drinking beer and gazing about. No hard labor for you. No beatings." His breath was sour against her face. "Does the nam feast on the zeh? Perhaps I will, too," he said as his hips pinned her, and his good hand squeezed her small breasts under her shawl.

She squirmed and shouted. Meptum slapped her hard and covered her mouth with his bad hand. "Do not squeal, zeh, or I will hurt you."

Her cheek burned and her eyes watered. His stink filled her nose. Her breasts hurt with his pinching. His hand left them and pushed at her goatskin skirt. She kicked out, but he did not move. She bit the hand at her mouth and screamed as he jerked away. His fist struck her face. The room dimmed. Blackness rimmed her vision. Meptum fell back. Her head light, Zeh watched as Šamaš, the soft-spoken gate guard, husband to the short, light-skinned cook Zimu, dragged Meptum to the hallway. Nin Aruru appeared in the doorway.

"Šamaš, take Meptum to the stables and tie him to the fence. Here," Nin Aruru beckoned a handmaid forward, "clean Zeh and see if he has taken her."

Zeh had not been taken. This did not seem to matter to many of the house servants—they had heard Meptum shouting and assumed it was the woman who had enticed the man. From her small room, Zeh listened when the first wife visited her husband that evening and reported what she knew of the disturbance. The law allowed an owner to kill a slave man who took a virgin slave woman, but only to fine him if the woman was not pure. Meptum had not taken Zeh; however, there were other complaints against him. Did Nam Eluti wish Meptum killed?

Something crashed against a wall. Zeh's fingers tightened on the blanket. Nin Aruru chastised Nam Eluti for breaking a good dish in anger. Another dish crashed and Zeh jerked. Nam Eluti asked Nin Aruru how anyone in his household would disobey his orders to leave his special sighted slaves untouched. She suggested household members were often susceptible to jealousies; demons indeed preyed on them—but what action did her husband wish her to take?

Nam Eluti told her he did not wish to be caught up in the vagaries of his house. He did not take life lightly—or the cost of labor—and would not injure a man based on one person's testimony. He left to talk to Meptum. Several moments passed, and the silence of the evening was broken by a goat bleating and then screams from the direction of the stables. Nam Eluti returned.

"Our third wife is jealous of Zeh. She does not understand the importance of the work we do." Nam Eluti sighed heavily. "She told Meptum that if he defiled Zeh, she would arrange his freedom. Please go to her, my most treasured Aruru, and find out if this is true. I trust you to take actions most beneficial to our household."

Aruru left and there was quiet for some time. The second wife and her handmaid came to Nam Eluti with balms and wine to sooth him. Zeh fell into a fitful sleep crowded with images of Meptum's attack.

The next day, Meptum was flogged. The third wife was moved to a hut and garden on the far side of the estate with two servants: a handmaid and Meptum. Her children stayed in the main house. Neither she nor Meptum came to the main house again.

The servants avoided Zeh. She heard them whispering—sometimes loudly when Nam Eluti was away—that demons made her a temptress to ensnare their men. She had cried to her brothers who shook her and said it was petty jealousies disguised in faith and should be ignored. Zeh tried to ignore the whispers, but they filled her head and made her body shake.

Nam Eluti began taking Zeh with him on his trips as his scribe. Strong, quiet Šamaš came as well. With them, Zeh's head cleared, her breath came easier, and her hands steadied. Each week they went to Adab to the temples for An, Enlil, and Enki where Nam Eluti prayed and visited with the doctors and scribes and Inanna's temple where he gave offerings to the city's favored god. Not as often they went to his brother Ursag Mundu's great house. Any trip into Adab ended with a walk through the markets.

## 15. Abulillum [Boxthorn berry]

The season's barley and wheat matured and was harvested, and people celebrated the bountiful harvest at the spring equinox and sacred marriage. The floods came weak and late. There was talk of drought. The slaves had prepared the fields for the second season, and the seeds they sowed were now short dark shrubs of chickpea, light straggly bushes of lentil, waist-high sections of flax waving its light blue flowers and round pods, and sesame with its spires of white flowers and thick pods. The field slaves' persistence at the shadufs, moving water from the river to the canals, ensured the crops would not all fail.

Zeh ran her hand over her bristly head to the shank of hair that indicated she was a slave. Her fingers sank into it and she began braiding by habit. She thought of Nam Eluti's new discovery: abulillum. A trader from the East had said it cleansed body wastes and improved virility, dizziness, fevers, and eyesight. Nam Eluti had taken samples of the plant's dried red fruit and dark crisp leaves to the temple to verify its properties with the azus and ašipus, but few had heard of it and none had used it in their practices.

He bought two bushels each of the abulillum's dried fruit, leaves, roots, and bark. He gave some to the temple doctors to investigate and brought the rest home where he started experiments on the field slaves. He was as excited as he was on the day of wonders. Zeh was told to work with the house doctors, and she found she enjoyed making abulillum experimental salves and teas. In the mornings, they went with Nam Eluti to the four slaves he had chosen and gave each one tea and applied salve to their bodies from only one part of the plant. Nam Eluti would have them describe the taste, their sensations, and their health, carefully considering changes. Nam Eluti noticed Zeh averted her gaze from the naked slaves. He chastised her—how could she document changes if she was too squeamish to look at a body? When done with the examinations, he would return to his rooms with Zeh where they updated the tablets describing the plant, its parts, how one could consume it, and its effects. Working closely with Nam Eluti reminded Zeh of working with her father making kisibs. She worked hard and savored each word of praise.

At the end of the first week, two slaves reported more vigor, one indicated a rash had healed, and the other urinated and defecated uncontrollably. The smells nauseated Zeh nearly to the point of retching. Nam Eluti and the doctors, unaffected, discussed the findings and doubled the dose.

At the end of the second week, the two vigorous slaves suffered bodily waste loss as the one had, that slave died, and the man with the rash reported increased virility. Zeh had seen the dead, but she had not touched a cold body or turned it in her hands inspecting it. She had glimpsed man's ardor, but she had not discussed a stout penis with its owner and with doctors. These things she learned to do. The names of the slaves, the fact they were men and had wives or children who ate the produce from her garden… all of this faded, and they became merely physical bodies she looked at and documented the effects abulillum had on them. Nam Eluti reduced the dose by a quarter for the remaining three slaves. He brought in a new fourth subject and started him at the first dose level. Each night, Eluti reviewed the findings with Zeh and contemplated the next action.

At the new moon, the temple doctors came to Nam Eluti's estate. They discussed their findings. Nam Eluti thanked them and gave them more abulillum.

Nam Eluti took more field slaves and gave them new mixtures of abulillum fruit, leaf, root, and bark. A few died. Nam Eluti's second wife became angry. She was in charge of the field slaves—and how was she to accomplish the sowing, weeding, and harvesting with half her labor force pissing and shitting and dying and the others walking around distracted with erections?

***

Zeh heard angry words from the wives and even some of the older children. Jewelry and perfumes could not be bought at market. Fine flour for cakes could not be acquired. Families would not show their daughters to his sons. The chest that held shekels and minas was empty.

Nam Eluti left them bickering, telling Zeh to continue his work with the slaves while he was away. He returned several days later with an entourage of doctors, priests, scribes, musicians; men carrying a gazelle on a pole ready for roasting, bushels of grain and vegetables, and jars of beer; men leading a line of slaves; and the great warrior Ursag Mundu, Nam Eluti's brother. As a feast was prepared, Nam Eluti reviewed his field slaves with the learned men. He described the plant part and dose each slave took and how it affected him. He discussed how long until certain changes took effect, dangers of death, and how some effects, though seemingly unfortunate, might be useful under certain conditions. The scribes marked their tablets so quickly their reed styluses whipped about like trees in a dust storm. The the priests led them in prayer. They feasted, drank deeply, clapped to musicians' songs, listened to Ursag Mundu's account of his latest victory over the mountain men who had pilfered the lugal's cattle, and slept. In the morning, Nam

Eluti gave his guests jars of abulillum. He gave his brother double. They gave him silver and gold minas and tokens of credit. They left singing and laughing.

The household was once again at peace. The rings of silver and gold and clay tokens for barley filled the chest. Nin Aruru made sure the needs of the wives and children were met. The new slaves were put to work in the fields. Nam Eluti, his research complete, stopped dosing the field slaves with abulillum. Confident of the doses required to improve sight, he started dosing Gibil. And then Dakum.

Dispassion left Zeh. These men were no longer subjects—they were her brothers; honorable men who had brought her into their family, helped her survive in Nam Eluti's strange household, and protected her. She crept down to their hut. Holding their hands, seeing the fear in their eyes and feeling it roil about in her stomach, she consoled them. "He will not harm us, our family. We are special to him. He did his work first on the field slaves to find the dangers. Some of them died." Here she let herself be weak and cry. She cleared her tears and shook Gibil's and Dakum's hands again. "The doses are known. He will not jeopardize a sighted one, experienced sighted ones such as you, my brothers. Tell him as soon as you feel a change. He will not let you die."

It took nearly a season, and Gibil almost went to the underworld twice and Dakum once, but Nam Eluti discovered abulillum could improve their ability to see An-mašĝik. He started the regimen with Zeh.

Her brothers found her weeping in the garden and consoled her. Gibil reminded her of her advice to them, and that it had been true. Dakum told her to be brave in weathering the experiment… for it was worth pleasing their master, and soon they would all see the An-mašĝik in this new way with abulillum. With hugs and encouraging words they walked with her back to the main house where Nam Eluti was finishing his prayers. He .asked how they were feeling.

"Nothing has changed, Nam Eluti," Dakum said.

"Our bodies are strong, and we see the An-mašĝik even now, in the weak morning light," Gibil said.

Nam Eluti nodded and gave Zeh a small bowl of abulillum fruit paste. "Eat it all, Zeh."

She stood staring at the bowl shaking in her trembling hand. Would her prayers to An, Enlil, and Enki keep Inanna and Ereshkigal from claiming her again? She remembered the cold underworld and shivered.

"Eat, Zeh," Nam Eluti said again.

"I am afraid, Nam." Zeh's voice quavered. Tears welled in her eyes.

Nam Eluti put his hand on her shoulder. "I would never harm you, Zeh." He shook her gently. "We do this for the gods, little one. Our work on the others has shown us the way, and now we must go down this path."

She nodded agreement, even though she was still fearful. Zeh scooped the paste with her fingers and put it in her mouth. The taste of the dried abulillum berry mixed with dates was sweet with a hint of bitterness, as she had documented. Ereshkigal did not claim her for the underworld.

When she drank the tea made of the bark, leaves, and root, she noted it was similar in taste, but more bitter. She knew what to expect at each dosage level, but still it was unnerving when her skin started to itch, her bowels loosened, and a strange yearning came over her. Finally, the day came when she saw An-mašĝik in the first light, in full light, and in the twilight of day and she cried with joy.

The An-mašĝik flowed through their world throughout the day, not just in the evening as Nam Eluti had documented. And there were sometimes large pieces of it that seemed to drift slowly across the landscape and not respond to her call. When she reported this, Nam Eluti began eating the abulillum fruit paste on his barley bread in the morning and drinking a cup of bark tea at midday and a cup of unumun tea in the evening like the rest of them. When he saw as they did, it was another day of wonder.

## 16. Saĝ ĝal [Advance against, attack]

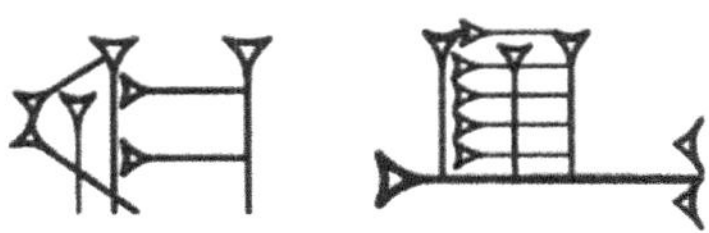

*Zeh age 13.*

Winter and Spring passed, and the Buranum River rose as the barley harvest was celebrated. The wheat was being winnowed when the river flooded. It was as the canals were being repaired and work started for brick month that the evil doers attacked Adab. The compact light-skinned men of the Zagros Mountains in the east came across the plains and the Idiglat River, and watched the wheat being threshed. They ran at the farmers, across the empty barley and wheat fields, tramping over the tender lentil shoots and sesame sprouts in their fields. Everyone in the households ran to the city. The young men, panting for breath, reached it first and alerted the army. The warriors assembled quickly and marched behind the chariots to the farms. The city closed its gates.

The mountain men were devious. The last time they had attacked, they set fire to the reed houses and this, they learned, alerted neighbors and the city to their presence. This time they did not set fire to buildings. They took the grains and silver, raped the women, killed the men, and moved on to the next farm, and then the next.

Ursag Mundu, with a fresh wound across his arm, told his brother of the skirmish as they sat in the shade of his courtyard wall. Zeh, at Nam Eluti's knee, had never heard such a story. She stopped watching black ants clear the dirt she had pushed over their tunnel and listened.

"It was easy enough to find them—just follow against the rush of people streaming to the city for protection. The poor weaklings, crying and limping—some carrying their boxes of shekels and minas, some with nothing. And us, pushing them away to get to the evil doers driving them away from their fields," Ursag Mundu said.

"Did you rush ahead in your chariot, brother?" Nam Eluti asked.

"Yes," Ursag Mundu said, grinning. "We have thirty and more chariots. They saw our strength and fled, the vermin! But we advanced like the rush of an oncoming storm and overtook them." Ursag Mundu paused to take a good swallow of his date wine. "From the chariots we let our arrows fly at them. Many fell, their blood staining the fields. They tried to hide in houses and barns, but we cut off their path. Our warriors on foot arrived with their spears. It was soon over."

"Brother, you have suffered." Nam Eluti pointed to the scabbed line of puckered skin crossing Ursag Mundu's muscled arm.

An ant bit Zeh. She moved a stone over their home and crushed several near her. She inspected one closely: glossy black like her hair, the round body segments, the thin legs. They could be eaten raw, but she preferred them in a soup or bread where their bitter taste was tempered by other ingredients. When, she wondered, had she ever been so hungry? Then she remembered: in her father's home with her mother. There had been an attack and the granaries had been looted.

Ursag Mundu laughed, not even looking at his wound. "In the end, their great man charged out at us with the few remaining savages. I met him on foot in the field. My spear splintered against his shield, and before I could draw my sword, he struck at me. It was a weak blow that got through. I delivered a great blow to his head and he fell. His men, the few left, begged for their lives." Ursag Mundu thought a moment. "I should only take fresh spears to battle."

Nam Eluti nodded, seeming to agree about weapons, and sipped his date wine. "Was the harm inflicted on Adab great?" He bit into a sweet, grimaced slightly, and handed it to Zeh. She ate it, not minding the sour goat's milk mixed with dates. A piece of An-mašĝik moving across the courtyard caught her interest.

Ursag Mundu shrugged. "Not much. A few farms ransacked, their harvest lost, their new crops trampled, some men killed. The temples will provide for them." He shifted in his seat. "The important thing, brother, is that we won! And the savages have told us some of their plans—with some persuading, of course. Our warriors will watch for them now. Adab will not suffer these evil doers to take our offerings to the gods for their own bellies."

Zeh's thoughts went to the An-mašĝik, and it moved. Nam Eluti reached down and pinched her ear. She closed her eyes so she would not be tempted to play, and she listened to the men. They spoke of war, which was so boring. And Nam Eluti—such a wise man—lost his sense and spent the entire visit staring in wonder at his brother and praising his every accomplishment.

"And you, brother, were your losses only this scratch and a spear?" Nam Eluti's voice held concern. Zeh was surprised for she did not often hear a tone of concern in his voice.

Ursag Mundu's voice was proud. "I have pleased Inanna on the battlefield and in my devotions. The lugal and high priestess know this. They have given me great favors. Speaking of such, I have several new slaves. Do you wish to see if any are to your liking, brother?"

Nam Eluti agreed. Before they left Ursag Mundu's house, Nam Eluti reviewed the recently acquired slaves—some purchased and some won in battle—and took one, a thin lightly bronze-skinned boy of about six years who seemed entranced by Nam Eluti's blue robes. His name was Idin, and he was from Kutha where they worshipped Ereshkigal, Queen of the Underworld. He had been taken from his father's garden during an attack by Kish warriors during the barley harvest. In Kish, Idin was put with the other young slaves threshing sheaves. His dour countenance and prayers to Ereshkigal frightened the other slaves who worshipped the Mother Goddess Ninhursag, so his owner gave him to his daughter as part of her dowry. After the harvest, the daughter married and moved with her husband to Shuruppak, where she traded the boy for a female handmaid.

Ursag Mundu provided a clay disk. Zeh marked the cool grey clay with Idin's story and the transaction detail. The brothers rolled their kisibs, Nam Eluti thanked his brother again, and they returned to the farm swiftly—Nam Eluti's excitement apparent in his quickened pace.

Nam Eluti put Idin to work in the kitchen. He told Zeh, and later Dakum and Gibil, how fortunate they were to find another sighted slave and explained it was necessary to acclimatize him to their ways before any work with An-mašĝik could commence with him. He made Zeh write Idin's name and story on their tablets before she slept.

Zeh prayed to An, Enlil, and Enki to silence the boy's prayers to Ereshkigal—just to think her name might bring unwanted attention! She wondered if Nam Eluti could convince the boy to change his allegiance and worship An, Enlil, and Enki instead. He had persuaded her to leave Inanna, so surely he could convince Idin to leave a less desirous god.

## 17. Namuš [Epidemic, death]

In the still heat of summer, Nam Eluti walked three paces ahead of Šamaš and Zeh as they headed to the market. The sun scorched their heads. The sand burned their feet. Black flies bit them. As they approached the sluggish Buranum River, a young muscled man in a coracle at the shore yelled to them, "Disease! Do not come closer. Disease in Adab!"

Nam Eluti stopped so suddenly that Zeh would have walked into him if Šamaš had not put out his arm to stop her. Zeh's mind raced: the man said disease, which meant death. Her mother had died by the evil hand of the demons who had brought an illness of red marks. Her father had locked her mother in a room to quarantine her—sliding food under the door. Cries and moans had often escaped and tortured Zeh. She had sat at the door of her mother's room and sung with her mother until her father finally caught her and sent her away to a neighbor's house. When she returned, nothing was left of her mother: not her hairbrush, not her clothes, not the cup she had drunk from. She was gone—buried deep beneath the house—and even though her father said he talked to her often, Zeh never heard her voice again.

"How are they dying?" Nam Eluti yelled back.

"Coughing and fever, Nam. Some bark, like dogs."

"Are there red marks upon their bodies?"

"Some, Nam."

Nam Eluti thought a moment and asked if there was diarrhea, bleeding, or delirium. The ferryman said no, he had not seen or heard of any of these. The man squinted. "Some had blood running from their noses."

Nam Eluti stood, his hand fingering his beard. They waited. Šamaš whispered to her as he peeled away her fingers clutching his arm, "Zeh, Nam Eluti is knowledgeable in diseases. There is nothing to fear."

She looked up at him, her body shaking, and tried to speak but nothing came out. He pulled her into his arms and comforted her like a child, humming a lullaby as he rocked her. She closed her eyes and hummed with him. Her body stopped shaking.

"How many are dying?" Nam Eluti finally asked.

"It does not seem like many, Nam, but it has only just started. Rumors are that the mountain men brought this evil upon us. The captured attackers have been killed and buried."

Nam Eluti nodded. "It is perhaps benu disease. We must pray to the gods to let them know we are still their devoted servants and to ask them to send away the demons who torture their faithful servants. Šamaš, Zeh, come here."

He led them in prayers to An, Enlil, and Enki. He told the ferryman to take no one across the river to or from Adab. Nam Eluti instructed him to go each day towards the city to learn if the gods were relenting in the illness and come tell Nam Eluti the state of affairs. In return, they would feed him. But he must not get close to anyone in Adab. Even if the wall gates were closed to contain the illness, those outside the walls could be afflicted. "Ask about the house of Ursag Mundu, my brother. I would like to know if this demon's illness attacks my family."

Nam Eluti told Zeh to run to Nin Aruru and tell her what had happened and to send servants to the other farms with the information and also bring to him bricks—they would build a small hut for a sentry to warn others of the illness.

Zeh ran. Her thoughts were of her father and family locked in the city. Would they disappear as her mother had?

She ran to Nin Aruru and the story spilled from her between gasps of breath. Nin Aruru sent runners to the other estates and slaves with bricks to Nam Eluti. She had the second wife inventory the food storage and the state of the gardens and fields and implement immediate rationing of food and water. Nin Aruru had the gates closed and guards posted. She sent word to the third wife that anyone who fell ill would be sent to her hut for isolation and care.

The ašipu began prayers and cleansing rituals. The azu began a daily check of everyone in the estate for red marks, fever, or a barking cough.

Nam Eluti returned. He had Idin tied to a date palm along with a slave who had been recently injured. If Idin carried the evil, they would both die; if he did not, then Nam Eluti would have time to determine whether he could see An-mašĝik.

Nam Eluti sent Zeh back to live with Dakum and Gibil, where the threat would be less, he told her. The family prayed, worked in their garden, and ignored the An-mašĝik floating by.

***

The farmers convened a council meeting by the river. The community had reacted quickly, spreading word of the illness and setting up a temporary market to exchange resources. Reports from the ferryman indicated the afflicted were being quarantined and the dead brought to the south market. The ferryman had no specifics about families or temples, but generally the disease was abating. Still, those outside the city would wait. Sometimes the demons struck them twice, or even three times, before finally leaving them in peace to bury their dead and repair the damages to their society. The granaries in the cities were enough to sustain the population for a moon's cycle. The estate resources were growing because of the rationing; they would be able to bring food to the survivors in Adab as soon as it was safe. Today the council discussed the traders.

A sentry had sent word that traders were approaching from the southeast. They would have timber, copper, and precious stones such as carnelian and steatite—and they would want to trade for grains. If the farmers sent the traders away, would they resume trade once Adab was cleansed? Would the traders encounter the mountain folk—who would then learn of the city's weakness and attack again? Was it ethical to give grain that might be needed to feed their own people in exchange for luxury items that were merely desired?

Profit could be made in these times, Eluti well knew. He had responsibilities to support his wives and children… and the more shekels and minas he had, the more land he could purchase, the more food he could produce for the gods. If the illness was short lived, the granaries would not be emptied. If the illness was great and few survived, the grain would not be needed. And, the farmers would help fill the granaries—to the north, east, and south of the city as well as he and his neighbors to the west of Adab. There were so many questions, it made Eluti's head ache.

The council prayed for guidance, debated, and then agreed to trade.

# 18. Uzudirig [Mushroom]

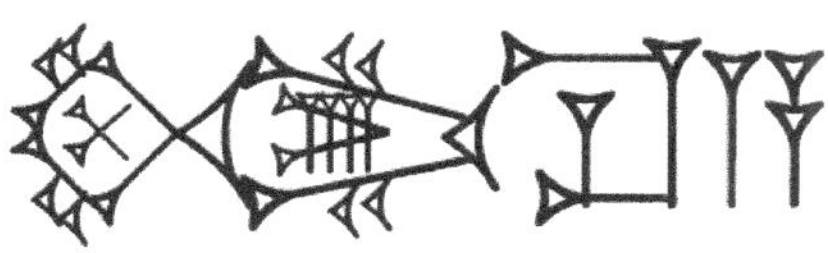

Zeh and Šamaš followed Nam Eluti to the new market. They stopped at their own stall, where Eluti's eldest son and a house servant organized the produce. They passed by the stalls of the other farmers; most had barley and wheat from this year's harvest. Some, the less prudent, brought from their stores: dates, lentils, chickpeas, flax, and sesame. This year's second crops would not be ready to harvest for two or three moon cycles.

Zeh liked the new market. It didn't have as many stalls as Adab's markets, but it gave her a sense of normalcy that was missing those first days when everyone stayed behind the walls of their own homes in fear of the disease.

Nam Eluti walked steadily past stalls, nodding to the landowners. His pace slowed when he reached the traders from the Southeast with their long, dark tents and foul-smelling pens full of camels.

Nam Eluti greeted the trader's guard with one of their foreign words and a gesture, then entered the tent, shaded from the sun but bright with the pungent smell of cardamom and musty goat hides. In the center of the tent, men sat on cushions on the floor around a brazier. They had black hair but did not let it grow long like free men. Their skin was as light as a mountain man's. Nam Eluti joined them, Šamaš and Zeh sat behind him on the ground.

Zeh had been through markets where foreigners traded, but she normally stayed well away from their tents, as her father told her they would steal her away and perform disgraceful acts upon her and leave her body for the lions in the mountains. Her hands trembled and she moved closer to Šamaš. She watched Nam Eluti and Šamaš closely for signs of fear, but they showed none. A man joined the circle who spoke both languages, and Zeh found she enjoyed the disjointed conversation… some she understood and some sounded like a garbled string of words she might know if the speaker's tongue did not warp them.

They were discussing types of stone she knew: solid and lined amber carnelian, black obsidian, green and white variegated steatite, and blue-green turquoise. They also had elephant ivory—from the elephants on whose hides they were sitting, they said. Zeh ran her hand across the floor. It was tough and wrinkled with scattered bristles. Nam Eluti motioned her forward. He asked her about the quality of the stone—did her father use material such as this for kisibs? Yes? How much would her father have paid for such unworked stone? She whispered what she remembered of her father's dealings. She took a deep breath and thought of how proud her father would be to see her using what he had taught her to help Nam Eluti.

The traders brought out metals—copper, tin, and the new metal bronze—and Nam Eluti turned to Šamaš with questions. No longer needed, Zeh took the time to look for new colors and watch An-mašĝik move through the fire, the traders, the elephant hide. There was nothing new here.

Nam Eluti asked the traders if they had slaves. They did. Nam Eluti indicated he and the other farmers would wish to look at their stock. Harvest was coming and they could use more hands in the field. Then he asked if they had unumun or abulillum. They had the latter; he purchased several bushels. They would bring the former on the next trip, they agreed, after discussing cost and quantity.

Someone from outside the fire ring, in a heap of animal pelts, cried out—or spoke—Zeh was not sure. The people around the fire nodded and brought forth a cedar chest, no bigger than a man's head, with intricate ivory inlay. The translator indicated they had a special item for Inanna's high priestess. Would Nam Eluti trade on her behalf and take this to her? They asked for six gold minas.

Zeh stared at the box. What could be so small that it would be valued more than anything she knew of?

***

Eluti hesitated. The risk was too great to be trusting. "I do know our most esteemed high priestess, and I would gladly bring her a gift from you."

"We do have gifts of pearls and ivory for the esteemed high priestess which we would be pleased for you to take to her with the uzudirig, should you represent her."

Uzudirig. It was not a familiar word. It might be their word for something he did know about. Eluti was sure, though, of their intent: this uzudirig must be paid for. Still, the price was high. Very high. Too high without understanding what this uzudirig was and its value. Even if it was only known to priests and lugals, if he was to trade he needed to know more. "I would be honored to represent our most esteemed high priestess. Yet, I would be a poor liaison if I did not trade well. Perhaps if I knew what I was trading for?"

The traders smiled and nodded. A bark of laughter followed by a stream of gibberish came from the old man in the pelts. The translator listened, then said, "You trade for insight, for a view of this world as perhaps only the gods see, the ability to touch the untouchable with your mind."

Eluti held himself posed in contemplation while his mind raced with the possibilities of how the uzudirig might help with An-mašĝik. He took a deep breath, seemingly unsure, but in reality, calming his excitement. He wished to openly discuss everything they knew of uzudirig—it would be helpful in his research—but if he was bartering on behalf of the high priestess, he could not show undue interest. Still, for that price, any man would want to know more. "I fear I do not understand your meaning."

***

When Zeh heard the translator's words, her eyes snapped to the heap of pelts. A way to touch An-mašĝik? Did they know how to do this? Did they know about An-mašĝik?

Nam Eluti spoke. Zeh knew his tone. Nam Eluti was intrigued. He also must have thought of the An-mašĝik. He would trade for the uzudirig. Her stomach clenched. She held herself rigid in disinterest while listening attentively to all that was said. Nam Eluti would ask her to help him write down the expected results and compare them to the actual outcome.

***

On the way home, Eluti's excitement set a fast pace. His thoughts flew ahead like a sparrow. Finally, something that might enable them to interact with the An-mašĝik! "The gods were good to us today," he explained to Zeh. "Thank you, An. Thank you, Enlil. Thank you, Enki," he said as he raised his hands to the sky. It was such a gift! He stopped them there in the path home to pray.

When they were moving again, the direction of his thoughts turned. He had shared unumun and abulillum with the clerics and doctors of many of the temples in Adab who had undoubtedly shared the knowledge with the high priests and high priestesses—but they had not shared the knowledge of uzudirig with him. Why not? While no one but Mundu and Aruru knew of the sight and

An-mašĝik, everyone knew he was an accomplished researcher of new plants. The temples had benefited from his work and knew it was important, and he was a loyal servant to their lugal and he gave devotions to Inanna for his wife, as well as to An, Enlil, and Enki. Why had none of the priests or priestesses shared this uzudirig? Maybe they already knew all of its properties. Maybe its only use was for the gods—or only for Inanna. He made their small party stop and pray again. This time he asked insight to do the work most important to the gods, and to beg their forgiveness that he would use the uzudirig without temple permission—Inanna's high priestess was isolated in Adab with the sickness the demons had brought upon them. Perhaps the gods had brought this gift to him because the high priestess had been taken away to the underworld. He assured them that he would use their gift to his best ability.

Once home, Eluti went directly to his rooms and hid the box under the floor beneath his bed. He called for his first wife. Aruru came quickly, concern on her face.

"My generous husband, I have come at your call." She bowed before him in appeasement. He took her hand and brought her to him.

Zeh sat in the corner by the window and guarded against eavesdroppers, as directed.

"Dearest Aruru, I am in good humor," he assured her. "Aruru," Eluti continued, "In my zeal to honor the gods, I may anger their most devoted worshippers."

"What have you done?" she asked quietly. She noticed Zeh and motioned for her to leave.

Eluti nodded. "Begin the tablets for today, Zeh."

* * *

Zeh went to her room. As she quietly prepared clay tablets for their knowledge of uzudirig, she listened to the words spoken between Nam Eluti and Nin Aruru in the next room.

Eluti explained to Aruru why he had spent all their wealth that day. When the city opened, they would make good profit on the precious stones and metal. The lugal would buy the slaves to fortify the army—when other cities found out about the illness, they might attack Adab in its weakened state: their devotions in decline, their gods dissatisfied. The temple would reimburse him for at least half of the uzudirig even if the high priestess was taken to the underworld—for this was a drug Inanna's temple used to communicate with the goddess, and, here his voice dropped to a whisper, how he intended to keep at least half for his work with the An-mašĝik.

Aruru voiced concern about the risks taken, but agreed her husband was shrewd to purchase the slaves and precious goods. She did not agree with and would not be mollified about the uzudirig. She called the purchase theft and the loss of funds robbery. How could her most devout husband participate in such sacrilege? Eluti explained if both parties were instruments of the gods, and the gods had allowed the demons to put the illness in the city, and because of that Eluti had discovered the uzudirig—might it not be theft but intended action by the hand of the gods?

They argued about good and evil, how to determine the gods' will, and what might befall their household should they choose wrongly. Zeh had never heard such a discussion of growing and diminishing wealth, of strategic marriage for children, or that the number of bushels one gave to the temples indicated one's devotion. She listened intently as they talked and prayed.

By morning, Nin Aruru had agreed to be silent about the uzudirig, and Nam Eluti had agreed to discuss the situation with Ursag Mundu before bringing the uzudirig to the temple when the city's gates opened.

The next days, Nam Eluti and Zeh marked tablets with everything they remembered from the traders about the uzudirig. If it was taken as a tea, it had to be steeped until the water turned wheat brown. If it was dried and eaten, one could only have a small bit of the cap, but twice as much of the trunk. Good reactions were a sense of wonder, of seeing the world in a different way, talking to the gods. Bad reactions were throwing up, intense anxiety and fear, and death. One should always have a disciple nearby in case of a bad reaction. If there was a bad reaction, the disciple should force the person's stomach clear and stay with the body as it thrashed about, fighting off the pull of the underworld.

They inventoried their product. There was not much: just dried stems and caps. All told, only a few handfuls.

"There is not sufficient quantity to learn its properties as I did with abulillum," Nam Eluti said as he twined his fingers through his beard. "We cannot discuss the properties of uzudirig with the temple priests in Adab until the demons and their illness is removed."

Zeh nodded agreement of his assessment. "What do the azu and ašipu say, Nam?" Zeh asked. She had been surprised they were not discussing this with the doctors and spiritualists as they had the abulillum.

"The two here on the estate do not have knowledge of this. You will not ask them any questions pertaining to uzudirig."

"But perhaps…" His hand slapped her across the face. She stifled a yelp.

"Insolent servant! You will not speak to them of this. Do you understand, little zeh?" Nam Eluti struck her again.

She fell to the ground, submissive. "Yes, Nam Eluti." Her heart beat heavily. They had been working companionably as mentor and student; he had encouraged her questions. What had changed?

"Never!" He loomed over her and she feared he would kick and beat her.

The strike across her face still burned. "Never, Nam. Never." She put her fear of his anger in her voice to convince him. She waited for another strike. What had changed, she asked herself again.

"Good." He stood back and took several deep breaths. A noise in the hall startled him. He went to the door, looked out, and came back rubbing his hands together. "Let us pray," he said, sinking to his knees.

Zeh scrambled to join him. She had never seen him so nervous, so… afraid, she realized. Fear? She wished she could talk to Dakum and Gibil to get their insight, but Nam Eluti had not let her go to her family for several days. He started a chant to An, Enlil, and Enki. Her voice joined his automatically, but her mind skipped back over the last few days looking for the source of his fear. She realized she was not attentive to her prayer, and Nam Eluti's voice was more strained than normal. His prayers. He was not asking for enlightenment down the path of discovery… he was at once asking for both the approval to take the path and forgiveness for taking the path. When had that started, she wondered? Thinking back, she realized it had started on the way back from traders after he had gotten the uzudirig.

She had thought he was elated. Yes, he had been. Then they had come home, and he had talked to Nin Aruru. That had been different: close, quiet talk, intense words, fear of being heard. Nin Aruru disagreeing with her husband. Zeh thought back over their discussion, and comprehension spread coldly through her: he was taking uzudirig meant for Inanna's high priestess. The punishment for stealing from the lugal or from a temple was death.

# 19. Kab [Test, experiment]

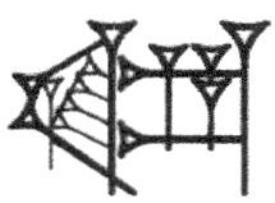

They went to the river the next day, early before many in the household were awake. Šamaš stumbled beside Zeh in the dark as they followed Nam Eluti down the quiet path. No birds sang. The breeze barely disturbed the grasses. They reached the river, and Šamaš yelled to the ferryman. The man waved and started across. Zeh watched the dragonflies dance above the water. She spotted a soft-shelled turtle, green with yellow flecks, and asked Šamaš why they did not eat its meat. He explained to her that many thought the animal belonged to the underworld and should only be hunted to add to the sacrifices to Ereshkigal. "Others don't eat turtle even though it is plentiful enough," he told her, "because it is an aggressive animal and the meat is poor."

Zeh didn't think the awkward moving animal looked aggressive, but she took Šamaš' word for it. If it had anything to do with Ereshkigal, that was reason enough to leave it alone.

The sky brightened with the rising sun. The ferryman arrived, and Nam Eluti gave him several shekels, asking him to send someone to the temple and ask the azus and ašipus and priestesses what was needed. Nam Eluti gave him barley flour and dried dates as well with a small clay ball with writing on it wrapped in cloth, asking if the ferryman could have someone take the message to the house of Ursag Mundu and bring back a response.

They prayed to the gods while the ferryman was gone. The day grew hotter and Zeh began to sweat as they moved from one prayer to the next. She saw fear and nervousness in Nam Eluti. The brown of his skin paled, his voice was slightly higher, his hand went to his beard more frequently, he was irritated more easily and more likely to strike out at her. She trembled.

Šamaš, on her other side, put a hand to her shoulder. He whispered in her ear. "You will get us beaten with your nervousness. Thank the gods for Nam Eluti: a kind, insightful master who treats you well."

She stared at Šamaš. Surely, he knew what Nam Eluti was going to do with the uzudirig and that the punishment for stealing from the temple was death? That a man as wealthy as Nam Eluti would have slaves take his place in the trial where they would be bound and thrown into the river? "I cannot swim," she whispered, her voice stark with fear.

Šamaš reached out and struck her on the back. "Sit straight, little Zeh," he said loud enough for Nam Eluti to hear. To Zeh he continued quietly, "You are too prized a possession to put into the water, little Zeh, and I can swim."

He understood! His words eased the knots in her back. She nodded and prayed harder. She wiped sweat off her face and out of the corner of her eye on her other side, she saw Nam Eluti's form stiffen, then relax slightly. Her prayers comforted him? She looked back at Šamaš with incredulity. His voice took up her intensity and they continued until the ferryman returned.

The information from the city was that the illness had taken one of every twenty. There were too many to allow families to bury their dead beneath their houses. The dead were being gathered at the south market, and when the city gates opened, they would be taken to a large grave and be buried together. The priests of the temple were praying to the gods day and night—the flickering of lamps in the temple could be seen at all times. Neither the lugal nor the high priestess spoke to the city, but the azus and ašipus brought their words: pray to Gula for healing and increase your devotions to Inanna so she does not become jealous.

The ferryman gave Nam Eluti a small tablet. He read it and thanked the ferryman with barley cakes smeared with honey and a few more shekels. They returned home in silence. Nam Eluti went with Zeh to the benches by the palms where they performed their rituals in the shade—drinking more beer than normal—and watched An-mašĝik. At the end of the evening, he had a quiet word with Dakum about Idin. The new slave Idin was not diseased and had resumed his place in the kitchen, but it still needed to be determined whether he could see An-mašĝik or not. Nam Eluti returned to the main house with Zeh, herself stumbling along, and sent her to her room. She heard him call for Nin Aruru as she fell into a deep sleep.

The next morning, Nam Eluti and Zeh cut the uzudirig stems into fine slivers for tea and weighed them out to equal portions. They went to the small reed house where her family lived, Zeh carrying beer and barley bread smeared with abulillum jam and Eluti carrying uzudirig for tea.

* * *

Nam Eluti, Dakum, Gibil, and Zeh sat around the small table eating. Nam Eluti recounted the traders' description of uzudirig and how its exorbitant cost resulted in their small stores, which impacted their opportunity to learn. With the abulillum and unumun, there was enough to learn plant properties using others; with the uzudirig there was enough for only one: Zeh.

Zeh's cup slipped in her hand and she barely caught it before it spilled—did he not mean Gibil? With the abulillum they had progressed from the field slaves to Gibil, then Dakum, then her. Why had this changed?

Her brothers were surprised as well. "Do we not start with me, Nam?" Gibil asked. "I am strong and willing."

"Or me, Nam," Dakum said. "I am old and weak. I can barely tend the garden. Why take Zeh? She is of more value than us, with her knowledge and youth."

Nam Eluti agreed about Zeh's value. "It is that knowledge and fine sight that makes her the best choice. Her body is more sensitive to the doses, her sight more discerning of An-maš̂gik. It must be Zeh." He emptied his cup of beer, had Gibil fill it with hot water from the fire, and added the uzudirig. He stared at it a moment, sniffed it, and pushed the cup to Zeh. "You must drink. You must tell us the effects."

A cold chill ran through Zeh. Nam Eluti did not promise to keep her from the underworld as she had once promised her brothers. No, she was the first: she knew there could be no promises.

"After you drink," Nam Eluti continued, "we will tie you to the cot. Until we know the reactions and their intensities, we must be cautious. We will untie you when the uzudirig has run its course. Drink now, Zeh."

Zeh took the cup in both hands. The uzudirig's fresh-turned earthy smell rose to her nose. "The smell is more pronounced," she said. Nam Eluti nodded. She did not want to drink, to be an experiment, to die. She felt her whole body tremble with fear; the cold that crept up her back came from Ereshkigal's world. Eluti has known he would do this and has kept it from me so I would not run away, she thought. Who would not run from death? She looked at her brothers, and they held her gaze. They would do it for me, she realized. They have asked, and Eluti has refused. But if I run away, one of them will drink this cup. Zeh lifted the cup slowly, looking from the dark liquid to her brothers, until the cup obscured them—they had not stopped her—and she drank.

"Tell us everything, Zeh," Nam Eluti reminded her.

She nodded. The better she explained the effects, the faster he would learn and the more able he would be to intercede should things go badly. She told them of the earthy taste of the tea. She did not eat the slivers of the trunk, but only drank the liquid. Nam Eluti knocked them out of the cup to dry. He would use the depreciated pieces for the paste they would make for her should she remain in the above world.

Her brothers took her to her cot in the hut and tied her ankles and wrists to the posts with slack lines. They sat by the cot with their eyes on the floor. Dakum held her hand. Nam Eluti was seated at the table with a clay tablet and reed and asked her questions.

There was nothing at first, and then, much like with an excess of beer, a change in the sense of the room. If she moved, she had more sensitivity about her clothes, the sheepskin on the bed, and the leather bindings. Her body felt a kind of dizziness.

Their voices started to echo as though they were in a large room like the priestess chanting over the worshipers in the temple. Her hearing was worse, or perhaps it was just her attention. Her family seemed so far away. Her sight seemed finer—lines were crisper, colors didn't blend but were definite transitions... a thousand lines of reed appeared in the ceiling from bright to shadow. A piece of An-mašĝik floated through, shimmering colors in its translucence. Her clothes were rough on her body. Her mouth was dry. They gave her beer and she reveled in its texture and taste. Nam Eluti's questions lasted much longer than the effects of the uzudirig.

There was a day of rest and then the dose increased. Each session found intensified sensations. They fed her tea and paste of the trunk, the cap, and both combined.

Her brothers kept her in the above world, emptying her stomach when the uzudirig made her body go cold, holding her when her body rejected the dose, and quieting her when it made her scream in terror at the demons she saw. They calmed her when she pulled at her restraints, cursing them or begging to be freed so she could swim in the fields, fly in the river, and walk in the sky. They prayed for the protection of An, Enlil, and Enki when she cried that she felt the presence of Inanna and Ereshkigal and trembled in fear that they were coming to take her. Always there was Nam Eluti's voice pushing her to feel the wretchedness and exhilaration, examine the fearsome and awe-inspiring, and describe it all to him… the real and the unreal, how it came to her, how it dwelt in her, how it left her.

Zeh came to desire uzudirig greater than she feared it, for among the distressing events, there were the wondrous and amazing. When the breeze told her of its journey from the sea, it had left one small drop of the saltwater on her skin as a gift. The fig trees waved and laughed at her, forgiving her for eating their fruit, fruit that when she bit into it she could taste the sun and soil that had soaked the tree with their essence so it might grow and reproduce. An-mašĝik showed itself having depth and filmy substance which she wished to reach out to, but could not.

One evening, Nam Eluti had Dakum and Gibil carried the cot, with Zeh fettered to it, to their spot beneath the trees where they sat to watch the An-mašĝik. Nam Eluti fed her a paste of stem and cap smeared on a fig. When the effects came to her and steadied, Nam Eluti asked her to move the An-mašĝik, which she easily did, explaining how it seemed to jump and turn and dance on her very whim. He asked her to bring it to her, close, and describe it in its greater substance. This, too, she easily did, telling him of the white and silver colors and all the colors that shimmered within them. He asked her to move the large blocks of slower moving An-mašĝik, and she could not. He turned their attention back to the easily moved An-mašĝik: he asked her to have it touch something of this world—the date palm they sat beneath.

Zeh beckoned the An-mašĝik and the tree, its branches limp in the summer's heat, to a shared space where they could meet, like Eluti and Mundu drinking in the garden. She asked lightly, like calling the ducks to feed. The An-mašĝik thickened. The tree leaves shimmered. As the An-mašĝik came close to the tree, a tingling echoed between them—a flash blinded Zeh and a crack pushed her against the cot's reeds. She blinked but only saw white. Nam Eluti's voice came to her from far away, demanding to know what had occurred. She blinked again. Slowly sight came back to her and she looked around. The An-maŝĝik moved on, across a field of lentil sprouts. The tree stood smoking: its leaves were gone, its branches blackened stumps, its bark in pieces on the ground. Her body was drenched in the burnt smell of it. Servants came running from the main house and the fields. The skin on Eluti, Dakum, and Gibil was burnished like men who worked in the sun. Dakum rubbed at his eyes.

Nam Eluti shook her. She looked to him and saw his mouth moving, but there was no sound. "What?" she asked. She reached out and pulled on Gibil's arm. He turned to her, and she saw across his breast a line of red, bubbling skin and ash. "You are hurt," she said.

"What are you saying?" Gibil seemed to be asking, but too softly for her to hear. Zeh shook her head. Gibil yelled, "What?" She pointed at his chest. He looked, then staggered. Dakum helped him to sit.

Eluti came to them and spoke but they didn't hear. Zeh yelled, "We do not hear you, Nam Eluti."

"Do not do this again, Zeh," Nam Eluti yelled. Blood trickled from his ear.

"We must be careful with this." His voice shook. He sent the servants away. As their hearing returned, he questioned her until they understood as well as she did—which was not very well at all. This was not a day of wonder. It was a day of destruction.

* * *

Eluti consulted the slaves who tended the orchard about trees losing their bark. One slave, recently acquired from the traders, had heard a tale of the gods arguing who was greater—the sky or the earth. An took the form of a desert storm, and Enlil became a great date palm bearing enough fruit to feed all his followers. The storm's winds battered the tree, ruining its fruits. The tree bent against the assault, and when it passed, Enki brought it water and it was fruitful again. An, angered, came again—this time striking Enlil deeply with lightning. Enlil's leaves and limbs erupted in flames, his skin burst from his body, and his power ebbed from him. An rejoiced in victory festivities that lasted a hundred years. When he noticed Enki filled their cups with water for there was no more date wine, An allowed Enlil's power to return so he might bring wine to the feast. So chastised, Enlil never argued with An, his omnipotent father, or Enki, his loving brother, again.

Eluti had the tree cut down. If it was such a rare event that it was only known in stories, he did not want men to come to his estate to see and discuss how it came to be. He most certainly did not want any curious minds asking about anything that could lead to uzudirig.

Eluti went to the river with Šamaš. The ferryman said that today there were no new dead in Adab. The illness was over. Eluti knew they would perform cleansing ceremonies before they opened the gates. He asked the ferryman if the city needed food. The ferryman said he had been told the stores in the temple would last another twelve days. He gave Eluti another tablet with Mundu's seal. His brother's house was in good health.

Eluti prayed to the gods and contemplated the day of destruction. The power of the An-mašĝik Zeh had drawn forth was terrifying and amazing all at once. He wanted to learn more and was afraid how damaging the learning might be. Surely his brother Mundu would want this power if it could be harnessed to defeat their enemies. But the state of mind Zeh had been in could have just as easily defied Eluti's command and brought the An-mašĝik to him, to herself—to anything—and destroyed it. Could he control Zeh? Could she control the An-mašĝik? Could he trust her? Her experience now far surpassed his own.

Memories of her strange rantings when they gave her doses of the cap came to his mind. Of her cursing of them, of screaming at things only she could see which surely could not be real… and it did not seem any loyalty would hold sway with her when she was in this altered mind.

However, they seemed to have found a good combination on the day of destruction for she had steadied. She communicated with them, there were no demons, she did not fight her own body, and she had somehow made an interaction with An-mašĝik.

A memory of their day of wonder where they had An-mašĝik pass through them came to his thoughts and he shuddered. Yes, it was safe without uzudirig, but if they had taken uzudirig, they would all be charred corpses in Ereshkigal's grey underworld.

Thoughts of death persisted. He turned it over and over in his mind before he realized the solution: Zeh may not be loyal to her master, but she would be loyal to the gods. They were all loyal to the gods. If he instilled that devotion into their work with An-mašĝik, they could proceed in safety. He hesitated. It was true that every day they prayed to An, Enlil, and Enki—but, like a man assuring his first wife of his love, their devotions had perhaps become rote over time. He must find a way to make them be like the first declaration—undeniable and binding—every time. He went to sleep with the puzzle heavy in his mind.

In the middle of the night he woke with the insight that unrestrained power was the reason for ceremony in religion! It was a control. He dressed and sent for Aruru. She came, wide awake with worry. He told her of the tree and his worries about controlling Zeh—or any person with An-mašĝik—and his epiphany to use religious ceremony. She accused him of heresy. He parried that the gods had not punished them for using the uzudirig. Surely, they had given him the access to An-mašĝik, and now the power to use it in service to them? Was that not similar to the temples that collected the grains and devotions for the gods? She begged him to stop such talk. He calmed. He asked her to pray with him. They prayed to An, Enlil, and Enki—and to Inanna as well—and waited for repercussions. She asked again for him to discuss this matter with the high priestess. He indicated they could not, for the high priestess would only see their use of uzudirig as unlawful; she would not understand how it could also be used to greater enrich the gods in other ways. He reminded Aruru that he had promised to speak to Mundu. Mundu would help them approach the temple. They returned to fitful sleep.

"In what ways will this enrich the gods?" Aruru asked the following day.

"I am not sure, yet," Eluti said honestly. "The tree is the first interaction. I believe this is a new tool for us. There is so much to learn, but without control, we cannot take the next step of discovery."

Aruru looked into his eyes. He reminded her that he was a good man. He had shared the abulillum with the temple. He tithed much of their wealth to the gods. He required each and every family member, servant, and slave attend the sacred festivals at the temple.

"All the fruits of this labor will go to the gods?" she asked.

"Yes," Eluti assured her.

Finally, she agreed.

Together they devised ceremonies for the taking of uzudirig. There would be three classifications of participants: the masmas, a new type of priest spiritualist who had the gift of sight; the gurum, one who also had the gift of sight, to watch over the masmas' actions; and the ennug, an armed guard. Because the work would be destructive, there would also be representatives of the lugal and the temple who would set the directive and condone the loss of life and property. Without divine approval, the ceremony participants would be punished according to the laws of the city for taking a life (death) or destruction of property (restitution or, in some cases, death).

The participants would begin the ceremony by praying to the gods and swearing loyalty to them and protection of their faithful worshippers: the lugal, high priestess, temple workers, warriors, scribes, and people of Adab. Next, the participants would avow the work was for the benefit of the gods and ask them for clarity in doing this work—to not be turned down the wrong path by demons and human imperfections of greed, lust, and loss of devotion. A sacrifice would be presented: an animal of the air—a duck or mallard.

The prayers finished, the masmas would state he would perform as requested and ask to be killed should he stray from the ordained work. The gurum would state he would watch for deviation from the ordained work and move An-mašĝik from the masmas' use to prevent wrongdoing. The ennugs, trained warriors with spears and blankets in hand, would state they would cover the masmas to remove his ability to see the An-mašĝik or kill him as the gurum indicated. Because the ability to see An-mašĝik was a rare gift, covering the masmas was preferred to killing him.

The masmas would remove his tunic, leaving only a small cloth skirt to cover him. This would be done so he could more easily be restrained or killed, as necessary. The gurum, wearing the traditional sheep skin skirt, would give the masmas the uzudirig paste in a fig. Only the masmas would take the uzudirig. It was required for him to be able to bring the An-mašĝik to an object.

Next, the ennugs would tie the masmas to a chair for security and the work would begin when the uzudirig took effect. The lugal's representatives would give commands. The gurum would monitor. If something was amiss, he would tell the ennugs to cover or kill the masmas. The gurum would move the An-mašĝik away from the masmas' reach. The ennugs would stand ready for action until the effects of uzudirig left the masmas.

Eluti told Aruru the ennugs must learn the indications of uzudirig use. It would be a safeguard against any trickery by the masmas or ennugs. She agreed.

"Will my husband take the uzudirig now to have a better understanding than the slaves?" she asked.

Eluti pondered her question. He did not wish to appear weak, but there were dangers to consider. "I was planning on dosing Dakum and Gibil first. If their reaction is similar to Zeh's, then I will follow."

"That will take more time and uzudirig."

"I will dose them with the combination that Zeh had taken when she destroyed the tree."

She tilted her head in agreement. "And if all goes well?"

"Then I will take the lead in experiments. If I am careful, it is less risk than making so much power available to a slave."

Aruru was quiet a moment. "If you spend more time with An-mašĝik, the matters of the estate will suffer."

"Yes, my Aruru. As always, you are mindful of the family responsibilities." He twirled a lock of his beard. "Perhaps it is time for our eldest son to assume management of the daily needs of the estate. Do you agree?" She did. He continued, "For our ennug, I think our second eldest, Imgur, would be a wise choice. He has a spiritual nature, like you, and it might work out well for us if the temple representatives developed confidence in his work and devotion. I would like Šamaš as an ennug for I have grown to trust him."

"These are all wise choices, my husband." Aruru smiled.

"And you, dearest first wife…" he faltered. He was going to say she should also learn the role of ennug or represent the temple, but a ripple of trepidation crossed his heart. Could he trust her? But didn't she already know everything—or would learn it from their son if not she was not included? She had helped him with the ceremony without guile. He kissed her hand. She looked at him, questioning. He smiled. She was good to him. She would be busy with the household; there was no need to fill her days with An-mašĝik as well as his and their son's. "You have been so patient with me. I will work hard to see your dedication rewarded."

The ceremony was explained the next day. Eluti dosed Dakum with the uzudirig, verified his mind's control, then questioned him about his experience—all without interacting with An-mašĝik — until the uzudirig had left him. The following day he did the same with Gibil. Their reactions were similar to Zeh's with minor differences. After a day of rest, Eluti dosed himself. The day after that he destroyed a row of date palms, one at a time, counting each just before it was consumed, and stopped before the last one. Eluti was in control. He understood An-mašĝik better than any of them. The days of destruction had begun.

## 20. Saĝ kešed [Take care]

Aruru went to the river to get an update of the illness on behalf of her husband who was engrossed with the An-mašĝik. She reported what she learned at the family evening meal. The house servants spread word, and by end of day everyone on the estate knew what the ferryman said. One in ten of the people of Adab had been taken to the underworld. The high priestess had been taken; the lugal had not. Many warriors died; the army was going to conscript farm slaves to fill the ranks. Nam Eluti's brother Ursag Mundu was well. Farmers to the southeast of town had dug a pit, and a mass burial rite was being performed there in a few days. After the burial, the city would open with a festival for An, Enlil, Enki, Inanna, and Gula who had saved them.

In their hut, Zeh sat, sullen. Gibil teased her as he rubbed ointment on his burn scars, "You are jealous that Nam Eluti no longer walks to the river or to the market with you in tow." She glared at him. "Poor Zeh. She wishes to be the teller and not the last one to hear of events."

"Poor Gibil," she retorted, "No woman will embrace him in the garden since rumor has spread that we are drugged religious zealots."

"Children!" Dakum reproached them both. "You act as children! Stop this bickering, or I will cut a reed and cane you both."

"Yes Dakum," Zeh and Gibil said dully. They made faces at each other and then fell into fits of laughter.

After their evening meal, they discussed their day. Again they had the An-mašĝik ceremony. Again only Nam Eluti took the uzudirig. He brought the An-mašĝik and items from this world together and everything An-mašĝik touched was destroyed: date palms, dried barley and wheat berries and flour, green lentil and chickpea stalks, sesame and flax flowers, river reeds, goat skins, flax cloth, ducks and snakes, the hair cut from their heads and placed on the ground… everything Nam Eluti could think of. Even though they had bathed, they could not remove the smell of burnt offerings or stains of the scalding burst fruit and animal blood from their skin.

"Why are we not taking the uzudirig?" Zeh asked aloud in the dark before she slept. "Why are we not all participating as we did on the day of wonder?"

"Be patient," Dakum told her. "We will come to understand soon enough."

The next day, Gibil suggested Nam Eluti experiment with water. The water seemed to jump, but they were not sure if it was the cracking of the bowl it was in or the touch of the An-mašĝik. They tried a larger bowl with the same result. They went to the stock pond by the cow barn when the slaves were busy dredging the sand from the season's floods from the canals. When Nam Eluti touched the An-mašĝik to the pond, the water shot up and jerked like it was trying to escape its earthen basin—reaching out like long fingers to scald Eluti's bare arms and Zeh's legs. Then it stilled and the fish floated to the top, dead. The water was hot. A few of the fish had black marks on them, but the rest were unmarked. Nam Eluti had them bury the fish in the barley field and sent them home.

"Children," Dakum called Zeh and Gibil to him as they weeded their garden under the hot sun, "come closer to help an old man with poor sight weed this row." When they were closer, he said with a lowered voice, "These times of destruction are dangerous for us for fear has entered Nam Eluti. We must be careful in our words and gathering about each other. We do not wish to raise his fear or have doubt in our loyalty to him and the gods."

Gibil nodded. He slowly and methodically broke up a clump of dirt with his hoe. Flies buzzed around them.

Zeh did not understand. "Why would he fear or doubt us? We helped find the way to using An-mašĝik."

"Precisely for that, little sister," Dakum said as he pinched off the tips off a stringy lentil bush to encourage it to fill out. "We know what he knows. We could do as he does. He fears we will bring harm to him. Masters are watchful of rebellion in their slaves."

Gibil grunted. "They take us from our homes, they treat us like goats, and they wonder why we are not thankful." He hacked at a weed.

"But...," Zeh started and thought. She swatted at a fly on her leg. "He knows so much more than we do." She took the weed Gibil had loosened and started a pile at the end of the row.

"No, Zeh," Dakum disagreed as he inspected the next lentil bush. "You have burned a tree."

"And he has burned seven, and other things," she insisted. "You and Gibil have not burned anything." She yanked a weed out by hand and tossed it on the pile.

Gibil smoothed over the hole she had made. "Burning one thing is the same as burning another," he said.

Zeh was about to argue the point more when Dakum held up his hand, stopping her. He explained, "Listen and observe. A good slave doesn't bring his master a date sweet only because the master has asked for one. The good slave learns the master likes the sweet after his devotions, that this is how his mother rewarded him when she taught him to pray."

"That is not the same as eating the date sweet yourself." Zeh remained obstinate. She pulled another weed and beat it against her side to loosen the dirt from its roots.

"No," Dakum agreed. He moved to the next plant and started pruning. "But, by this I know how to mollify this man into feeling he's done right, I know in his inner heart he does not worship the gods willingly, I know the reward to use to change his behavior—and I know how to eat a date sweet like an owner of men and land."

Gibil, hoeing weeds the next row over, nodded his agreement. A cow lowed.

Zeh shook her head. "I don't understand."

"It is so easy to see…" Gibil started.

"You have seen more of this life than Zeh," Dakum said to Gibil. He motioned Zeh closer, as if to explain pruning to her. "When Nam Eluti saw you kill the tree with An-mašĝik, he feared one of us could easily kill him, destroy his home, escape and bring Adab to ruin. He realized he had no control over us. This is why he has made the ceremony. We must act as though we are bound by the ceremony and we believe in it. But we know, for we have seen, that this ceremony is not needed to work with the An-mašĝik. Look at the ceremony's purpose: state what the master has told you to do with An-mašĝik, and have others around to prevent you from doing anything else. Kill you if you diverge from the master's expectations."

Zeh fingered a small lentil pod, soft with two small bumps, as she considered Dakum's statements against her understanding and saw he could be right. "But, Nam Eluti himself is bound by the ceremony," she said.

Gibil whispered, "His son and loyal servant are the guards. I have seen that they are inattentive when he works. They are much more attentive to our actions."

Dakum nodded and handed branches to Zeh for the pile. "I have observed that as well."

Zeh took the branches to the pile. She felt resentment well inside her chest. She wanted to understand as they did, but this new view of Nam Eluti felt awkward to her. She returned and tugged on another weed.

Gibil's hoe drew lines in the dirt. "Because they are afraid, they may judge and kill us for a perceived act of insubordination. We might be killed for no reason at all."

"Yes," Dakum agreed. "We must act as though we believe in their ceremony."

Gibil agreed.

Zeh shook her head. "I don't think Nam Eluti would do this to us. We are favored. You have both said this."

Dakum moved down the row. "Yes, we are valued highly for our sight, but we work his garden—we are possessions to a master, and that master will always choose his wellbeing above ours." He pinched off a few dead leaves. "Have you forgotten you are Marat and not an animal to be slaughtered for his feast?"

Zeh startled at her name. She looked across the landscape and sighed. The flax was in full bloom, the rows were deep green covered in light blue flowers with a yellow center. The sesame was just starting to flower: white flowers dotted the bushes. The dates in the trees were turning from their unripe deep green to a yellow that the sun would later burnish gold. "Nam Eluti has shown me colors and An-mašĝik. He has taught me to write. I have helped my master; I have shown him how to interact with An-mašĝik. We work together putting our knowledge of An-mašĝik on tablets." Several pieces of it moved through the farm. Zeh beckoned one to her silently.

Dakum thrust branches at her and broke her concentration. "You may tell the master you are grateful for all he has shown you, but do not think working with him makes you his equal, and do not tell him you have taught him something—especially about An-mašĝik. This, I am trying to tell you: what you do is his, and he sees it as that. The slave Zeh did not discover it—the master Eluti did. Gibil and I know you where the one who led us to this discovery, but if you claim it, he will punish you."

Zeh was tired of gardening. She stomped back to the end of the row and threw branches at the pile. She missed and had to pick the branches out of a bush. She felt the urge to kick the pile, but she would only have to clean it up. Tears welled in her eyes. She wiped them away and returned to Dakum and Gibil. "I do not like what you say." A memory emerged: Nam Eluti praying feverishly in gratitude for the uzudirig he had just gotten from the traders. "But"—she pulled a weed—"You would not speak falsely to us." She told them of Nam Eluti's praying and discussion with his first wife.

Dakum thought on Zeh's words a moment. "He carries much fear of possessing uzudirig—and now of what it can do."

"Of what we could do," Gibil added.

Dakum nodded. "It is a harsh truth. If any one of us makes a mistake, he might kill us all. We must be devout to his plans."

"At least for now," Gibil added.

The words felt awkward in Zeh's mind. They were to follow the ceremony to protect themselves, but at some point Gibil intimated they might not. Would they not be in danger at any point they deviated? Yes, of course they would be. The only thing that could change the danger would be if… Zeh faltered. "You would leave?"

"I would." Gibil hacked at a weed. "I dream of my true family every night. I would return to them if they were not in the underworld. Still, I would leave this place to be free, to go back to my people."

"I am old. I came to slavery to pay off debts," Dakum said. "Like you, Marat, my price is too high to ever buy freedom. And here I eat every day and sleep peacefully. Yet," he fingered a leaf, "I would like to be free to wander, to go with the traders and see other lands. Dilmun, perhaps, if it exists."

Zeh remembered her stepmother's words from the day she was bought. And here Dakum was saying the same thing. Gibil said he would leave. That meant run away. Even though he had been taken into slavery as a prisoner of war, he, too, could buy his freedom. She asked him, "You would go against our laws? Instead of buying your freedom, you would run?"

Gibil spat. "How could any of us buy our freedom? Nam Eluti does not give us grain or shekels for our work. And if he did, he could easily claim them as his own. Everything a slave owns is his master's. I have never seen a slave walk to freedom."

"Children," Dakum took their hands, "There is no good talking of things we have no control over. I wished us to understand we have danger with this ceremony. Do we all see this, now, and agree to be careful?"

"Yes," Gibil said.

"Yes," Zeh said. She weeded slowly. "What of Idin?"

"He works in the kitchen. Nam Eluti has put him with Šamaš' family to raise," Dakum answered. "Idin is a willful child. I think Nam Eluti hesitates to introduce one so unruly to a force so destructive."

Both Gibil and Zeh nodded. They finished the row and started another.

"I still don't see why you say we can do what Nam Eluti does," Zeh said.

"Everything that can be done is written down in great detail on the tablets. It is like the farmer's advice to his son," Dakum explained. "If we knew what Nam Eluti knows and consumed the uzudirig, we could do exactly as he does."

"We need to know the writings on the tablets." Gibil looked to Zeh.

Zeh hesitated. Nam Eluti had said they put their knowledge in clay so it would not be lost. The knowledge was nothing more than their daily practice. Eluti did have a set of tablets that Zeh did not help with. She had assumed they were for household management. If it was about their discoveries, shouldn't they know? Even if it was just as gurum in the ceremony, she reasoned, they should know so they would be better able to oversee the masmas' work. "I will read all that is written and share it with you."

# 21. Silim [Healthy, completeness; well-being]

Nam Eluti's household made the pilgrimage across the river, past the walls of Adab, to the burial site for the victims of the illness. The family wore long fabric tunics that reached to their ankles. Nam Eluti and his older sons with freshly curled and trimmed beards led the way. The wives and daughters followed, their gold and silver rings, bangles, and earrings shone warm and bright in the sun.

Unlike being at Nam Eluti's side for trips to the market, Zeh's place in religious and festival pilgrimages was after the family and house slaves and before the field slaves, with Dakum to her right and Gibil to her left. The male slaves wore belted goat skin skirts that fell to their knees. The women wore the skirts with short tunics that covered their breasts. The slaves and servants, even the children, had freshly shorn heads with one lock hanging to the side.

When they were crossing the river in coracles, Zeh startled, nearly forcing the passengers off balance and earning a dark look from the ferryman, when she noticed Meptum with Nam Eluti's third wife ahead of them. Her breaths came in short gasps. She tried to calm herself, to loosen her hands locked on the boat's reed rim.

Dakum's warm hand covered hers.

Gibil's concerned voice was in her ear. "You must be strong, sister. Do not let your fear of a lowly field slave show We are gurum now and will be masmas. You are protected against those lower in status."

Zeh wanted to believe his words, but she had been under Nam Eluti's protection when Meptum had accosted her. No matter her status, she was vulnerable. She tried to not look upon him, but the coracle turned in the current and she found herself staring at him again and again. He looked up and as he realized who looked upon him, his eyes turned as cold as a snake's. Holding her gaze, he spit into the water. His coracle turned, and Zeh turned her gaze upstream to those coming after her and met the master slave's scrutiny. They had an uneasy peace, Dakum had told her. She bobbed her head to him, acknowledging his rank, and his demeanor seemed to relax. Zeh decided to study the reeds along the shore and watch for turtles and birds.

By the time their coracle landed, Nam's family had moved ahead and there was no sign of Meptum. On land again with her brothers close at hand, Zeh finally breathed more fully as they walked to the burial site.

The ceremony was like one Zeh had seen performed a few years ago to rid the city of the benu disease that demons had hidden on caravans from the West. The people of Adab gathered at Inanna's temple; the lugal and High Priestess spoke to them from the first level. The smoke of the sacrificial pyre drifted through the crowds, its white-grey essence flecked with black cinders and brilliant water droplets. The smell of burning wood and reeds; roasting sacrificial sheep, goats, and aurochs; and perfumes of the wealthy and perspiration of everyone wound around her. Even though Zeh had grown taller, she could not see the lugal or priests or hear their words clearly. She saw a piece of An-mašĝik and threaded it among the worshipers until Gibil stole it and made circles in the sky and Dakum reached over and pinched them both. The An-mašĝik moved on. Zeh watched the back of the house slave in front of her, noting the colors of her dark hair, white and brown goat fleece, and dark skin as the voices droned on. When the devotions started, she joined in the chanting.

After the ceremony, the field slaves returned to the estate and the remainder of the household filed through the crowded streets and visited An, Enlil, and Enki's temples before turning to Ursag Mundu's home. Zeh watched the crowds for her father's face—or her brother's or stepmother's. Dakum caught her looking and told her to comport herself before someone accused her of trying to run away which, he told her, many would be happy to do as snitching was rewarded.

Zeh affected a visage as blank as an unused clay tablet. Shame rose inside her—she knew better than to gawk about. Nam Eluti had slapped her back into place several times when she had first accompanied him to the markets with Šamaš. The shame and hurt was not worth stepping out of line. She could still see, just in a restrained fashion.

Finally, they reached Ursag Mundu's home. Nam Eluti's slaves were given makeshift quarters in the courtyard, the family was provided rooms. Zeh stayed within the protection of Dakum's shadow.

***

The last meal eaten, the women gone to tend their concerns, attendants within calling but not hearing distance, Eluti was finally alone with his brother. He explained his progress and results with An-mašĝik. Mundu had been incredulous to the point of disbelief. "Come to my home and I will demonstrate."

"Do it here, now." Mundu challenged.

Eluti shook his head. "It is too dangerous here. And I do not have the uzudirig. It would not be good to take it after consuming such a large meal and wine."

"This sounds like the excuses of the charlatan," Mundu taunted.

"Come to my house and let me show you. You will be amazed. Fear and wonder will fill your heart, brother."

Mundu shook his head. "Eluti, I love you, but you have been talking of seeing things since before you could grow a beard. You are prey to demons and their delusions. Mother and Father should not have allowed you to continue in your delusions. It is not good for the family name."

Eluti was well aware his family humored him. The estate had been a gift to move him away from the city and everyone they knew. It was their wealth and influence—and his eventual farming success—that had kept people from calling him crazy and the temple from tossing him in the river for demon possession... Damn, the river again. He tore his thoughts away from its cold depths. "I was right about the abulillum, wasn't I? That was no trick of the mind."

Mundu was quiet a moment. "True. That has been helpful."

"Come then, in that faith," Eluti pleaded.

"All right. After the next moon. I'll gather the same party..."

"No," Eluti interrupted. "You must come alone. Just you—or you and your personal guard... Maybe one of your officers, a nubanda." His head fell into his hands and he shook. "Brother, I am in trouble." The river was close again. Tears rolled down his cheeks. Mundu looked at him with incredulity mixed with shame. Words flowed from Eluti. He told his brother of coming across the uzudirig, how he felt compelled to see if it would help him with his An-mašĝik even though he knew it was for Inanna's High Priestess and he might face strict reprisal from the temple for using it. He told him of the experiments—and of Zeh destroying the tree, and of himself destroying plants and animals. And he told him of promising his beloved zealot of a wife that he would tell this story to the temple. "I am afraid Inanna's High Priestess will kill me for sacrilege… for using the uzudirig. That they will not see the wonders it can do." He wiped the wet from his face. "Or… or, they will understand the wonder and will want it for themselves and still kill me." Eluti knew he was a coward. He felt it keenly, here, begging his brother for protection. "Please"—his throat thickened and voice broke— "come soon. Claim An-mašĝik for the army. I am not sure how it can be used, but when you see what An-mašĝik does, you will know how it can be used." He sniffled and cleared his throat. "Protect me from the temple." His disgrace continued as tears streamed down his face. He closed his eyes.

Warmth enclosed Eluti—his brother's arms: one hand on his back and the other cradling his head. "I will come the day after tomorrow, little brother," Mundu whispered in his ear. He held him a moment, lips at Eluti's temple, and released him. "Now, let me tell you a story of a man who was enamored of his auroch cow. It will make you laugh so hard you'll cry."

***

The next day, Eluti woke late with the headache too much wine brings. He instructed the new slaves and his azu and ašipu be left with Mundu to reinforce the army, and he sent his family home except for Šamaš and Zeh. They visited several shops where he made good profits trading the precious stone and metals he had acquired from the traders while the city was closed.

They went to his gods' temples, gave devotions, and prayed. Then they went to Inanna's temple and spoke to a priest who arranged for a fair exchange for the box of uzudirig and discussed how many bushels of wheat and barley were needed to restock the granaries. Eluti committed to more than his share. He also agreed to send their first harvest of dates, lentils, chickpeas, flax, and sesame at the autumnal equinox. The priest was so pleased! Eluti felt some of the heaviness of his guilt lift. He knew Aruru would be proud of their donations. His heart beat heavier: she would not be happy that he had not told the priests the full story of the uzudirig.

He returned to the priest and arranged to have statues of his family made and placed in the temple to increase the continual devotions to the gods. Eluti hoped it would be enough for Aruru.

## 22. Dim [Bring forth, create]

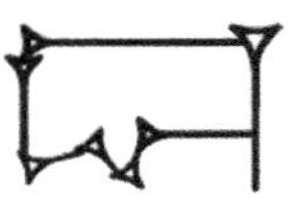

True to his word, Mundu came two days later with a small contingent of his own men. As was customary, Eluti gave him a tour of the improvements to the estate first. One detachment of slaves was clearing the irrigation canals and improving their banks with the silt being removed and with bricks. Mundu agreed baked bricks would be better but were costly. Another detachment of slaves was knocking out bird nests and was inserting sticks into the palm tree crowns to support the heavy strands of dates.

Eluti led his brother and men to a new two-story building that had no openings other than a door. "This is where we perform the An-mašĝik ceremonies. There is no real need for a building other than privacy. There are no openings for ventilation, but the walls are thick, so it stays relatively cool."

Mundu nodded and followed Eluti into the building. Inside, it was as plain as the outside. There were wall sconces where lamps burned brightly, a stone chair near the middle of the room, and cushions on the floor near the walls—and no other furnishings. In front of the chair were several slaves, Eluti's son Imgur, baskets, pots, and rope.

"We will begin the An-mašĝik ceremony now. Imgur, show my brother where he and his men may sit."

* * *

Mundu kept a neutral look upon his face. He wanted to laugh at the ornate prayers Eluti had devised. Sweat trickled down his torso in the room's growing warmth. The sacrifice was a nice touch—the army usually sacrificed a bull before marching to war. When they tied Eluti to the chair, his fist clenched—his brother was allowing slaves to bind him? Even with his son in the room, this was not a sensible act.

The watchers—gurum, he called them—moved to the dark corners, and the guards—ennugs—took their positions with spears leveled at Eluti. Mundu frowned. Eluti had explained the ceremony and the reasons for it—and maybe it did make sense if the person in the chair was a slave—but it was not sensible if the master was in the chair. He heard his men murmuring that the farmers held their spears like hoes.

Eluti spoke, his voice weak. Imgur brought a basket of dates and chickpeas for Mundi and his men to see, then he poured the contents out into a pile in front of the chair and moved back into place. Eluti mumbled. A flash of lightning and crack of thunder hit the room—Mundu was on his feet, swearing and blinking his eyes, drawing his sword and yelling to his men to defend against attack.

Imgur's voice came to him, "Uncle Mundu, uncle… be at peace."

"What the…" His eyes and ears started to clear. The scene was the same as before the lightning with the exception that he and his men were standing, weapons drawn, ready to fight. He shook his head.

"Be at peace," Imgur repeated. "This is the An-mašĝik. Father wanted you to experience the lightning. In our next work, I will warn you so you may protect your eyes."

Mundu swore again and wiped his eyes. His nostrils flared. Something was burnt.

Imgur pointed to the blackened pile of dates and chickpeas scattered in front of the chair.

Mundu went to the pile. He touched his sword to the fruit and moved it about. He looked around the altar. Had someone come in and switched the pile of ripe fruit for burnt? It did not seem possible, yet lightning striking exactly here was… was… not possible. He turned and pointed to one of his men. "You, go guard the door. No one in or out. Keep your eyes facing out."

Imgur had them sit again. This time he showed them a basket full of wet clay. He swept the burnt food away, formed bricks in front of the chair, and moved back into position. Eluti murmured. Imgur shouted out "Cover your eyes!" Mundu had barely raised his hand to his face when the lightning struck. Then he was up and went to the bricks—they were baked and cracked. He inspected the basket; it was nearly empty. He ordered his men to search the room for wet clay. None could be found. He asked the sentry if anyone had entered or left the building. No one, his sentry reported.

Mundu went back to his place and paced. "He is doing this? My brother Eluti?" he asked Imgur.

"Yes."

Mundu went to his brother. "Eluti, you swear you have done this?"

Imgur pulled at Mundu's tunic. "It is not wise to talk to the masmas when he has taken the uzudirig."

Mundu's nubanda pushed the boy away. "Do not touch the ursag!"

Mundu leaned into his brother, held his face with his hand and searched for signs of lies. "Brother, tell me."

Eluti's eyes were glassy and wandered. They came back to Mundu, and Eluti smiled. "There is more work for me to do," his voice slurred.

"Please uncle," Imgur said, spear in hand but point down. "My father wishes to show you more."

Mundu let himself be taken back to his place. He sat. He closed his eyes when instructed. Bread and feathers and wood were burned. Water boiled. A live fish—a small turti—in water was killed. A snake—a poisonous musgiri—in a basket and a pigeon in a cage burst when they were killed, their guts splattered across the room and guests, the containers destroyed as well. Several men picked wood and bone splinters from their skin.

Mundu did not believe this was possible, yet it happened. He asked for this An-mašĝik to be touched to metal. Nanar, his nubanda, took a sword from one of the men and offered it to Eluti. Eluti brought the flash of light. The metal glowed red like it had just been in a metal worker's forge. When it cooled, Mundu tested it; it shattered as metal does when overheated. He gave it to Nanar to inspect. "By the gods!" he heard him whisper.

He agreed silently. Out loud he noted these were all small things. "Can this An-mašĝik not be brought to anything of size?" he challenged. Imgur conferred with Eluti a moment before leading everyone outside. Eluti told them the uzudirig was leaving him, so he quickly destroyed a date palm and a nearby hut.

Mundu felt his pulse quicken. This force against an enemy… He caught the gleam of comprehension in Nanar's eyes. "A man. I wish to see it used against a man." He envisioned a battlefield. "An onager. I wish to see that. And a chariot."

Eluti collapsed to the ground. Imgur rushed to his father and barked at the other ennugs to bring the masmas to his rooms to rest.

"He has done more than ever before," Imgur said.

Mundu frowned. "Have you done this with a man—or an onager?"

"No," Imgur answered.

"This uzudirig does not seem to last long." He walked over to the burning hut. It had been struck in the middle of the roof, which had left a hole that was widening as the fire worked its way outwards. He ordered his men to study this and the tree.

"My father has done many experiments. He can tell you of doses and durations."

Mundu nodded. "How long must he rest?"

"We will eat. He will join us after."

***

Eluti joined his brother at the smoldering hut. He had not meant to destroy the sighted ones' quarters, but it was expedient. Zeh lived in the house and Dakum and Gibil could live in the ceremony building.

"Good evening, brother," he said as he approached Mundu. He had eaten a bland meal, yet his stomach churned. He thought of how he had shown great weakness—crying and begging—to this man who had suffered in battle without complaint. Eluti's chest tightened. "What are your thoughts of what I have shown you?"

Mundu turned. His face split into a smile, and he took Eluti into a tight hug and rocked him. "Eluti, brother! It was magnificent!"

The anxiety drained from Eluti and his brother's excitement filled him. A smile took over his face.

Mundu held him at arm's length, pulled him in, and hugged him again. He whispered in his ear, "Adab will crush her enemies!" He released him. "Tell me everything."

***

Mundu returned to Adab with a light step even though questions buzzed about his mind like a swarm of dragonflies on the river. First, he would go to the lugal. He would explain he was investigating a new weapon and needed special dispensation to kill several slaves and onagers to verify its effectiveness. He would also need permission to purchase and use uzudirig. And, he would have to convince the lugal that the weapon fell under the purview of the army and the temple was not to be included, even though this new weapon, if it worked, was truly a gift of the gods. Mundu smiled to himself: the lugal and the new high priestess were already in disagreement on several points where government and worship overlapped—he did not think the lugal would mind keeping something from the temple.

Second, he would send several trusted warriors to be trained as ennugs immediately. It was a miracle Eluti had not been killed by his slaves—allowing them to bind him to a chair of all things! "Nanar!" he called his nubanda to his side. "We must have true warriors protecting Masmas Eluti. Send four loyal men." Nanar nodded and Mundu fell back into his planning.

The lugal's purchaser would be able to find supplies of uzudirig.

Third, he would have all of his men tested to see if they had this special sight needed to see the An-mašĝik. Eluti had indicated he had three slaves, maybe four, that had the sight. One was a woman. Mundu frowned. Eluti said the ability was rare, but he did not have the resources for a thorough search. With the lugal's help, Mundu could screen Adab's entire population.

In the meantime, if Eluti could determine an optimal dosage of uzudirig and their consumption was staggered, he could have maybe half a day to wreak havoc on the enemy. If used strategically, it might be enough to win. Having more who were masmas, preferably warriors who knew a good target in war, would ensure victory.

The ceremony. Fourth. Mundu sighed. He understood now why Eluti had created it: controls on power. It was too much like a religious ceremony, though, and would cause trouble with the temple. They would modify it for the army.

Once they had his men in place as ennugs, and possibly some trained as the masmas, they would begin training in earnest. He stopped walking. He had forgotten something.

The lugal! Yes, he snapped his fingers, he would need a demonstration. That would be third, he thought as he started walking again.

## 23. Gi [Turn, change status]

Aruru came to Eluti as soon as Mundu left. "What does your brother say?"

Eluti muted his joy before he turned to his first wife. "He thinks it may have some value. He is going to talk to the lugal."

"And the temple high priestess?" Aruru's voice held a tinge of accusation.

"This is the first step: show my brother and take his council," Eluti explained.

She bowed her head. "This is not what you promised," she said in a low voice.

Eluti could tell she was displeased—her skin color lightened slightly. "Would you have us disgraced in front of the high priestess herself if this did not work?"

Aruru was quiet a moment. "But you are willing to be disgraced in front of the lugal?"

He folded his hands. He felt a tinge of exasperation. "As agreed, we were cautious and took it to my brother. His recommendation is to take it to the lugal next. I trust him to know what is best."

"Did you tell him you stole the uzudirig? That you are obligated to the temple for your sacrilege?"

"I did not steal…, he started. "I told Mundu everything. Everything," he repeated. "And his council is to approach the lugal. The lugal will decide when to tell the temple."

Aruru scowled.

"The lugal and the temple are equally accountable to the gods. The purview of one is nearly the same as the other. What does it matter if I go to the lugal first?" He wished a child would cry out so she would go tend it.

"What does it matter?" Aruru's voice rose. She turned and quieted herself. "What do promises between us matter, husband?"

"Aruru…" He watched the skin tones on her face change to reddish brown. The color spread down her neck.

She would not be quiet. "I am not a fool. The lugal and Inanna's high priestess do not serve the gods equally. The temple is pure of heart and intention. The lugal is a warrior, a brutal man risen to power…"

"Woman…" He warned her. "The lugal has the approval of the gods to protect us! What he conquers he gives to the temple to offer to the gods…"

"You twist words to suit your desires," Aruru turned and left.

Eluti stared after her. Such insubordination! He stamped his foot. "May the demons take her!" He swore.

***

Zeh walked with Šamaš and Gibil behind Nam Eluti, guarded by Ursag Mundu's men wearing their metal studded skirts and armed with spears and knives. The warriors had arrived the day after Ursag Mundu had left and were fixed at Nam Eluti's side wherever he went. At night they guarded his door. She was not sure if she liked this change. On the one hand, they were terrifying, on the other, they kept Nam Eluti safe and herself as well since he kept her close. Unlike other men, they did not steal glances at her or insinuate why Nam Eluti kept her close. She felt a lessening of tension in her body she had not realized had become pervasive.

They passed the fields where the chickpea's purple and white flowers bobbed in the slight breeze and the late flax blooms dotted the expanse of green. The dark green sesame bushes had grown to knee height. The lentils were still so young that there was more dirt brown to see in the fields than their light green shoots. Most of the slaves were assigned to repairing the canals and working in the orchard; however, the women and children were in the fields weeding, killing grasshoppers, and swatting at flies. Their voices floated across the fields.

An-mašĝik drifted by in abundance. Zeh would have braided them, but a quick glance at Gibil caught his slight head shake. Nam Eluti did not believe one should be frivolous with a gift of the gods. Dakum had warned it was dangerous to play with something others cannot see. Gibil would play with her, but only if there was nothing else demanding his attention—and they would not be caught and punished. She slowed the pace of several drifting ahead of them imperceptibly, adding more and more until it was almost too many, and then she let them go one by one.

As their party neared the river, the flies thickened so even the warriors swatted at them. Zeh saw the river filled the banks and she was thankful they would not have walk through mud to get into the boat. The crossing was calm, as was their walk into the city. She noticed people turning to see which important man was passing with his guard.

Zeh wondered if she felt safe and decided she felt more like a goat being herded. She did not know where they were going and could not change their direction or pace. The guards were for Nam Eluti. If they were attacked, she was sure she, Gibil, and Šamaš would have to defend themselves. Her feet padded quickly along the soft warm sand. There was no need for fear: they were in Adab, not in the outer holdings where mountain men attacked the farms. The guards turned to the right at the market; they were going to Ursag Mundu's house.

***

Eluti gave Zeh his blue tunic and directed her to determine if any of Mundu's household had the sight. Gibil was to help her.

Mundu's tailor came and fitted Eluti for several linen cloth tunics suitable for appearing before the lugal. Eluti envisioned the meeting and decided Zeh and Gibil would accompany him and therefore should wear something less pungent than their goat skirts. He would have them bathed and oiled as well. He would have perfume and wear his rings and earrings and a necklace. He smiled. He was going to meet Lugal Daudu.

In the afternoon he worked with Mundu and his nubanda on the ceremony. They practiced it the following day. Their audience with the lugal was the day after.

***

"This is impossible!" Zeh complained to Gibil. "They believe we have an elevated status, so the servants have told each other what to say so they might become gurums." She took a bite of grilled kunzi fish with roasted onions on wheat bread. She closed her eyes. The food in Ursag Mundu's house was greatly pleasing.

Gibil sucked on his beer and spat hulls out on the plate. "We could give them abulillum and unumun, but it would take so many days to take effect."

Zeh laughed, thinking of the servants defecating uncontrollably or with erections. "They would not think our status was worth attaining after enduring that."

Gibil snorted. He sipped his beer and ate another piece of fish. "What do you think, Zeh… I was visiting a kitchen maid last night and as we walked through the kitchen, she stumbled on a pot left out that I could plainly see."

"What do I think that you will have more children than a man with five wives?"

He shook his head. "No, no." He lowered his voice and whispered, "She is from my people, a Gutian. We spoke of home in our own language."

Zeh stilled. This was more dangerous than getting a woman pregnant. She wanted to admonish him, but Dakum and Gibil had discussed this many times and Gibil would not be dissuaded from creating a network of Gutians. "You saw the pot and she did not. Is that the question?"

"Yes. Is this also the sight?"

This had not ever been discussed or considered. "Is she old? Her sight poor?"

"No, she has had children but is not old. I do not know if her eyes are poor."

"Has she worked in the kitchen long? Perhaps she is awkward?"

"She has been in Ursag Mundu's kitchen for several years. She is not awkward."

Zeh picked a date and chewed it slowly, enjoying its sweetness. She looked at the two windows letting light stream into the room. "If we covered these would it be dark enough?"

Gibil stuffed reed mats and cushions in the openings. The room grew dim. They made a game of touching every item in the room without stumbling or knocking anything over. Laughing, they sat back down to finish their meal in the dark.

"That was too easy," Gibil laughed.

A guard opened the door and stepped back. "Why is it so dark?"

"We have covered the windows," Zeh explained. "The room was too warm."

"Ursag Mundu did not give orders for the windows to be covered." The guard remained in the doorway.

"Would you bring the next servant?" Gibil asked politely.

The guard grunted and left.

"He did not come into the room," Gibil noted. "Perhaps it is darker than we realize?"

Zeh jumped up and arranged some bowls by the door. When the guard returned, they asked the servant he brought to close his eyes until the door was shut behind him. They asked him to walk into the room. The man hesitated.

"I cannot see—it is too dark," he complained.

"Just a few steps," Gibil cajoled.

Zeh took a date and stood a little in front of the man. "I have a date sweet for you. Take it from my hand."

He would not. They gave him the date and sent him away.

"Could it be the abulillum and unumun have enabled us to see in the dark?" Zeh asked.

"I have never…" Gibil hesitated, then whispered, "When sheep wandered from the herd, my people would send the children to find them. I always found them—even at night." He inhaled sharply. "I was younger than most in the scavenging parties. They put me in the lead, scouting ahead. I had thought it was because I had not learned to use a spear, but it must have been my sight."

"You attacked at night?"

"Yes. In the dark, we could not be easily detected. The attack was a surprise. Afterwards, we would slip away into the dark and no one could easily follow us." He shook his head. "And you?"

Zeh thought. She never stumbled when she woke in the night and used the chamber pot in the washing room. "No. Not like that. I thought the others were careless in the dark."

Gibil nodded.

"We should tell Nam Eluti." Zeh knew he would be excited to learn something new about An-mašĝik. They would discuss how to test the new property, carry out the tests together, and add the results to the clay tablets.

Gibil grunted. "He is busy. Perhaps we should discuss this with Dakum first."

Zeh's stomach twisted. "We share all knowledge about An-mašĝik."

"Nam Eluti does not share everything with us. We are possessions to him, not partners—do you forget just this morning he had us cleaned like animals to be shown?" Gibil threw a date pit across the room. "We are his possessions, Zeh. He destroyed our home, too, don't forget."

Zeh touched her linen tunic. She had never had something so fine. The cleaning—women scrubbing her and oiling her—had been invasive. The hut, their home, burning. She had seen Nam Eluti stagger from the ceremony building, looking for something to destroy to please his brother. His eyes had passed the cow shed and landed on their hut, and he had decided in that moment.

"If we are wrong, he would be angered. We must not interrupt him in his work for the lugal," Gibil added.

"The servants will tell him we've darkened the room." Zeh offered token resistance.

"We'll do both the tunic and the darkened room. Like an experiment," Gibil said.

Zeh did not like withholding information from Eluti. But she enjoyed discussing the test with Gibil. Some of his ideas were so bad that they laughed, but others were good.

They tested Mundu's servants—even the women and children. Some stumbled into the bowls, a few were able to take the date from Zeh's hand, but none could differentiate the colors on Nam Eluti's robe.

# 24. Lugal [King]

Eluti walked with Mundu to the Lugal Daudu's palace. Their entourage included a full complement of warriors, Eluti's two slaves to help with the ceremony, and several of Mundu's servants carrying objects to be destroyed for the lugal.

The lugal's men met them at the gates and took them to the gardens where tall walls held carved scenes of Gilgamesh's story of the defeat of the giant Huwawa in relief. A flock of sparrows, disturbed by their arrival, flew past in a flutter of wings. The plants were more lush and varied than Eluti had ever seen: several varieties of date palms, flowers with strange and colorful blooms of red and yellow, and small shrubs the darkest of greens. The open area and paths were paved with white brick with a zigzag design. Mundu called him to his side for he had wandered into the green shade.

Several warriors in studded armor and helmets came into the garden and behind them Lugal Daudu, resplendent in a long red cloth tunic, a gold and lapis lazuli crown, gold and lapis lazuli earrings, and gold arm bands and rings. His dark curly beard fell squarely down his chest. Everyone bowed to him. The lugal bade

Mundu rise, and then he embraced him. They talked briefly, and Mundu brought Eluti forward and introduced him.

Eluti was nearly overwhelmed. He felt his legs weaken, but he stood firm.

"You have something special to show me, Eluti?" Lugal Daudu asked, his deep voice sounded clearly.

Eluti bowed, "Yes, my lugal."

Servants brought a cypress chair inlaid with lapis lazuli and gold. Lugal Daudu sat and motioned for them to proceed.

Eluti took the uzudirig. It seemed in his nervousness that the effects came upon him quickly. Mundu explained the ceremony and instructed the lugal on the need to avert his eyes the moment of destruction. Eluti calmed as the ceremony began. Much like the demonstration for Mundu, an item was shown, destroyed, and inspected: clay, fish in water, wheat, and dates. Instead of a pigeon, Mundu had him destroy a sheep. Instead of a house, Mundu had him destroy a chariot.

"One more item, brother, for our lugal?" Mundu asked.

Eluti nodded.

Mundu beckoned, and his nubanda, Nanar, brought forth a man bound at the wrists. "This man," Mundu explained, "has stolen from the lugal and is condemned to the underworld by our laws."

Lugal Daudu nodded.

Nanar took the man to the blackened chariot and tied him to the wheel.

"Kill him," Mundu commanded.

A cold sweat broke over Eluti. They had not discussed this. Mundu's stare was hard on him. He didn't dare look at the lugal. Kill the thief. He looked at him, tied.

"Quickly." Mundu's voice was like gravel.

Eluti looked to Mundu and saw not the gentle brother who held him when he was weak, but the warrior who ran into battle—who killed those who would attack their city and take their food and spoil their women—who brooked no dissent. Eluti swallowed. His ears filled with a high pitch. He felt the uzudirig ebbing. He turned his head, the beginning of refusal, and caught sight of Nanar, smirking at his fear. There was An-mašĝik just behind him. He pulled it to the chariot, to just in front of the chariot, to the man.

* * *

Mundu was proud of his brother. It had been a risk to ask for the kill. He nodded to Nanar to take charge while he talked to Lugal Daudu. The lugal was greatly impressed. He, like Mundu, saw the applications for war immediately.

"You have done well to bring this An-mašĝik to me," the lugal slapped Mundu on the back as they walked in the garden away from their men. "In the hands of warriors, it will bring many victories."

"My lugal, it can only be used by those with the gift of special sight. One must be able to see and control the An-mašĝik to bring it to the target. The gods have given the gift sparingly to men. We will have to train those warriors who have the sight how to use the An-mašĝik."

The lugal's brow creased. "How many with this sight do we have?" He fingered a waxy green myrtle leaf as they passed medicinal plants.

"My brother and three of his slaves—and possibly a fourth slave who is too young yet to train. Eluti tells me it has taken him years to find them. He has tested my entire household—none have the sight."

"We must find more with the sight. Has he tested them well? Or is he hoarding the power?

"His greatest desire is the power be used for the good of Adab and the gods we worship." Mundu responded in plain honesty. He chuckled. "He loves to investigate, research… you saw he could barely kill that thief."

The lugal laughed. "He is not a warrior, no. The others—will they kill?"

"We can train them, yes. But my lugal, they are slaves, some from other lands. We must find means to control them." Mundu inhaled deeply. They were in the herbal section of the garden now, and the fragrances were wonderful.

"Ah, yes." Lugal Daudu was quiet a moment. He pulled off a sprig of thyme and rolled it in his fingers. Its scent wafted up from his hand. "Does the ceremony achieve control?"

"Some," Mundu admitted.

"Breaking their spirit? Holding loved ones hostage?" The lugal moved on down the path.

"Would they kill us in anger as soon as they took the uzudirig?" Mundu asked.

The lugal thought a moment. "So, they must be content."

"My lugal?" Mundu asked.

"Feed and clothe them well. Give them spacious rooms. Allow them women—or a wife of choice." The lugal chuckled as they passed into the shade of fig trees. "Rewards for compliance."

Mundu nodded. He remembered the other items he must resolve. "My lugal, what of the supply of uzudirig and the priests?"

"I will take care of it," Lugal Daudu said. "I will talk to the High Priestess Siduri. We will have more demonstrations—for them and the ursags. They will need to know its abilities." The path turned again and brought them back to the open courtyard. "You may leave me now."

Mundu bowed.

"As soon as we show the ursags, we will test the warriors. There are more with this sight," Lugal Daudu's tone was firm.

***

"How many events have we been to?" Gibil asked Zeh from where they stood against the courtyard wall.

"How many people have we tested for the sight?" Zeh smiled. This was a game they played to alleviate boredom.

"How many… oh, they are ready to begin the ceremony." Gibil straightened and they headed to the front of the room to play their parts as gurums in the demonstration. This one was for the temple priests.

Nam Eluti brought the An-mašĝik to clay, wheat, dates, a pigeon, a goat doe, and a small cart that was to represent a chariot. The priests inspected the items before and after and conferred amongst themselves. They asked to see what Nam Eluti had eaten; Ursag Mundu said they could talk in detail later. En Siduri, the tall thin high priestess in blue linen robes wished to talk to Nam Eluti; Ursag Mundu said he was in a warrior mind set and was not to be disturbed until later. She asked about the ceremony; Ursag Mundu explained it as the passing of orders from an ursag to his nubanda and the specialist: the masmas.

"He asks our goddess for her favor," En Siduri noted. "This is the domain of the temple."

"We all ask the Most Powerful Inanna for her favor," Ursag Mundu replied. "Before battle and in the midst of it, from the lugal to the foot warriors—we all ask to succeed in her name."

"The herb this man uses… we believe it is ceremonial and forbidden to all except the high priestess," she said. The priests at her side nodded in agreement.

"Masmas Eluti uses several herbs. The lugal approves of his work and supports his methods." Ursag Mundu said blandly.

The high priestess was quiet as stone. She signaled her entourage and they left.

Zeh walked over to Gibil. "Another demonstration completed," Gibil said and yawned. "Just like the others."

"I am thankful they did not request Nam Eluti to kill another man." Zeh shivered as if a cold breeze from the underworld blew across the courtyard. It had been horrible, seeing that man die. Every time she saw revulsion on Nam Eluti's face, she remembered and her own stomach twisted.

"Killing…," Gibil started then stopped. He turned his head from her and drank the wine from his cup.

"The high priestess left quickly." Marat observed. "When we showed the ursags, they stayed and drank and talked."

"Yes," Gibil turned away from the gathering and lowered his voice, "this is not good."

"Why?"

"Ursag Mundu's answers to their questions has angered them. When warriors and priests fight, it is not good for the people."

"But why do they fight? We all serve the same gods." Zeh could not believe someone would argue with a priest—they were the eyes and ears of the gods.

Gibil laughed lightly. "It is not so simple, little sister. As long as there are men and things for men to possess, there will be fighting. My people attack Adab because you have food and we do not. Ursag Mundu, representing the lugal, and the high priestess argue over who should rightly control An-mašĝik."

Zeh thought about that. They could not control An-mašĝik; they didn't have the sight. "And that is us?" Zeh ventured.

Gibil nodded. "I will ask Šamaš to bring this information to Dakum. He returns to the estate almost every day."

"You trust Šamaš?" Zeh herself trusted Šamaš somewhat. If Gibil trusted him, then Šamaš could be trusted completely.

"Yes, he is family."

***

Eluti's stomach cramped and again he wretched into the clay pot. It had been several days and many demonstrations since the An-mašĝik touched the man tied to the chariot, yet every time Eluti closed his eyes he saw him, the moment before the strike staring back and the moment after, charred. The smell of burnt flesh filled Eluti's senses and he wretched again.

He wiped his mouth. Thankfully, Mundu had not asked him to do anything as horrible as that since the demonstration for Lugal Daudu. Now it was snakes, pigeons, and sometimes goats.

Eluti went to the table and drank some wine. He eyed the tunic laid out for him to wear to the celebration this afternoon: blue with some red, full length, made of fine linen. He fingered it; soft, fine quality indeed. There were random color variations in the material and thread, but they did not create hidden images. The wine was grape, not date. Very fine indeed. He called for a servant to help him dress.

They rode in chariots to the celebration. Mundu explained this was often done for military events. They could have ridden together, but again Mundu explained protocol. He was in the leading chariot with Eluti following and the servants behind them on foot. They arrived at Ursag Hammi's home in a grand procession. As Eluti stepped from the chariot, Šamaš and Zeh joined him, and they followed Mundu past guards and into the building.

Immediately Eluti was greeted by the ursags he'd come to know. They welcomed him heartily. He was greeted by land owners he knew and was introduced to a few more who had quite large estates. Several priests nodded their greeting. A small knot of doctors asked him if he was researching any new herbs.

Eluti parried several questions about his rise to prominence. The lugal and Mundu did not want word of An-mašĝik to spread among the general populace and possibly to other cities and their enemies. He looked for Zeh—she was not to speak one word of their work—and saw she stood amongst the servants by the musicians. He noted several gazes followed his, smirking. They thought he kept her close by as a concubine. He thought a moment. Countenancing that perception could put her at risk. It would be safer to keep her and Gibil under guard at Mundu's home.

* * *

The music reminded Zeh of the evenings on the rooftop of her father's home. She wondered if he was prospering. Her thoughts turned dark—had the money from her sale been enough, or had he sold any of her brothers to stay solvent? Šamaš came up to her and under the guise of adjusting her tunic gave her a date cake.

"They taste better than any I have ever eaten," he murmured.

She turned away from the crowd of doctors, warriors, and priests and quickly ate. Flavors filled her mouth and warmed her throat—they must have soaked the dates in wine. She licked her fingers. "It is very good," she agreed.

Šamaš nodded. "Many are quite interested in our Nam Eluti," he said. "His social status has risen. He attends more functions. He is granted favors by men of power. Some know why, some wonder."

"The priests?" Zeh asked. "Their eyes are hard and their skin is tinged red. It is not the flush of beer and wine."

"I think they are angered," he responded.

"Gibil thinks so also."

"Watch Nam Eluti and his brother. See how they maneuver among the guests so they are never alone with the priests. When they talk, they never speak of the ceremonies. You will see that no warrior does."

The song ended and the musicians rested on their mat.

A priest stopped in front of Šamaš and Zeh. "You are Nam Eluti's slaves?" he asked.

"Yes, my priest," Šamaš bowed his head as he answered. Zeh bowed as well.

"You were both in the demonstration with Nam Eluti." He moved nearer. "Can you remind me of the significance of your roles?"

"Only our master speaks of such things, En," Šamaš said.

The priest addressed Zeh, "I have heard you helped your master in his research on abulillum. What other plants have you researched?"

Zeh froze. She was not to talk about anything related to An-mašĝik, which definitely included the uzudirig which rightfully belonged to the temple. Her eyes darted to Šamaš. She did not know how to reply. A priest had never before spoken to her or looked at her other than as a worshiper in the crowds. Priests talked to the gods… to Inanna, who Nam Eluti had rescued her from in the underworld. Had Inanna told this priest to bring her back? "A-all pr-praise Inanna," she said and dropped to her knees, head bowed. "All praise Inanna, goddess of the sea above and the earth below, fiercest of warriors, righteous judge…" Zeh took a breath and heard the prayer continue around her. She joined her voice to the others in devotions as she had every morning and evening since she was born, every holy day since she could remember, and as an offering before work every day she had made kisibs with her father.

***

When the sun was taking away the night's darkness, they returned to Ursag Mundu's home. Nam Eluti and Ursag Mundu questioned Šamaš—did he know why the priest had suddenly started prayers to Inanna? Zeh swayed and pinched herself to stay awake. Nam Eluti asked her something, but she must have dozed. She looked at him blankly.

He slapped her cheek lightly. "Why did you start devotions to the goddess Inanna?" He held her chin so she must look into his eyes.

Zeh bit her inner cheek to wake up. "A priest has never talked to me before, Nam. I was afraid."

"You were afraid?"

"Yes, Nam."

Ursag Mundu's deep voice broke in, "Next time I have a pesky priest to deal with, I will remember that trick!" He laughed and slapped his brother on the back. "The whole celebration stops for impromptu devotions! The priest could hardly do anything else, with your girl leading everyone in prayers."

"You did well, Zeh." Nam Eluti's fingers curved along her jaw. He pulled her into a hug. Abruptly he released her. "Šamaš, take our devoted little pig to her pen."

# 25. Me [Battle]

The celebrations and functions continued, but Nam Eluti no longer took Zeh with him. Her days were spent practicing the ceremony, testing people for sight, and preparing new supplies of unumun, abulillum, and uzudirig for consumption.

The new moon came. The air cooled. The river shrank back from its banks. The sesame then lentils, chickpeas, and flax flowered their whites and purples, and their fruit grew. The fields greened. When they yellowed, the slaves sheaved, threshed, and winnowed the harvest. The noise in the streets grew as drivers yelled at their onagers to pull wagons full of bushel baskets and clay pots to the temple granaries. Children, their parents busy with the harvest, ran laughing and shouting in the streets, which made the dogs bark and run after them, which made the old men sitting in the shade and talking of earlier times yell at the hoodlums. Shopkeepers helped keep the streets clear—the produce, once received by the temple, would be counted by the scribes who would settle accounts—grain spilt meant waste, and waste meant someone would not get full payment.

Fall equinox came, and all of Adab celebrated. At Inanna's temple, the priests sacrificed aurochs: two bulls and several cows. The lesser temples sacrificed goats and doves. The people prayed and rejoiced their thankfulness for a bountiful harvest.

In the early light, shouts echoed in the deserted streets. Zeh tried to block her ears. There was so much noise in the city! She had grown accustomed to and preferred the quiet of the estate.

The door burst open and Šamaš ran to her. "Attack!" he yelled. "We're under attack. We must perform the ceremony!" He pulled her up off her pallet. He saw a pitcher and threw the water on her face.

"I'm awake!" she sputtered. "Let me get my tunic." She put it on and followed Šamaš through the house to the roof closest to the southern city wall, her chest pounding as loudly as her feet on the brick. Nam Eluti, yawning, was pulled in by two warriors. Everyone else was there.

Nubanda Nanar rushed them through the ceremony. Once Nam Eluti had taken the uzudirig and they had to wait for the effects, Nubanda Nanar explained that the army, while on watch for an attack from the mountain men, noticed estate fires to the south were extinguished when they should burn well into the day for the festivities. Scouts were sent and reported seeing warriors from Umma, the city to the south that worshipped Sara—Inanna's son who was a minor god of war. It was possible the people of Umma were making a pilgrimage to Adab to praise their god's mother, but it was perhaps more likely they were coming to establish their god as superior to his mother—to take her grain and temples and people for his own. The lugal of Adab was wise: he was sending the army out to greet the Umma warriors, and he was closing the city gates until he was sure of their intent.

The night's darkness began withdrawing to the west. From the rooftop, Zeh could see well past the city walls. Nubanda Nanar pointed out the armies. In the city below, Adab's chariots and foot warriors glided slowly like a snake through the streets outside the wall. On the shimmering plains to the south, Umma's army seemed unmoving, thick across the land like a wall of bricks. A layer broke free and moved forward.

"It is an attack!" Nubanda Nanar yelled at the same time horns began sounding throughout the city. He ordered everyone in the ceremony close to the roof's edge.

Everything became crisp in Zeh's sight, yet she felt disoriented. She had lived through attacks on the city before, but never had she seen the warriors fighting. She felt the urge to run to Inanna's temple and give devotions to make the goddess strong—and at the same time wanted to stay and watch and be a part of the goddess' will. Gibil pulled her to his side. She felt herself calm. She belonged here, with him, with Eluti and Dakum and Mundu's warriors.

Below them, as the snake of warriors cleared the city's surrounding buildings it split into smaller snakes—the ursags in their chariots spreading out across the plain with foot warriors running behind. At the same time, Umma's first line of chariots and warriors thinned and spread, as though it was a rope meaning to spread around Adab and then tighten its hold.

Nubanda Nanar pointed. "Destroy their chariots."

Zeh watched Nam Eluti take wisps of An-mašĝik down to the plain. He missed the first few, adjusted for their movement, and tried again. One, two, six, twelve, and more chariots flashed and crumpled. Through the dust and smoke, onagers emerged, still in their yokes, running without direction, dragging remnants of chariots behind them.

"Give Masmas Eluti more uzudirig," Nubanda Nanar ordered.

Zeh watched as one of the foot warriors pushed a date into Nam Eluti's mouth and he chewed. This was their most recent research: extending the effects of uzudirig in order for the masmas to perform more work. She smiled.

"Wait for the dust to clear," Nubanda Nanar directed.

Nam Eluti began to laugh hysterically. He pulled another An-mašĝik from the sky. Zeh would have gone to Nam Eluti, but the ennug kept her in place. She looked to Gibil. His head tilted briefly, unsure. Zeh looked back at Nam Eluti, and she moved the An-mašĝik away. "Nam…" she started.

He turned to her suddenly.

Gibil spoke out loudly. "The nubanda has said to wait, Masmas Eluti," he said in the commanding warning of the watchful gurum he played instead of the supplicating whine of the slave he was.

Nam Eluti whipped around to Gibil, his face changed from glee to rage. "How dare you! You insolent…"

Zeh turned to Nubanda Nanar. "Slap him! The uzudirig does not go well."

Nubanda Nanar looked at her blankly.

An-mašĝik began swirling about them, Nam Eluti pulling it towards Gibil, and Zeh and Gibil shunting it away. Zeh yelled at Nubanda Nanar, "He is mis-directed. Bring his mind back to task or he will kill us all in his anger!"

Nubanda Nanar finally went to Nam Eluti and slapped him. "Warrior, compose yourself!" he barked.

Nam Eluti's hand went to his cheek. Emotions crossed his face: anger to hurt to shock. He looked at Nubanda Nanar. "Why would you…"

"We are under attack. You must bring the An-mašĝik to our enemies. Come with me to see where to strike. The dust has settled enough to find another target." Nubanda Nanar's stern voice of command settled Nam Eluti. They turned back to view the armies. "There, the rear support. Bring the An-mašĝik to their wagons and animals—anything in the rear. See. They are like little clay warriors you and your brother played with as children. Bring the An-mašĝik to them—bake the toy people for Mundu."

Zeh quickly brought the An-mašĝik towards the target so Nam Eluti would not have to search for it in the confusion of warriors, dust, and the rising glare of the sun—or feelings. Sweating profusely, Nam Eluti took it to the target. Gibil copied Zeh's actions so there was always An-mašĝik near at hand. Nubanda Nanar remained near Nam Eluti, murmuring encouragement and suggesting new targets.

Finally, Nam Eluti slumped in exhaustion. Nubanda Nanar looked to Zeh and Gibil. "Shall we feed him another date?"

They both shook their heads. Zeh spoke, "His mind and body are exhausted. He would withdraw into the fantasies of his mind. He cannot do any more work this day."

Nubanda Nanar nodded. A smile flashed on his face. He turned around and surveyed the battlefield. He raised his arm and the warriors on the rooftop cheered. Zeh looked out. Chariots crossed the fields running down men and creating lines of dust as they moved. Men on foot everywhere were fighting. She did not know who was from Adab or from Umma. She looked back at Nam Eluti. He smiled at her like a lost child and clutched at her leg. She sank down next to him and rocked him slowly to ease his mind.

* * *

Eluti woke in the comfort of an embrace. He opened his eyes and saw it was Zeh. He frowned. Yells and shouts reached him, and he realized he was on Mundu's rooftop. He had been working with An-mašĝik. "Why am I not doing the work of the masmas?" he asked Zeh.

"Your work is done, Nam Eluti. Nubanda Nanar is greatly pleased with what you accomplished for it has helped Adab's warriors bring victory to Inanna," she explained.

"How long have I been recovering?" He winced at the pain in his head.

"The customary period," she said. "You were given a second date, perhaps too soon after the first, so you may still feel disoriented. Do you wish a light meal?"

He started to rise, and she helped him. "Bring me wine and a honey cake." He shooed her away. He took a steadying breath and walked slowly towards Nanar, his steps becoming firmer as he went. He did not wish to appear weak to the warriors—but Zeh had said his work with An-mašĝik was a success, and everyone understood the masmas needed to recover from the effects of the uzudirig. "How goes the battle?" he asked Nanar.

Nanar turned to him and smiled broadly. "We are decimating them! Come see!" He yelled to the other warriors, "Cheers for our masmas!"

The men turned and shouted cheers for Eluti. Pride filled him. An-mašĝik worked! Nanar described how his work with the An-mašĝik had weakened and scattered the attackers so Adab's warriors could kill and capture the stragglers at will. They stayed on the rooftop watching the warriors until after the sun peaked and the Adab warriors returned with prisoners and treasures for the lugal's review. Nanar took Eluti to join them in the lugal's courtyard.

Everyone in Adab was in the streets cheering. Eluti saw shopkeepers and scribes he knew waving and yelling their praise to the warriors—to him—passing by in chariots. Nanar waved and shouted back. He bumped against Eluti, and shouted into his ear, "Yell! Wave! You are a victorious warrior! Accept their praise!"

Eluti smiled broadly: he had been instrumental in the victory and deserved to be part of the celebration. He started yelling and waving back at the crowd. When they arrived at the lugal's courtyard, the noise was even louder. The warriors on the walls and those lined along the base were chanting as more warriors poured in, yelling in response. The lugal's chariot broke from the rest and stopped in the middle and the noise roared to a crescendo. Eluti knew he was yelling but could not hear his own voice. Lugal Daudu raised his sword to them, acknowledging their victory, and somehow it became louder still. The lugal lowered his sword and brought his hands together as in prayer, turned, and raised them to the figure of Inanna above his door. In an instant, the courtyard went quiet as night. The high priestess came through the doorway, bowed to the lugal, and led the warriors in prayers to Inanna, revered goddess of war, righteous judge, powerful influencer, and giver and taker of life. Servants brought food and drink, the onagers and chariots were taken to the stables, musicians and dancers began their entertainments, and the spoils of war were displayed and documented.

Nanar took Eluti to Mundu and gave an accounting of the masmas' work and everything else he had seen of the attack from the rooftop vantage. Mundu took them both to the lugal where they repeated the story. The lugal embraced Eluti and the deafening roar of the army filled the courtyard again.

"You have brought us a great weapon, Eluti," the lugal told him. "You will be well rewarded."

"May all I do always benefit Adab," Eluti said. The lugal took a step back and suddenly Eluti realized the lugal, Mundu, and nearly every warrior except Nanar and himself were covered in blood and sweat. The tang filled his nostrils and lungs. He felt his throat restrict and repressed his body's desire to retch.

* * *

The celebration continued through the night. In the morning, the warriors staggered home. Mundu called Nanar to his room to discuss the day's events as was his custom after every battle.

"Tell me, Nanar, did my brother perform as he did in the demonstrations?" He offered a cup of wine.

Nanar accepted the cup with a slight bow and took a sip. "Yes. There was one point, after we had given him the second date, when he and Gibil seemed to lock horns and the woman ordered me to intervene."

"That little mouse? Zeh? Ordered you?"

"There was desperation in her eyes. I don't like that I cannot see this An-mašĝik. I wouldn't believe it exists except for the damage it does."

"I dislike that disadvantage as well," Mundu agreed.

"I stepped in, ordered your brother about like a new foot warrior who doesn't know one end of a spear from the other."

Mundu laughed.

"With firm direction, he did well."

"No hesitation killing?"

"I think the distance helped. I told him the small figures in the distance were toys. In his altered state he might have believed it. With the first dose he took out chariots. When our men were too close for him to distinguish defender from attacker, I concentrated on their rear support. Their ranks broke quickly."

Mundu nodded. "How did the warriors in your squad comport themselves?"

"Like old women at first, bitching at being held out of battle and losing out on the glory and the rewards." Nanar chuckled and nearly spilled wine from his cup. "You should have seen when they realized the orders I was giving Eluti were actually being carried out on the battlefield! They turned into a cheering squad—men encouraging their best friend on his wedding night." He laughed again. "And when you returned, they ran among the men congratulating them on their great feats and claiming victory with them." He shook his head. "They will serve in this new squad without complaints. Your idea to use injured and old warriors was brilliant."

Mundu smiled. "Well, what else would we do with them? Tell me about Umma's style of attack."

"They came in square as a brick. At the front were chariots that broke off immediately to take the lead in the attack, much as we do. Eluti's work disrupted their attack early—I could not discern any strategy once he brought the An-mašĝik to their rear lines."

"Well, victory is the important thing. I could wish to learn more of our attackers." Mundu refilled their cups.

Nanar drank. "Do we not have survivors we can interrogate?"

Mundu rubbed his jaw. "Yes. The lugal has them. Send someone to see if we may participate in the interrogation. Perhaps with our elevated status with the An-mašĝik, the lugal will seek our company more." Mundu took another sip of wine. He had done well for his lugal. But the lugal was wary of his ursags, concerned they would rise up against him. A thought flickered through his head—while the An-mašĝik was an advantage to the lugal, would he also see it as a threat? "Are my brother and his slaves well-tended and guarded?"

"Yes, my ursag. The wine and food flows freely. Warriors guard the doors."

"I think my brother should take up residence here permanently. If he had been on his farm, the advantage of the An-mašĝik would not have as been as swift and decisive."

Nanar nodded in agreement.

"Send for those other two sighted slaves of his…"

"Dakum and Idin?"

"Yes. I want them all here, under my sight."

***

Gibil poured another cup of wine and brought it to Zeh. "Now taste this—it is wine made of grapes. It is much sweeter than the wine made of dates."

Zeh felt her head tip to the side. She had drunk more wine than ever in her life. She was more used to beer. She took the offered cup and sipped. It was smoother. She frowned. "You have been drinking this all night and only now let me taste it? After I am drunk on date wine?"

Gibil laughed. "Of course, little sister!" He stumbled on a rug. "I had to make sure it was safe for you to drink!"

They both laughed.

He wiped tears from his eyes. "You must learn to be more observant of things beside the An-mašĝik —but later after I have drunk all this grape wine."

Zeh laughed again, then suddenly turned somber. "Did you see Nam Eluti when he returned from the celebration? I heard he retched in his rooms, would not eat anything, and immediately started drinking."

Gibil plopped down next to her on the cushions. "I think our master does not kill easily."

"No?" Zeh thought he had killed many people easily.

"I have been in battles and fights. Some men revel in the carnage; most are disgusted by it—it sickens them until they have done it so much that they are hardened to it," he explained.

"I think I will be sick," Zeh said.

"Here," Gibil grabbed an empty carafe, "use this."

"No!" Zeh cackled. "I mean, when I am masmas and bring the An-mašĝik to men."

Gibil put the carafe down. "Yes, probably."

They both nodded.

"It goes easier if you remind yourself that you are doing this for your god," Gibil said and sipped his wine. "And if you think of them—the people you must kill—as demons, or something other than men you might share a meal with."

Zeh nodded. She looked at her fingers, playing with a cushion tassel. "I saw a house servant today who had been at my father's shop to buy a kisib when I was young. Now he works in Mundu's store house. He told me one of my brothers and my father's second wife died in the illness and that my father has taken another wife." A tear fell to her cheek. "He said my father does well."

Gibil pulled her into a hug and kissed her hair. "We are hostage to the will of the gods and powerful men." He whispered in her ear, "But do not despair, little sister, there is hope."

# 26. Idlurugu [River ordeal]

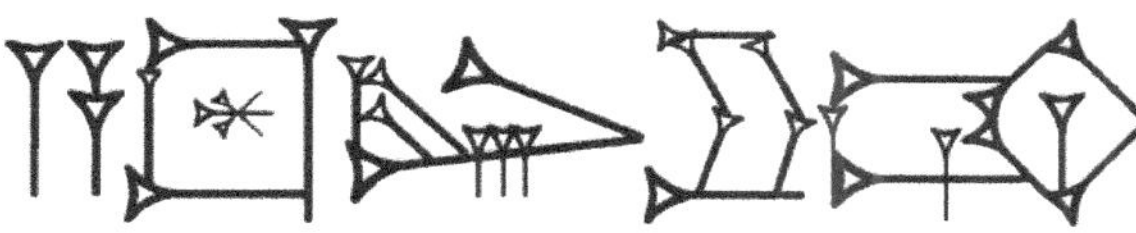

En Siduri stood, resplendent in blue linen, lion pelt robe, and copper headdress, in front of Inanna's blue temple high above Adab, watching the city's army overcome Kissura's attack a few days after Umma had attacked and lost. Kissura was craven; like vultures they waited for their prey to be weakened by others, and only then did they circle to feast.

En Pakum came up the stairs to her in his plain long blue priest linen tunic, his beard square on his chest. "High Priestess, is the Goddess Inanna with us today against the aggressors?"

"Yes. She is reprimanding the arrogant minor goddess and her followers." Lightning struck across the plain. It was odd how it moved horizontal to the ground and not from the sky as it should come. She looked about—there were no rain clouds in the sky or darkness of a sandstorm on the horizon. "The wrath of Inanna is distorted. This is the work of Eluti."

"I fear so, En."

They watched in silence as lightning took out most of Kissura's chariots. Siduri's thoughts wandered to the man beside her. He had entered into the service of Inanna a few years after her, but had mastered the rituals so quickly that he was nearly her equal. If this had been a temple to one of the male gods, their roles would undoubtedly be reversed.

"Have we learned any more about his means and methods?" she asked him.

"A great deal more, En. Our devoted worshipper in Ursag Mundu's home has brought us the information we need."

Siduri motioned for him to continue.

"They have a special vision, as you know, to see this essence Eluti has named An-mašĝik." She nodded and he continued, "They drink teas of abulillum and unumun to improve their vision. They talk of seeing the essence move about. They take the uzudirig to interact with it. Without the uzudirig, they can only watch the essence."

"Do we know how they came by the uzudirig and its use?"

"It was during the illness, En, when the city walls were closed. Traders from the east came. In a hurry to make their trades and continue on, they bartered with Eluti. My understanding is that they told him the box and contents were the sacred domain of the temple."

The lightning stopped. Siduri held her hand up, a sign for Pakum to be silent. She studied the battle. Kissura's warriors were in disarray. Adab's chariots crisscrossed the battlefield unimpeded. She nodded for Pakum to continue.

"Eluti is no fool. He would not trade for so dear an item he knew nothing of. The traders told him of some of its qualities. He purchased it and when the city walls opened, he brought the box to us and we repaid him. However, he kept a portion of the uzudirig for himself." Pakum took a breath. His voice lowered. "Eluti is a careful man. He researched uzudirig on servants before consuming it himself. I am told he did this with the abulillum as well. He would do well as an azu."

"It would have been better for him—and us—had he been an azu," Siduri said. She admired Pakum's ability to find devotees who were witness to crucial events. "Will our devotee come forward at the judgement?"

"If he does, we will no longer know what transpires in Ursag Mundu's home."

Siduri had learned from the previous high priestess that knowing the habits of the ursags was necessary for the temple's survival. She did not wish to lose insight, particularly into Mundu's home. He was a strong ursag, rising in power—a potential ally. She knew how much uzudirig was required to reach the state of mind she had seen Eluti in at the demonstration. It would have taken much more to learn of the states of mind, give demonstrations, and participate in battles… more than the amount missing from the trader's box. Eluti had gone to his brother Mundu, and Mundu had gone to Daudu. Lugal Daudu had acquired uzudirig for them.

Siduri pondered their acts of impiety. Stealing from the temple. Misuse of the sacred. She wondered that The Most Revered Goddess Inanna did not punish them for misappropriating her wrath. It was not likely she had not noticed—Eluti had given many demonstrations, and now he used it in a battle. Siduri took a deep breath and closed her eyes.

Inanna's thoughts entered Siduri's mind: power, victory. Strength from the goddess entered her, filling her lungs, expanding her chest, warming her core and limbs, flowing out of her nostrils. Siduri looked with Inanna's eyes out from the temple, across Adab, its fields and river, the fallow plains beyond. She heard the men and women talking, the dogs barking and cattle lowing, the insects chirping and buzzing, the wind brushing by.

Yes, these men had committed heresy—and Inanna had allowed it, but only to show to Siduri the power Inanna wished her high priestess to command. Reprimand the devotees harshly so others would not presume to steal from the goddess—and take the power, for Inanna's wrath as well as her love belonged in the temple.

Siduri lingered in the essence of Inanna. Below her, Adab defeated Kissura's warriors. She debated whether to reprimand the minor goddess and raze Kissura or show benevolence and send them grain. She considered motives. This goddess had thought Inanna was weak because her followers in Adab had the illness and had been attacked by Umma. The opportunistic upstart! She would send warriors and take away her little city.

She turned to Pakum and asked for a honey cake. The warriors would return soon and she would greet them—and ask them to make plans to avenge this assault. As she ate the sweetness, Inanna's thoughts and power ebbed from her. Pakum stood by her side. "Eluti's first wife is a devotee. Go to her now and invite her to an evening of prayer. She will wish to see the statue carved in her likeness that has been placed in the temple."

"Yes, En."

"Talk of rising impieties and how they anger our Goddess Inanna. This will bring out a confession. Steer her towards her husband's faults."

"Yes, En."

"We will have judgement in the morning at the river. See that our priests prepare."

"Yes, En."

"I will go now to praise our victorious warriors."

***

Aruru checked her pace. Again, she was walking too quickly. If she continued this way, the heat would pull moisture and odors from her body and overpower the perfumes she had applied. She called her handmaid, who did not have a quick step, to her side, and asked if she had the gift for the temple. She slowed to her pace.

"Yes Nin Aruru. Imgur carries the copper bowls with lapis lazuli stones," she responded.

Aruru glanced back. Imgur was conversing quietly with the young acolyte sent to invite them to the temple. "Is my hair in place?" she asked her handmaid.

"The jeweled pins still hold it, Nin. It is lovely."

"Am I not beautiful?"

"Nin is beautiful but wished to be modest on her visit to the temple."

Aruru nodded. She kept the girl talking and her pace moderated until they reached the river where a ferryman and coracle were quickly secured and they crossed peacefully. On the other side, she asked the young acolyte to lead them to the temple. She motioned for Imgur to come to her side. A lock of his hair was out of place; she smoothed it back.

At the temple, the acolyte introduced them to a priestess. Aruru presented the bowls which were received with proper reverence. It was not a gift as generous as her husband's, but it was appropriate for the occasion of being invited to the temple. She bade her handmaid remain in the lower level when the priestess asked them to ascend in prayer. Her voice and her son's joined the priestess' recital of a poem to Inanna's benevolence as they ascended the steps of the temple's black base. In the cool shade of the chamber at the top of the stairs, En Pakum greeted them.

"Nin Aruru, Nam Imgur, may the Goddess Inanna smile upon you."

"May we be worthy of her," Aruru and her son responded in unison.

"This is your second son that you bring to the temple?" En Pakum asked.

"Yes, En," Aruru's demeanor and voice became acquiescent. "The eldest oversees the estate. Imgur's interests and talents are more spiritual."

En Pakum nodded. "It is wise of a father to set his sons on their paths early."

Aruru felt her mouth tighten.

"As your son is spiritually minded, please allow our priestess to show him Inanna's temple and share a prayer with him while you and I visit, Nin?"

"That is most gracious of you, En." Aruru turned and motioned to Imgur to go with the priestess.

After they left, En Pakum said, "As we ascend each level, we must clear ourselves of impurities. Priests drink a special tea that lends the mind to insight. Would you share in this ritual with me?" He motioned to two beautiful silver cups on a pedestal.

Aruru's heart beat faster. She was being asked to participate in a sacred ritual and ascend to the higher level of the temple? "Yes… yes, of course." A smile came to her face. "I would be honored, En Pakum."

He recited a poem of the Gods, their power and knowledge, their creation of demons to perform the baser earthly tasks, the revolt of the ungrateful demons, and the subsequent creation of humans to fulfill the gods' needs.

He encouraged her to join him in the refrain after he had said it a few times. "The Gods created us. From nothing they created us. To serve them they created us. And we serve them. Inanna, to you we give all our effort, all our lives. We are yours, most righteous and powerful Inanna."

She joined in and they started to mount the red stairs. "I wake that I may serve you. I work that my efforts may increase your power. All that I am is yours."

He encouraged her efforts as they climbed. There were many stairs. They moved higher and higher.

En Pakum ended the prayer with: "All that is yours, Righteous Inanna, is most holy and to be held reverent. We come to you today with Nin Aruru, first wife of Nam Eluti, both who have given greatly to you through this temple. You rewarded them by sparing their family the illness, and they in turn have given more barley and wheat and minas than anyone else of their station. They are your most loyal devotees."

Aruru stumbled. Thoughts of Eluti and his work came to her mind.

While she struggled with her thoughts of impiety, the priest's prayers changed. He asked forgiveness and mercy of Inanna. He told her they were in a troubling time—for the high priestess she loved had been taken to the underworld in the illness, and now Adab's high priestess, En Siduri, as devoted as she is to Inanna, perhaps did not yet have the trust and ear of the goddess, the most wondrous Inanna.

Aruru felt lightheaded. The tea. The heights. The insight.

En Pakum stopped and turned to Aruru. "Now we must work to ensure the gods do not turn away from Adab in its time of need. The priestess was talking to the Goddess this day about enemies who attacked us. She saw your husband, Nam Eluti, working with the army. This was something new. His brother Mundu is a known warrior. Eluti is known for farming and researching medicinal plants. Now he is in the ranks of the army."

Aruru felt a chill rise up through the heat of her body. Her bond to her husband was sacred. He told her of his work and had asked for her help because of the trust they had between them. Her faith, though… was not the goddess who sanctified her marriage more sacred? She believed, as the priest said, their purpose was to serve the gods. Had she betrayed them in helping her husband? Yes. She knew this in her heart. But he had said he would bring his An-mašĝik to the temple. But he did not. He had taken it to his brother Mundu—and Mundu had taken it to the lugal Like children sent to the market to get sweets who ate them on the way home… Eluti was breaking his promise to her; he and Mundu and the lugal were breaking their promise to the gods.

"Sometimes people try things that are out of their area of expertise. The outcome may appear to be good, but in fact is not. Think of the man who unceasingly takes water from a low river to his garden—he will have a bountiful harvest with large seed pods, but his neighbors' harvests will wither and there will not be enough food for Adab," En Pakum said. He confided in her that their low supply of uzudirig was hampering the high priestess' ability to talk to the gods. And if she could not talk to the gods, then the gods listened to other people—like Adab's enemies. Even if it were right for Eluti to work with this thing he calls An-mašĝik, the war would perhaps never have occurred had the temple had the uzudirig to talk to the gods.

Tears came from Aruru's eyes. She had put her husband above the gods. A cry broke from her, and she confessed the theft of the uzudirig, the destruction of plants and men, and the creation of a ceremony for the gods by herself and her husband. She told En Pakum this An-maŝĝik didn't belong with farmers and traders, but with priests—but her husband would not listen, and what was she to do? There had been illness and she could not come to the temple for advice.

En Pakum calmed her. They prayed.

Aruru wept and castigated herself over and over.

"I will lead you back into Inanna's good graces," En Pakum said. "Stay here, in the temple, and cleanse yourself." He took her down the stairs. "I will talk to your husband. Where may I find him?"

"He stays at his brother's house." Bitterness filled her. He stayed distant from her and his family obligations to his wives and children. "He will be tired after using the An-maŝĝik in the war." Aruru thought of how different he was, like after physical intimacy, open to her, sharing. "He will be most approachable in his fatigue."

***

As the sun was leaving the sky, Inanna's temple warriors came to Eluti's estate. Word spread quickly among the slaves that the family was being collected in the main house and the priests were looking for subversive tablets and stolen herbs.

Dakum, working alongside Idin in the kitchen gardens spreading manure in preparation for the next crop, heard of the activities and went to the master slave. Quickly he explained what he thought was happening: there was a power struggle between the lugal and the temple, the temple would take Eluti's family to judgement and whether the family returned or a new family was given the land, the slaves would most probably remain to work the fields and orchards. But the power struggle was over Eluti's work, and everyone who participated in the ceremony was now caught between the wishes of the lugal and the temple. If the master slave would hide Dakum and Idin from the temple priests, Dakum would make sure his good deeds were made known to Ursag Mundu and the lugal.

The master slave hesitated. Dakum knew the special treatment Eluti gave the sighted slaves rankled him. "You could take your revenge upon us now, or you could win higher status—maybe even your freedom. I tell you the truth: there is something special in us who have the sight. Use that to your advantage."

The master slave hid them. His command among the field slaves held when the priests came looking, when family and house slaves said two sighted slaves were missing, and when the priests threatened them. Not a word was spoken of the man and the boy in the manure pile.

The priests finally left. They had found tablets on the use of uzudirig and the ceremony for An-mašĝik, a supply of uzudirig, and family members and house slaves willing to discuss Eluti's impiety.

* * *

The sun rose.

En Siduri stood by the river in her judgement vestments. Priests, priestesses, and acolytes stood to her side chanting quiet praise of Inanna's wisdom. En Pakum stood with Nin Aruru, her family and house slaves behind her.

The sand warmed.

A messenger in a temple tunic came running from Adab. He spoke briefly to a priest, who came to En Siduri and said, "Eluti is coming now. He has been told his wife is not well."

The sun chased shadows a hand's width. Eluti approached with Šamaš at his side and two temple guards in his wake.

En Siduri watched him come to Aruru. She raised the staff of judgment and the chanting stopped. "Eluti, you are brought to the river to be judged for heresy by Inanna, most righteous goddess, who walks in the sky and the underworld."

Eluti spoke to his wife who did not reply. The temple guards lowered spears between the husband and wife.

En Siduri raised her voice and repeated her pronouncement. Eluti remained focused on his wife. Siduri motioned for the gathering to kneel. Everyone went to their knees, even Aruru, but not Eluti. The motion was enough to break his focus on his wife. He turned slowly until he faced the only other standing person: En Siduri.

She spoke again. "Eluti, you are brought to the river to be judged for heresy by Inanna, most righteous goddess, who walks in the sky and the underworld."

"My wife is unwell," he said, not comprehending.

"You wife has told the Goddess Inanna of your theft of the uzudirig from her priests. She has told of the sacrilegious misuse of the uzudirig and the blasphemous creation of a ceremony calling upon the goddess. Do you acknowledge these discretions?"

Eluti turned back to his wife. "You…?" he questioned.

"Most righteous Inanna, I serve you," Aruru said, eyes fixed on En Siduri.

Eluti turned full circle, taking in the temple priests and guards, the crowd of people. "Send for Ursag Mundu," he commanded of En Siduri.

His presumptuous order did not surprise her; few people remained calm under judgement. "He will not come," Siduri told him.

"The lugal…" he started.

"You, a farmer, demand the high priestess of Inanna send for men?" Her voice carried across the crowd.

"Yes! I do," Eluti's voice raised. "They will come. My work is important."

"What you have done is sacrilege." Her voice was even, stern.

"You don't understand..." He turned back to Aruru. "Tell her, tell them..."

Aruru was still as stone.

Eluti turned back to Siduri. "You saw the demonstration," he pleaded. "Did you not see my work against Umma? And Kissura?"

"I saw a heretic usurping the wrath of Inanna."

"We were victorious."

"That is not relevant."

"It is! I can save us..." he raised his voice to the crowd.

Siduri motioned and a guard swept his spear against the backs of Eluti's legs, bringing him down. "You stand when others are kneeling before me, the High Priestess of Inanna. You call for great warriors and the lugal when we already have the all-knowing goddess Inanna among us. You tell us you, a farmer, can save us when you have no knowledge of the council of the gods or the impact of your misuse of Inanna's wrath."

Eluti tried to stand but was pressed down. "Please send for my brother... he will..."

"Silence, heretic!" Siduri felt the power of the goddess in her voice. When Eluti made to speak again, she motioned for him to be quieted and a guard struck him in the chest with the butt of his spear. "Bring forward the witnesses," Siduri commanded.

Aruru came forth and told how her husband had stolen the uzudirig and used it for his own benefit. His son Imgur told of the ceremony they created that called on Inanna. Servants told of his prayers to gods An, Enlil, and Enki—but not to Inanna. While they spoke, Eluti wept. They brought forth his clay tablets and he cried out and was silenced again.

Siduri had him raised to his knees. "What do you say to these charges?" she asked.

"Do not do this, En. Do not kill me and lose this great power," he said softly. "I admit my transgressions, but I swear all was done for the safety of Adab."

"You do not pray to Inanna. You did not come to the temple as you should have done. As you even promised your wife."

"An and his sons Enlil and Enki are the gods of my family and the city of Uruk where my parents lived and taught me to pray. Inanna is the granddaughter of the sons…" His voice grew hoarse. Tears streamed down his face. "I was afraid. My brother understands me; I went to him."

"You chose the wrong path."

"Please," he begged. He was sweating profusely. Sand stuck to his oiled body. But he saw in her eyes and stance that she would not be persuaded. He started to shout, and she had him gagged.

The judgement continued: she called on Inanna to judge this person who had wronged her but asked forgiveness, she had Eluti tied to Aruru, and they were put into the Buranum River.

***

Šamaš knew Eluti's fate. One could be absolved if one survived the river ordeal. Eluti did know how to swim—but to be gagged and bound to another… the high priestess had decided his fate before he was put in the water.

He wondered if Eluti had been submissive before her, the high priestess would have been more benevolent. Instead, he had enraged her. Šamaš watched as the priestess had his wives and children bound and put into the water and had the tablets broken into pieces. He scanned the household slaves and did not see Zeh, Gibil, Dakum, or Idin. Did the high priestess wish to punish Eluti's blood line and not those who participated in his sacrilege?

The priests and crowd ran down the river, documenting the distance those judged were able to swim. Eluti's family was fortunate the river was at its lowest and the current was slow. His two eldest sons and a daughter came out of the water after having swum an acceptable distance and came to shore on their own.

The survivors were brought back to the starting point, and En Siduri began the closing of the judgment when a thundering pack of onagers and warriors burst onto the riverbank. Ursag Mundu pulled his onager up in the clearing before En Siduri and jumped down.

"What is the fate of my brother, Eluti?" His breath came in huge gulps.

"Inanna has judged him guilty of heresy," En Siduri said calmly. She motioned to her right. "Inanna has judged these three of his seed free of guilt."

Rage built on Ursag Mundu's face. It turned red, with white where the muscles were most tense. His eyes bulged. He was about to speak when Nubanda Nanar stepped in front of him and bowed to En Siduri. "As uncle to the guiltless, Ursag Mundu asks for ownership of them. He ensures they will be raised to worship and follow the laws of the Most Righteous Inanna."

En Siduri contemplated the man bowing before her and the ursag barely able to check his rage behind him. She remembered that she may need him as an ally. "The second eldest son has shown interest in the priesthood. The daughter is needed as well. You may have the eldest son."

"And my brother's lands and slaves?" Ursag Mundu's words were like a growl.

"You may have the eldest son." She met his glower. She began to turn, stopped, and faced him again. "The Goddess Inanna has seen you defend her city and is proud of your fierceness. If you need slaves, you may take six field slaves."

Nubanda Nanar, still bowed before her, said, "We are most grateful. The Goddess Inanna is righteous and compassionate."

En Siduri lifted her hands, the priests and crowd moved into alignment, and they closed the ceremony with prayer. Ursag Mundu and his men participated. When it was done, Ursag Mundu and his men mounted their onagers and watched the people file back to Adab along the path.

"This man," Ursag Mundu pointed to Šamaš. "He was Eluti's slave. I know he would make a good warrior. I choose him as one of my six."

En Siduri allowed it.

A warrior pulled Šamaš into their ranks.

After everyone was gone, Ursag Mundu and Nubanda Nanar went to the river. They called Šamaš to them and had him recount the morning's incident. Ursag Mundu sent men to watch the riverbank and bring back his brother. He asked Šamaš about the sighted ones. Šamaš told them he had not seen them. They were perhaps at Ursag Mundu's, on Eluti's estate, or with the priests. Mundu nodded. Nubanda Nanar suggested Ursag Mundu go home, look for the sighted ones, and make preparations for his nephew and new slaves. He, Nanar, would go with Šamaš to Eluti's estate. This was agreed to.

They went quickly to the estate. The hesitant priests standing guard were persuaded with a few shekels that the warriors had the approval of the high priestess to six slaves even though they did not have a tablet indicating the transaction. The field slaves were gathered.

Šamaš walked behind Nubanda Nanar who was accompanied by a priest.

"Which is the master slave? I will need to know the skills of these people. Ursag Mundu does not need slaves to weed his garden!"

The master slave came forward. Šamaš gave him a slight nod. It was returned.

"I am Nubanda Nanar. I represent Ursag Mundu, who desires slaves who would make good warriors."

The master slave barked out names and men came forward. Nubanda Nanar looked to Šamaš, who shook his head. None was Dakum or Idin.

"These are all your men who would be good at killing? They have seen death and destruction and will not faint like women at the sight of blood? My master, Ursag Mundu, needs exceptional warriors or men with prized skills and he rewards them well."

"There are some others, but they are ill," the master slave said.

"Bring them here. Bring every man. I will conduct a review." Nubanda Nanar turned to the priests. "This may take the afternoon. Shall we bring the ones that meet our needs to you in the house?" The priests agreed and left for the comfort of the house.

The master slave stepped forward. "Nubanda, Dakum promised I would be rewarded for hiding him from the priests."

Nubanda Nanar nodded. "What do you ask for?"

"Freedom for my family." His voice was strong, his stance strong.

"How many are there?" Nubanda Nanar sighed.

"Nine. My wife and me. Two sons and a daughter. My sons' wives. Two grandchildren."

"Nine! And Dakum and Idin." Nubanda Nanar swore. "I am allowed five. You ask for much, master slave."

"The two you want are sighted. I know their value."

Nubanda Nanar kicked at the dirt. He turned to the main house and back to the men. "Gather your family. Bring Dakum and Idin. I will discuss this with the priests."

"Nubanda Nanar, I have a wife and daughter who are Eluti's house slaves," Šamaš, seeing kindness in the warrior, asked for his family.

"Thirteen! Gods!" Nubanda Nanar swore.

Šamaš watched the barter with the priests. Nubanda Nanar was sly with his words and generous with Ursag Mundu's shekels. The slaves gathered their belongings. Soon the warriors and slaves were standing outside the estate walls.

"We will return quickly to Ursag Mundu's home," Nubanda Nanar told them. "Take Šamaš, Dakum, and Idin as quickly as you can to Zeh and Gibil. The rest we will take to Ursag Mundu. A scribe will document Ursag Mundu giving this family freedom, and a barber will remove their marks as slaves."

# 27. Dud mu [Start a quarrel]

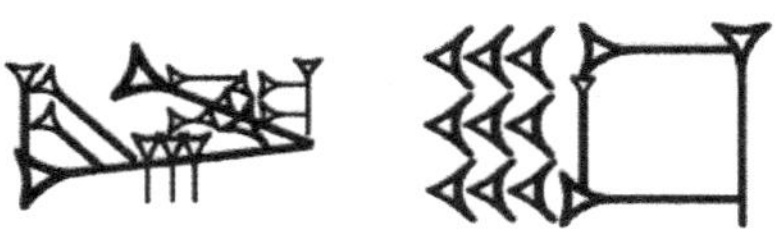

Mundu did not forget that the High Priestess had killed his brother. He told himself the political game was much like war: who was the enemy and who was the ally often changed depending on circumstance.

He had found out who in his household were loyal to the High Priestess. In doing so, he uncovered some loyal to the lugal as well as other ursags. It was unnerving that outsiders had influence over people he thought were loyal to him. He was a trainee in a deadly game. Working with his most trusted men—who he confirmed were loyal to him—he rectified the situation. Infiltrators in his household were noted and put in positions where information could be filtered to them more easily yet did not alert them to his knowledge of their true masters. As Nubanda Nanar said, they were not to be punished, but used—an advanced strategy in political skirmishes.

It took time, but he gained infiltrators in the homes of his enemies and allies. It cost him dearly, for two or three in each household were needed—unaware of each other's presence—so their stories could be corroborated and they watched each other, unawares.

He and his men trained with information. They determined something close to the truth—if not the truth itself but just unknown to others—in the ears of the infiltrators would be best.

Mundu slept with his second wife and told her his troubles: he wished to have more chariots but did not have the shekels to get them from the best chariot maker. Two days later Ursag Hammi, whose third wife was Mundu's second wife's sister, invited him over and discussed spears—and well-made chariots, of which he had several he would be willing to sell for a good price if he was assured a place in Mundu's next war party.

To test the temple infiltrators, Mundu's inner circle created conflicting stories. While inspecting his cattle, Mundu and Nanar debated in front of his master slave if a bull or two auroch cows would be best to gain Inanna's blessing in their upcoming exploits. Later, while practicing weaponry with the house guards, Mundu complained that somehow they had an excess of grape wine and did Nanar think it would garner Inanna's favor if they gave it to the temple? That evening his temple infiltrator told him the priests had mentioned his name while discussing their warehouse holdings. The next day at a celebratory dinner, a temple priest happened to mention in conversation with Mundu that the temple wine stores were low and the cattle pens were full.

And then there was the most powerful man who Mundu thought to be a friend but who had an infiltrator in Mundu's home: the lugal. It seemed disloyal, so he thought of it as a game of twenty squares amongst friends. When word reached them from their palace infiltrator that the lugal was going to ask Mundu to lead their forces in retribution on Kissura, Mundu brought his eldest son into their strategy meeting where they debated the merits of attacking the city. They agreed the ursag with a victory there would surely be the next lugal. But would the lugal allow such a possibility—or would he send his own army augmented by men from each ursag? Later, in confidence, Mundu told his son he hoped the lugal did not send him to Kissura alone. He could not say this in front of his men, but Mundu did not feel he was ready to become lugal—he was content to follow their current leader. In the lugal's next war meeting, he laid out his plans to attack Kissura: he would lead an army augmented with warriors from the ursags' ranks.

The political machinations reminded Mundu of An-mašĝik. The high priestess and the lugal thought it had ended with Eluti's death, and Mundu and his trusted men worked to maintain that false assumption. The sighted ones were confined in Mundu's home with instructions to never leave unless Mundu or Nanar was in the escort. They were not to discuss An-mašĝik outside themselves. They were put to work preparing the herbs they used and writing in new clay the knowledge that was on the tablets destroyed by the temple. The image of Eluti, dragged from the river, Aruru holding him tight, and he pushing away from her with his mouth gagged, filled Mundu's mind. He felt his eyes water and he swept the tears away. Eluti had been smart, but he had not been cunning. Mundu would not make that mistake.

***

En Siduri and En Pakum sat in the temple's inner sanctum and listened to their scribe read the last of Eluti's tablets.

"Eluti's documents provide great insight to the An-mašĝik," Pakum said.

Siduri nodded. She did not understand Eluti's obsession with colors. He had written tablet upon tablet of the colors of things and seeing colors better. Apparently, it was part of the training to see the filmy An-mašĝik —a sharpening of the mind, of perceptions. "He spent great effort on the subject of colors."

Pakum laughed. "The man was obsessed! In the dark of night is black not just black?"

"Yes," Siduri agreed, chuckling. She sobered. "I think we could introduce the teas—abulillum and unumun—into the daily diet of the acolytes, and once Eluti's tablets are proven true by the reaction of the acolytes, we will add the tea to the temple's meals for everyone."

Pakum nodded his agreement. "How shall we watch for the An-mašĝik? We cannot have the priests sitting on the temple stairs, drinking beer, and looking out vacantly at the sky!"

She smiled. "We must make sure each person receives only one cup of tea, for we cannot have them all sick or aroused either. Mundu may become suspicious that not all of his brother's tablets were destroyed if he hears priests are suffering the same symptoms his brother discovered of abulillum's properties."

Pakum nodded.

"Perhaps a new prayer to the Goddess in the sky realm? It could be said while walking the steps, stopping to take in the sky, its clouds, its colors—" Siduri nearly laughed at the word "—and the An-mašĝik as Inanna makes it known to us."

"Yes," Pakum agreed. "And this affords more exercise. Some of the priests are getting fat. It is not good that some huff and puff up the stairs during sacrifices while the people watch."

"Agreed. You will select someone to acquire the herbs, prepare them, and prepare the tea?"

"Yes, En."

Siduri thought a moment of the fat priests. There were many sacrifices to Inanna—birds, fish, goats, and pigs for weekly ceremonies, antelopes, aurochs, and even lions for special occasions. After the goddess consumed the essence of the animal, the priests distributed the earthly remains among themselves and a privileged few of the city's elite—who had of course given impressive devotions to be part of the ceremony. "And find some more merchants or farmers who would like to participate in the sacrifices. That will reduce the portions for the priests and increase our coffers as well as good will."

"Yes, En."

* * *

Zeh was almost happy. Dakum and Gibil were with her and they worked with herbs, named colors, played with An-mašĝik, and wrote about it in clay. Her belly was full. She had a soft bed. The house was well guarded. They gave small offerings to An, Enlil, Enki, and Inanna. But the memory of the last time she had seen Eluti haunted her. The servant had come and told Eluti that his first wife was injured. Zeh rose to go with him, but he pushed her away, saying, "No man brings a zeh to his beloved wife's sickbed," and he was gone. Every time she slept, she dreamed of Eluti's death. If she tried to save him, the crowd attacked her. If she did nothing, his family and servants pointed her out in the crowd and she was judged and thrown into the river—and when she sank below the water, she saw Eluti staring back at her, angry eyes bulging.

Dakum tried holding her in sleep, and she dreamed she was tied to Eluti—she clawed to get away from his livid stare as they sank into the dark cold.

Dakum or Gibil would shake her awake from her terrors, and she would pray to Inanna. Sometimes they would sit up and drink tea with her until she was able to sleep again. Usually she drank alone, playing with An-mašĝik, until the room's colors brightened with the rising sun.

Šamaš and his family were sent to work with the household servants. Before he left, he gave Zeh the kisib her father had made for her. "I found this in Nam Eluti's house before they took us. You are Marat, not an animal."

She ran across the room and rolled the kisib her father had carved for her across a piece of clay. Marat, devotee of Inanna, appeared with a sun over a river full of fish. She cried and embraced Šamaš. They found a length of leather and she tied the kisib around her neck. The tears continued as she smiled, joyful, to have her name and the memories of her father. Her feelings turned mournful and she sobbed as she thought of everything Eluti had taught her, how kind he was, how intelligent.

Dakum and Gibil expected her to lead their family in understanding, but she did not think she could—it was Eluti who had questioned his ability to see colors as others could not, Eluti who had found herbs to enhance their sight, Eluti who knew it was a gift from the gods. She was just a girl who had seen Eluti's blue robe and had been taught by him. She confided her worries to Gibil and he shook her: it was Marat who first moved An-mašĝik, it was Marat who discovered its destructive powers—Marat, not Eluti. She was not convinced, but realized she was perhaps the most able to continue as Eluti would have. She determined to try.

Idin was not sent away with Šamaš' family. He stayed, and Dakum taught Marat and Gibil to accept him as a brother. Marat found Idin wary, like Gibil, but quieter. Dakum told them Idin was troubled: he missed his father and his faith, but he would improve with their acceptance. As a family, they discussed night vision and agreed to keep the knowledge amongst themselves until it could be further studied. They would use Eluti's blue tunic to find others with the sight. Marat continued writing what was known of An-mašĝik on tablets for Ursag Mundu. Dakum and Gibil instructed Idin in processing unumun, abulillum, and uzudirig. Marat realized Gibil kept a store of uzudirig hidden behind a loose brick in the wall. When she questioned him, he told her, "You should do the same."

## 28. Halatuša [Apprentice]

The rains came to nourish the barley- and wheat-sown fields and to fill the Buranum River to its banks. Marat bled for the first time, and Šamaš' wife Zimu counseled her on womanhood. Ursag Mundu sent her a handmaid who never left her side. Marat grew weary of her new shadow and finally yelled at the girl for following her to the latrines.

The girl cried. "They will kill me if you lay with a man. You must not have a child."

Marat stared at her. "I must not have a child?" A weakness came to her knees. Eluti had forbade male contact, but she had thought it was because she was young. Now she was a woman. "Why?"

"Nubanda Nanar says you must not."

"Is it because I am a slave? Šamaš is a slave. He has a wife, children."

"I do not know, Marat. Only that they will kill me if you do."

Marat asked Dakum and Gibil if they could think why she would be refused children. "The gods have made me fertile—surely they want me to have a husband, and children, and lead them in devotions each day?" She wiped tears from her face. "Šamaš is a slave. He has a wife and children. Why is it forbidden to me?"

Gibil thought a moment. "Many women die in childbirth. You are valuable; they do not wish for you to die."

"A woman is made to provide children for her husband and the gods. How would we continue if women did not bear children?" Marat countered.

Gibil laughed at her. "I forget you believe so strongly!"

Dakum chided Gibil, "Do not aggravate your sister." He turned to Marat and held her. "It is a burden they ask you to bear for the sake of An-mašĝik," he whispered in her ear. "Nam Eluti forbade any man to touch you. He instructed us to protect you. His brother Mundu demands the same. You may never have a husband, Marat, but you will always have us."

Marat cried. She later asked Zimu if Gibil's statement of women dying was true. Zimu confirmed it, but she also spoke of women with husbands who did not have children and other ways to serve the gods. Still, Marat cried.

***

Ursag Mundu came one drizzly day, Nubanda Nanar beside him, to the rooms for the sighted. "Adab has seen peace since the attack from Kissura, but this will not last. I have told the lugal and the high priestess that my brother was the only one who could wield An-mašĝik." He stopped and looked at each one of them before coming to rest on Dakum. "But I know each of you can do this."

Before he could continue, Marat spoke. "That is not true, Ursag Mundu. We cannot use it as Nam Eluti did."

His eyebrows drew together as he regarded her. He addressed Dakum. "Is this true?"

"Marat used it once, upon a tree, Ursag Mundu. After that day, only Nam Eluti took the uzudirig," Dakum said.

Ursag Mundu paced in front of them. He came to a stop. "I need this power for my army." His voice rose. "I did not save you just to have you crush herbs and write some words upon clay."

Marat spoke again. "Ursag Mundu, we could wield it, as you say…" Gibil threw a coil of An-mašĝik around her—a signal for caution. She ignored it. "But we would need to practice, to learn to use the uzudirig before we could do this for you."

Gibil's shoulders slumped slightly. He released the An-mašĝik and turned his face from her. She did not understand his actions—surely, he didn't think they should hide everything they had learned with Eluti?

Nubanda Nanar stepped forward. "You did practice. We drilled on that ceremony."

"Yes, Nubanda Nanar, but always with Nam Eluti as the masmas," Dakum said, his voice soft. "None of us have used An-mašĝik to boil water or strike a chariot from a distance. We need to learn."

"Of course," Ursag Mundu said. "Of course." He started to pace again. He stopped. "This must be done in secrecy. The An-mašĝik is like lightning from the sky. How will you learn without every child and his dog knowing about it?"

"Nubanda Nanar could take us out on the plains where your army practices. We could work there." Dakum's suggestion broke the silence.

Ursag Mundu shook his head. "That is a good idea, but still you would be visible from Inanna's Temple. The high priestess must not know what we do."

They were silent a moment. Nubanda Nanar spoke. "Our guards go beyond the sight of the temple to watch for attack from the mountains. We have set up sentry posts. I will take them there to practice."

Gibil straightened.

"I do not like you so distant." Ursag Mundu frowned. "Your counsel is invaluable."

"Warad is trustworthy. Let me take him and train him in that role. With four who can wield and two who can command, we will have two groups that could be placed strategically in an attack. I will return with one unit and Warad will remain with the troops with the other."

When they were alone again, Marat tried to get Gibil to explain his actions. He refused, saying only, "Maybe some good will come of it."

In the dusk of evening in a light rain, the group was taken in chariots to the sentry post northeast of Adab. Marat clung to the chariot as it lurched over the plain. She was sure none of the warriors were sighted as they did not steer the onagers away from the stones and muddy ruts.

Nubanda Nanar had a tent set up for them. Marat remembered being with Nam Eluti when he traded for uzudirig and how enamored she been with the foreigner's tent. Gibil remembered also and teased her when the water dripped through the roof, the wind blew through the openings, and ants and fleas bit them: "Such fine living, to be in a tent!" She retorted that he was in a foul mood because there were no women for him to chase after, and he laughed in response. Idin sometimes smiled at their bantering. Dakum allowed it until he tired of it, and then he would give them tasks to fill their idle hands.

Nubanda Nanar's training filled most of their days. Hot with the sun beating down or wet with rain, they practiced the ceremony, marched with the warriors, and learned how to handle a spear and knife. Nubanda Nanar taught Warad, a thickly muscled warrior with a short beard, to instruct them and the guards—using criminals as examples—to kill the sighted ones quickly should they not obey.

The man standing next to Marat was disgusting. He stank and told her things he would do with her if he was not bound. The warrior behind them thrust his spear through the man and he fell quiet to the ground. Marat looked at her example. His red blood settled darkly into the sand. She wondered if Ereshkigal would use the spear hole to hang him on a hook in the underworld. A convulsion took over her body and she wretched, her meal of flat bread and goat stew spilled onto the sand. Nubanda Nanar yelled at her to remain in her place. The warrior next to her nudged her with his spear. She wiped her mouth with the back of the hand, shakily straightened, and stepped back into place.

She looked up and saw dead men at Gibil's feet, and Dakum's, and Idin's.

Gibil stood calmly. He nodded at her. Dakum stared ahead, his watery gaze unseeing, his skin pale. Idin trembled in place, tears running down his face.

The dead were removed. New criminals were set at their sides, and this time they were killed as they all walked. And again, as they crouched. And again, as they ran. Nubanda Nanar called for a change: each sighted one called out to have the other killed, as they would do when they were gurum and the masmas did not obey orders. Gibil called her name, and the man at Marat's side died. She called Dakum's name and the man at his side died. Dakum called out Idin. Idin called out Gibil. They stood in a circle of blood.

That night they sat in their tent not able to eat or sleep. Dakum said, "Red like blood fresh. Red like blood dried." Everyone nodded.

Marat spoke. "The skin living color. The skin as the person dies. And when they have gone to the underworld. It is different for each color of skin, but each has these variations."

"Ereshkigal will be pleased with our work today. She will not take us if we send her men." Idin's voice was oddly dispassionate.

Dakum pulled the boy into an embrace. "No one will take a sighted one. We are too valuable."

"They took Nam Eluti," the boy said, his voice muffled in Dakum's sheepskin skirt.

"Eluti was not of our family. Our family protects each member. Did I not hide you when the temple warriors came? And take you with me to Ursag Mundu's home where we are well cared for?"

"Yes, Father Dakum, but today they scared me."

"They scared all of us today." Dakum looked at Gibil and Marat and inclined his head, asking them to share.

"You saw my fear," Marat said. "I could not contain my meal. I stepped out of place."

"I felt fear," Gibil said, "as they intended. This was intimidation. They wish us to learn to obey orders. As long as we do as we are told, we will not be harmed." He ate a date and paused. "Do not think of them as men—they are animals like a fish or a snake."

They discussed this and other observations into the night.

The ennug training was repeated the next day. When Nubanda Nanar was sure they understood the consequences of disobeying an order, practice with uzudirig started.

Marat was masmas first. As the uzudirig filled her, she started to drift—but Nubanda Nanar was there commanding her. She brought the An-mašĝik to the items before her: the water boiled and the fish died, wheat and dates were charred, the clay baked and cracked. She tired but continued bringing An-mašĝik to each thing Nubanda Nanar brought her until Dakum saw she was trembling with fatigue and called a stop to practice. As she rested, Gibil took his turn as masmas. When he tired, they ate a small meal and marched with the warriors. When they returned, Dakum was masmas. When it was Idin's turn, they had him find and manipulate the An-mašĝik —he was not proficient enough yet to take uzudirig. Dakum worried he was too young for such violence.

Each day Nubanda Nanar found different things for them to destroy. He began to put the items further away. When he saw they could destroy a target without harming things around it, he put warriors around their targets so they learned precision. He put the targets on moving chariots, or drug behind a warrior, or carried between warriors. The three sighted ones learned quickly and their endurance grew.

Nubanda Nanar introduced a new target. A pile of rags in the distance. Marat easily brought An-mašĝik to it. A similar target was moved closer, and it was even easier to strike. Marat wondered at this reversal of difficulty. The target was moved closer again and she saw it was a man covered in many sheep skins. He moved. A cold entered her and she felt ill. She had killed two men. Nubanda Nanar had done this purposefully—had her kill unknowing. She thought of Nam Eluti and the first man he'd killed for the lugal. Marat had asked Gibil how it would be to kill. Now she knew.

Warad commanded her to strike.

Marat stared at the man on the dirt before her. Her breath came heavy. She felt a spear point at her back.

"Strike!" Warad commanded.

Fearful, she pulled the closest An-mašĝik to the sheep skins and it jumped at the shock of connection and smoldered.

Warad ordered the man cleared and another placed closer. "Strike!"

The man in rags lifted his head and looked directly into her eyes. Bile rose in Marat's throat. She fell to her knees and wretched.

"Strike!"

A spear rested on her back.

She looked up, found An-mašĝik, and brought it to the man.

"When you told Ursag Mundu we could be taught to wield An-mašĝik, this is what I feared," Gibil told Marat as they walked back to their tent.

"I did not think…," she started. "I only thought of Nam Eluti's work going to waste… All he did, all he sacrificed for it." Her steps slowed, and she stopped.

Gibil put an arm around her. "I understand." He kissed the top of her head. "This path was inevitable. I wish it was not. I am sorry I blamed you."

She leaned into him. "I am sorry, too."

That night, sleepless again, they talked of killing, of the smell of sheep skin burning, wood burning, flesh burning. Gibil assured them killing men was the hardest to learn to endure. But he was wrong. The next day the targets were women. The day after, they were children.

# 29. Lulul [Liar, one who is false]

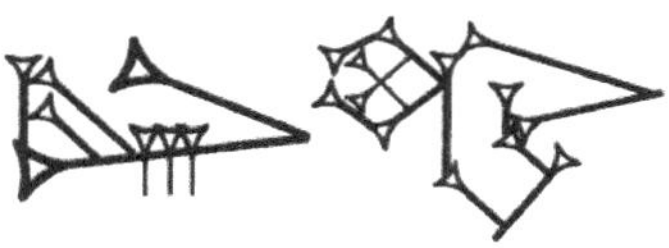

*Marat age 14.*

The rains had stopped. The days were cool and the nights cold. Idin had finally begun to see all the colors and could move An-mašĝik with agility. Warad said it was time to train Idin as masmas. Dakum felt he was too young at six, and Marat agreed; their concerns were not considered.

A servant brought the hot water and Gibil made the uzudirig tea. Marat explained to Idin the sensations the plant brought to her. Dakum and Gibil added their experiences. They explained the tying was necessary, that they all endured this for safety.

After the tea had steeped sufficiently, Marat gave Idin a small portion and he drank it without hesitation. They tied him to a chair. He told them he had no sensations, so Marat gave him a few more sips of tea. Eluti and she had consumed approximately the same amount, but Gibil and Dakum required more—perhaps this was true of Idin as well, she thought. They waited for drug to take effect. Again, Idin told them he felt no change. Marat was about to give him more tea when Idin brought An-mašĝik to the warrior guarding them and struck him dead. Gibil and Dakum immediately began moving An-mašĝik away from Idin, but there was much and it proved difficult. The boy alternately cursed them and prayed to Ereshkigal—asking her to free him of the ties so he might bring her more dead. At one point he pulled a wisp of An-mašĝik to Marat's thigh. She screamed in pain and jerked back away from its touch. She slapped the boy, breaking his concentration, and then Dakum put his hands over Idin's eyes so he could no longer see the An-mašĝik to move it. Idin bit at Dakum, cursing. Gibil pulled the helmet from the dead man and put it over Idin's head backwards. Idin tried to throw it off. They tied him more securely.

Dakum went to Marat and pulled the sheepskin skirt up and looked at her injury. She cried out at his touch and cursed Idin. "If I'd had any uzudirig, you'd be dead, boy!" She clenched her teeth as the pain pulsed in her leg and hip. Definitely, she thought, she should have her own uzudirig as Gibil did. Her body spasmed in pain again. "Ahggrrr," she cried out. She swore to herself she would pay close attention to every movement the masmas made and limit his access to An-mašĝik.

Dakum called to Gibil. There was no blood or bone visible, only a red fern of raised skin unfurling from the point of contact. Dakum touched a tendril and Marat shrieked.

When Warad learned of the incident, he sent for Mundu's azu, who gave Marat herbs for her pain and poultices for the blisters that flowered across her thigh. Warad and Nubanda Nanar discussed Idin's punishment for killing a good warrior and injuring a sighted one—normally it would be death, but Idin was sighted. In the end, they caned him.

In the days after, Marat felt pain even as the blisters healed and the fern faded to white against her brown skin. The family found it difficult to make Idin understand he must follow their instruction. He only wanted to kill others for his goddess or be killed himself so he could meet Ereshkigal. It was Gibil, finally, who got through to him. He explained that the gods had given them a great power and they expected great things to be done with it. If Idin went to the underworld with such a paltry devotion—one or two lives—

surely Ereshkigal would punish him. But if he would learn their ways, he would become part of the army and kill many, many men and when he went to the underworld the gate keepers would kneel before him and Ereshkigal would embrace him.

Gibil recounted that Nam Eluti had been in one war and had killed almost sixty men for the glory of Inanna. Did Idin wish to meet Ereshkigal with only one body for her? Surely she would be angry if he did not at least bring her more bodies than her sister had received?

Idin agreed.

Gibil took over his teaching. Marat was the best teacher, but she refused—and Idin did not respect her capabilities Dakum was too lenient.

Idin was a quick, impatient student. He could move An-mašĝik, but his focus was intense, not relaxed, so his movements were jerky. He was reluctant to perform tasks not directly related to An-mašĝik, such as marching with the warriors, which impacted his endurance and, from that, the length of time he could work An-mašĝik under the influence of uzudirig.

Marat did not push to make Idin obey. Not because he was a child—Dakum's excuse for the boy—but because she feared him. If anyone was truly Ereshkigal's devotee, it was Idin: his eyes were as cold as the underworld and his skin as pale as the sickly things that lived there. He did not care about the people he killed—or even the people he did not; they were all a sacrifice he would give to his goddess now or eventually.

Marat shared her concerns with Gibil. He laughed and told her Idin was a natural warrior with no fear of death; however, she did notice he only taught Idin basic technique and was on his guard when Idin practiced. And Gibil kept scrupulous control of the supply of uzudirig.

The distant brown fields turned green with barley and wheat shoots. Ursag Mundu came to judge their progress. After the demonstration, he conferred with Nubanda Nanar and Warad. That evening they feasted on roasted goats and pigs. Great vats of beer were provided and everyone drank freely. Ursag Mundu announced Warad was now Nubanda, and presented him with a necklace of shekels. He commended both Nubanda Nanar and Nubanda Warad on their work with the warriors and decorated them with ivory earrings. The sighted ones he praised and gave them necklaces of carnelian. Marat did not think Idin should receive any reward, but did not complain to anyone. The warriors were given copper arm bands and shekels.

The sun set with laughter, music, and dancing. In the morning, Ursag Mundu took Nubanda Nanar, Gibil, and Marat back to Adab.

# 30. Kadra [Gift, bribe]

Marat missed Dakum but enjoyed the comforts of Adab. While in either Adab or the sentry post, the grain came from storage and needed to be sifted of meal worms and mouse droppings, the dinners were more varied in the city. In the country with the warriors they had the same beer, flat bread, and goat stew with onions and garlic every day. Now, she and Gibil sometimes had fish, sometimes duck, sometimes goat or pig or auroch, and date wine or beer.

Ursag Mundu had also given them more rooms in his household—one sleeping chamber each for her and for Gibil with thick straw pallets scented with sweet grass and covered with soft gazelle hides, and the main shared room they had before in which they prepared herbs and wrote on the clay tablets.

Their protector's azu was fascinated by Marat's scar. When the pain came, she limped. The azu determined it was minor demon tormenting her who could be banished with more sacrifices to Inanna. Marat complied, and the pain faded.

Marat and Gibil studied her scar and discussed the size of An-mašĝik that had caused it, the pain upon contact, and the lingering aches. They experimented teasing out smaller and smaller strands of An-mašĝik until they had refined it to threads, and then threads shorter than a hand's length—a scrap.

One day on a march with the warriors, they passed a weaver's shop and the large piles of fleece reminded them of An-mašĝik. They went back, accompanied by their personal guards, and spent a day watching the workers card the sheep's wool into alignment and rove it into long fine strands that was then spun to become yarn and the yarn woven into cloth. They went home and applied some of the weaver's techniques to the An-mašĝik.

Threads from different sources could be combined like roving. Roving could be twisted to become denser and thinner strands. Weaving was not possible—when the strands were brought together, it assumed its original fleece form. And, whenever their attention left the An-mašĝik, it returned it its natural state and path.

The application in battle, they thought, would be more efficient use of the An-mašĝik. The gurums could find the An-mašĝik and rove it into a continuous thread, ready for the masmas to use. Manipulating the An-mašĝik was not wearing; so it would give the gurums more to do and save on the masmas' energy. It would also be a source of control: if the masmas used only the thread provided by the gurums, it would be easier for them to remove it if the masmas did not follow orders.

On days when the An-mašĝik was not plentiful, the gurums could find it, ready it, and bring it to the masmas for use.

Next, they began researching how powerful each amount of An-mašĝik was using Gibil's hidden store of uzudirig. Obviously, a smaller thread of An-mašĝik would do less damage than a complete fleece. They had worked with large pieces at the sentry post. Here, in the city where secrecy was essential, they worked with scraps.

They touched a scrap to a handful of hair they had gotten from a barber. There was a small pop like wet wood in fire, and the hair became fine ash on the floor. With reeds, they discovered the amount and state of material changed the outcome: older grey reeds and those broken into strips were destroyed more easily by a scrap of An-mašĝik than a whole green reed. Wet clay baked; a baked brick cracked. Dry sticks of wood were destroyed; green logs were singed. Water in a cup evaporated, in a bowl boiled, in a pitcher warmed. Food burned, but if you put it on bricks and warmed the bricks—you could bake.

Copper, silver, and bronze warmed easily. If touched with many scraps, it heated and could be bent and shaped; if touched with too many, it became brittle. They did not have gold but decided it would react similarly.

"We know enough to share our discoveries with Ursag Mundu," Marat declared once they had exhausted their supply of uzudirig and things to experiment on.

"There is no need to tell him."

"He is our master. He has provided a roof over our heads and food to eat," Marat reasoned.

Gibil shook his head. "We are slaves. He treats us as he must. This we discovered on our own—with my uzudirig."

"A nice roof. Large rooms. Good food." Marat said. "Uzudirig you stole from him."

"He would not be impressed by these findings," Gibil countered. "He only cares about what will kill an enemy."

"If he is pleased, we will convince him to give us more uzudirig... more materials to work with... It will be a furthering of his brother's work."

Gibil was silent.

"It does not matter if he does not care about our discoveries. We care. We can use it." Marat pushed.

"Oh, yes. It would be so useful. He would assign us to the kitchens to boil pots of water." Gibil mocked her.

Marat stood up and walked away. She tried to think of a way to make him understand. When Nam Eluti found a new plant, he wanted to know everything about it. Was it edible? In what ways? What parts of the plant? Was it medicinal? For what ailments? In what quantities? Was it harmful? Could any ill produced be reversed? Gibil did not care that way.

Behind her, Gibil started humming. It was the song the Gutis sang to their children to quiet them. He did this when they argued. She stomped her foot. She would not be placated like a child. She turned and marched back to him, feet slapping the clay floor.

He looked up at her, humming still. He smiled.

Marat turned away again. She took a step towards the wall and stopped, staring at the wall. The battle of Umma stood before her. Ursag Mundu had artists paint it after the victory. The colors were bright, but not varied. The words told of Lugal Daudu's devotion to the Goddess Inanna, her approval through the granting of the victory, and the riches they gained in slaves, chariots, and shekels.

"Is there any figure on the wall boiling water?" Gibil's voice taunted her.

Marat clenched her skirt and jerked it down. "Are there any figures on the walls in Guti?"

He hissed. "You know nothing of my people."

"Do they eat their meat raw? Bathe in cold rivers? Live in caves? Are they animals?" she taunted him.

A clay cup zinged past her ear and broke against the mural. The shards clattered to the floor. The beer bled down the wall.

Marat bent her head. Dakum was not here to yell at them for fighting and to make them apologize to each other.

"They are people." Gibil's voice was soft by her ear. He touched her shoulder. "I have been rude, little sister. Forgive me."

She pulled his hand to her mouth and kissed it. "I forgive you, brother. Please forgive me."

He hugged her and slowly rocked them. The rocking became more exaggerated, and they laughed as they nearly lost their balance and separated before falling.

Marat pushed her braid to her back. "Brother. I wish to learn everything An-mašĝik can do. Does it boil, does it burn, does it… what? I need to learn—whether Ursag Mundu cares or not. I hope he cares so he will give me uzudirig so I may continue."

"He will care for what brings him victory in battles."

"Maybe he will wish warm water to remove the grime and blood from his face before he kneels before the lugal and high priestess."

Gibil laughed. "You are much like Nam Eluti."

"Yes." She smiled.

Together they went to Nubanda Nanar and requested uzudirig. He refused. They told him they found a way to use it undetected in the city and reminded him warriors must continue to train even when an attack is not imminent. He said he would speak to Ursag Mundu.

* * *

During council with Ursag Mundu, Nubanda Warad reported Dakum and Idin were improving their endurance with uzudirig and becoming proficient with spears. Nubanda Nanar brought the request for more uzudirig for Gibil and Marat, with the information they had learned a refinement that would enable them to practice undetected in the city. He indicated they also were not drilled with the warriors and therefore they would not be able to perform as well as the other pair in battle.

"I do not like this An-mašĝik. I do not like what I cannot see and feel," Warad complained.

Nanar nodded. "It is worse than training warriors a technique you yourself are not proficient at. You have to rely on others. In this case, we have to rely on slaves to train each other."

"Yes," Mundu agreed. He could not remember an instance when Nanar was not a master of all aspects of war. Mundu shook his head. "An-mašĝik is sharper than a sword with a longer range than an arrow."

"It is a dangerous situation," Nanar said.

"Yes, but the rewards are great," Mundu said. "Lugal Daudu suggested rewarding good behavior with trinkets and comforts."

Nanar thought a moment. "It is like training a feral animal. It will respond to easy food and other comforts—but if you beat it, you will most likely be bitten."

Warad nodded.

Mundu agreed to provide Nanar uzudirig as soon as his pair provided a demonstration to Mundu showing their refinement. He ordered an immediate change to their schedule so they would march and practice weapons daily.

Mundu was wary about the demonstration. If this refinement did not work, the spies in the city would quickly learn he was using An-mašĝik. He decided he needed to review his troops at the outpost, and took Nanar, Gibil, and Marat with him. There, away from the duplicitous eyes in the city, Gibil and Marat showed their discoveries. It was as they said. Mundu demanded this new knowledge was shared with Warad, Dakum, and Idin. While Marat and Gibil taught Dakum and Idin the use of An-mašĝik fleece, thread, and scrap, Mundu and his nubandas worked on uzudirig dispensation rules.

After a few days on the plains, Mundu tired of the blowing sand. Before returning to Adab, he held a small feast. He rewarded his warriors with beer and trinkets. He gave praise, shekels, and the promise of more access to uzudirig to Marat and Gibil for their discoveries. Marat gave half of her coins to Dakum, ignoring Idin's cold stare. Gibil gave the boy a few coins and teased him about gathering enough for a wife.

***

Marat and Gibil brought everything they knew of—reeds, sand, dirt, stones, hides and cloth, plants—into contact with An-mašĝik scraps in their training sessions. Each day, they secreted away a pinch of uzudirig for their own stores.

The barley and wheat harvest came, and also the floods. On the feast day, Ursag Mundu held a great party. There was beer and roast pig and wheat bread and figs for everyone. In the large hall the ursag sat at the head table with his nubandas. Musicians played harps and drums, and women danced. The kitchen servants replenished the platters of food and cups of beer as soon as they were emptied.

Ursag Mundu bellowed. The musicians and dancers stopped. The warriors put their cups down. "My special warriors," he said and commanded the two sighted units to the middle of the room. Everyone stomped their feet as they wound their way there. "You have done well and I reward you!"

Servants came to them and put copper bands on their arms and earrings on their ears. Šamaš led a line of women into the open space.

"Choose a servant, and she is yours. May she make your days go easier as you have eased my days." Ursag Mundu a cup to them and drank. Again, the warriors stomped their approval.

Marat stood uncertain. The warriors moved to the women and quickly selected among them. Gibil waited, selected a woman and brought her back to his place by Marat. "Go choose," he told her. There were several left.

"How do I choose?" she whispered.

"Someone who is pleasing to your eye and does not have a sharp tongue." He laughed.

"I have never…" She started.

Gibil leaned into her and whispered, "You must. Not to choose would be an insult to Ursag Mundu."

Marat went to the remaining women. She immediately discounted the older ones—they would order her around. The younger ones she discounted also: she did not want to raise a child as she had her brothers. That left two. One stood beautiful and defiant, the other with her head bowed. Marat asked the second one, a thin light-skinned girl, her name. "Whatever you wish, Nin." Marat chose Tuda, as she found she was called.

# 31. Adamin [Contest, dispute, debate]

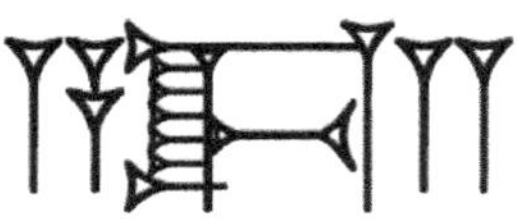

*Marat age 15.*

Adab was alive with festivities. They had suffered floods that overran the irrigation canals and heat that baked its way through the thick walls of their homes. But now the air turned cooler, and they harvested the crops that had survived: dates, lentils, peas, chickpeas, bitter vetch, flax, and sesame.

Mundu tuned out the noise in the streets as he listened to the reports of his nubandas. Their infiltrators' stories brought some amusement—the priests in the temple were drinking abulillum tea so they could see An-mašĝik, but all they were getting were wet bowel movements and erections, which resulted in hilarious couplings—and the stories brought some concern: a young ursag rising from the ranks of warriors was questioning Mundu's loyalty to the lugal. It had to be the machinations of the temple, Mundu and his men thought, but there was no word from their infiltrators confirming the theory. Still, something would have to be done about this Ursag Bulalum.

Mundu went to Ursag Hammi for advice. Much as expected, Hammi was not subtle: he suggested a bribe. Instead of following that strategy, in the next lugal's council meeting Mundu suggested a tour of their sentry posts. Their warriors' spirits would be improved with a visit from the lugal and ursags, and it was festival time after all. The lugal declined to go, but agreed to send his son in his place with a temple representative, En Pakum, to bless the festivities and lead them in prayers. Every ursag was represented either in person or with a nubanda. Bulalum went with six of his men.

The ursags sent riders out to their sentry posts to announce the festivities and order their men to ready the camps for visitors. Mundu's man had an additional order that An-mašĝik should not be discussed or used during the event. Dakum and Idin were to be assigned to the kitchen for the duration.

After the last harvest feast in Adab, the entourage set out for the first sentry post due south of the city. They brought with them musicians, dancers, singers, cattle for sacrificing, bushels of fresh produce, and beer for the men. Upon arrival at the post, they inspected the men and received a report of enemy activity. A sacrifice was performed, and the entertainments began and lasted through the night. The ursags woke late, praised their hosts, and moved on to the next sentry post.

On Mundu's orders, Šamaš mingled with Ursag Bulalum's servants. Shared beer and stories around the fire while their masters feasted led to an easy comradeship as the tour progressed. Mundu gifted several of the young ursags with carved stone spear points. Bulalum refused the gift, indicating he had fine bronze spear points and neither he nor his men had need of stone weapons. Šamaš, as instructed, nearly got into a fight that evening with Bulalum's men in defense of Ursag Mundu, who Ursag Bulalum had obviously slighted. He allowed himself to be calmed by new friends who appreciated his jugs of beer, if not his stories. Bulalum's men calmed as well. After several more cups of beer, they were singing and complaining about their masters. Šamaš told them Ursag Mundu mourned his brother and no one was allowed to speak his name. Ursag Bulalum's men complained their master was too religious for a lugal's bastard son. The information made its way to though the web of command to their masters who pondered it as they made their way to the next sentry post.

***

En Pakum brought En Siduri all he had learned of Adab's enemies and sentry posts, the allegiances among the ursags, and the rumors he had heard in the entourage.

"Has Mundu determined Bulalum is supported by the temple?"

"I believe he is unsure if it is the temple or the lugal who supports Bulalum. But he will know soon enough. He is no longer the naïf warrior he once was."

En Siduri nodded. "Did you find evidence of An-mašĝik in use?"

"A spear warrior of Mundu's mentioned special training. Unfortunately, he was bitten by a viper and died later that night."

"Such coincidence."

En Pakum shrugged. Obviously, it was not coincidence at all.

En Siduri let out a heavy sigh. "We have not progressed with An-mašĝik. The teas are not helpful." En Pakum remained silent. En Siduri continued, "Encourage Bulalum to discredit Mundu's fealty to his lugal and Inanna more."

"Surely this will cause Mundu to strike out at Bulalum?"

"Yes."

"You sacrifice a lugal's son?"

She stared hard at him. His status did not allow him to question her. Yet, he was her closest confidant and helper. She relented. "He's a bastard son. There are plenty of those. Our lugal will not mind this sacrifice if it exposes an overambitious ursag."

"Would Inanna ask anything more of me in this matter?" En Pakum asked.

"Continue to watch for An-mašĝik —talk of it, use of it, or anyone looking for uzudirig, abulillum, or unumun. Send priests out on the trade routes to intercept anyone with these herbs. If anyone following Eluti's instructions is practicing An-mašĝik, they will soon run out of resources."

"They will be forced to come to us, then?"

"I am not sure. But whatever they do, we will notice."

***

Šamaš brought an update of Dakum and Idin to Marat and Gibil. "Dakum is pleased with Idin's progress even though the boy is still sometimes too eager to obey commands to kill. Idin was given responsibility of a dog and a goat and both were found to have met a cruel death. All this Dakum says is expected in a young man separated from his family, surrounded by warriors, and living in an isolated place."

Gibil asked Šamaš his thoughts. Šamaš knew of masters who treated their servants no better than their animals, and their animals not good at all. These were not good men. An-mašĝik in such a person's hands would be ill-used.

"Can we plot against our brother if Dakum believes he will improve?" Marat asked. Her hand dropped to her thigh where the An-mašĝik scar lay hidden beneath her linen skirt. Just the thought of Idin seemed to make it burn.

"Dakum hopes he will improve," Gibil said. "But we must observe and be wary until we know we can trust him completely."

Marat wondered if Gibil trusted her completely. Did Šamaš? Surely Dakum trusted her if he already trusted Idin. She trusted them. All of them, except Idin. And of course, she did not trust Mundu, Nanar, Warad, any warrior, or any house servant—except Tuda, maybe.

***

Just before the rains would come, the mountain men attacked. Mundu's warriors at the sentry post quickly killed every enemy and then ran to the aid of Ursag Hammi's warriors to the south. Stories of lightning from the sky striking men dead reached En Siduri's ears. She took the stories and her concerns to Lugal Daudu.

Mundu's supplies of uzudirig, abulillum, and unumun were low. The traders who normally brought the herbs came empty handed. Double the usual barter price gave him access to their reserve supply, and sixty bushels of barley were enough to find out it was Inanna's temple taking the herbs his sighted warriors needed. It made sense: En Siduri had every priest and lay person in the temple drinking the teas every day. He would have laughed at their folly—not one of them had the sight—except for the impact on his forces. Mundu had wanted to wait until his position was stronger, but his council advised something must be done now. He took his complaints to Lugal Daudu.

Daudu brought the temple's high priestess and his best warrior together after the victory feast.

"He is using An-mašĝik which is forbidden to all but the temple," Siduri pointed at Mundu.

"I am using every resource Inanna provides to defend her temple and the people who worship her," Mundu countered. "If Inanna does not give the same resources to the temple, am I to blame?"

"You dare…" Siduri started, rising from her seat.

"You acquire all the abulillum and unumun and waste it on your priests." Mundu spoke over her.

"You bicker like an old married couple!" Daudu roared. "Sit! Both of you." He took a deep breath, and a sip of wine. He bade them do the same. "Eluti found the An-mašĝik and shared its knowledge with his brother, Mundu. They showed its great force to me. It was first used to thwart the attackers from Inanna's son Sara and his devotees from Umma.

"Eluti told us this An-mašĝik can only be wielded by one who sees it, and people with that sight are rare. He used teas to improve the vision of those who can see it, but if one does not have this gift, they will never see the An-mašĝik. Is this true, Mundu?"

"Yes, Lugal Daudu."

The lugal turned to Siduri. "This An-mašĝik must be from the world of the Gods. The sighted see it, but they must eat uzudirig to bring it to our world to meet it with water to boil it, wood to burn it, and animals and men to kill them. The use of uzudirig is forbidden to all except a high priest of the temple, for it is used to speak to the gods. For any other to speak to the gods is heresy. Is this true, Siduri?"

"Lugal…" Siduri began. The lugal gave her a cautioning look. "Yes, what you say is true," she finished.

"This An-mašĝik has proven useful against the attacks from Umma, Kissura, and mountain men. It is a weapon we cannot put aside." Daudu turned to Mundu. "Send your servants to the temple and test everyone there to see if any are sighted."

"Perhaps my lugal does not remember," Mundu said. His gaze went to Siduri and he nearly spat. "The Temple killed the first sighted person, my brother Eluti. The sight is indeed rare as you say. I will not send a gift from the gods to slaughter."

"Eluti stole from the temple. From the Goddess Inanna herself…"

"You were at a demonstration of An-mašĝik in this very room. You knew my brother's activities were condoned by the lugal—and you killed him out of greed and jealousy!"

"An-mašĝik is ours to discover and use," Siduri retorted. "You do not understand the politics on the council of the gods, how carefully we step to appease Inanna. The gods would have punished us—all of us—for your brother's intrusion in their world. We would have suffered another plague, more wars…"

"Enough!" Daudu yelled over them. He pointed to Mundu. "My warriors will come to your home tomorrow and you will give them a sighted person to take to the Inanna's temple." He turned to Siduri. "They will come and speak to each person at the temple and determine if any have the sight. No one will be harmed." He sat back down. "Call your servants and tell your people this is to be done. You will both stay here. When everyone is returned safely, you will return to your homes.

"If a priest is found to be sighted, he will be trained." Daudu sipped his wine. "A priest will become part of the ceremony. They will lead the prayers and provide the uzudirig." He swirled the contents of his cup and drank again. "This is a warrior's weapon, but the spear must be blessed by the temple."

# 32. Saĝ šum [Go against, oppose]

*Marat age 16.*

Marat opened her mouth and waited for En Pakum to give her the date palm sweet laced with uzudirig. Since the ceremony had been altered to include the priests, they had practiced and fought together through the floods and the heat of summer. Now they were defending Adab from Kissura, again, in the rains. Still, Marat did not trust the priests. Their prayers thanked Inanna for the gift of An-mašĝik but asked her to forgive the ignorant servants who wielded it. When they provided the uzudirig to the masmas, their affectation was that of a parent forced to give their child's food to a beggar.

During the ceremony, the nubanda still gave the order and the masmas followed it—but now the priest injected praise to Inanna for each feat accomplished. It took more of the masmas' drug-compromised concentration to listen for the next order through the priest's exultations. Marat bowed her head and prayed to Inanna—for she did not mean to offend her—but the priests were no warriors! She said another prayer for insulting Inanna's priests.

When Marat's sighted family had been brought together for the training with the priests, they agreed they did not trust the temple in the preparation of the uzudirig. Marat suggested to Nubanda Nanar that the gurum aid in uzudirig preparation to ensure the team could continue even if the priest became injured in battle. Ursag Mundu and Lugal Daudu approved, En Siduri acquiesced. Working with the priests, Marat learned more precise measurements of cap and stem that could be used in the paste and how to make a honey cake that provided the masmas a swifter recovery.

The family had also discussed Idin's use of large pieces of An-mašĝik instead of threads when Ursag Hammi's sentry post was attacked by the mountain men. Marat complained that it was this action—with the lightning—that had alerted their activities to the priests and now put them in more danger. Idin indicated his actions were necessary: Nubanda Warad had been directing him to bring An-mašĝik to many men in a small area. To accomplish the task without overtaxing himself, he had to use a larger piece of An-mašĝik. Discussion was irrelevant. The priests were here now so it no longer mattered. Marat's eyes went to Dakum. The old man looked away. Later, Marat walked alone with Dakum away from the tents, and still he would not say Idin had used more force than was necessary—only that the masmas might make a judgement others did not understand.

Marat had brought this information to Gibil, who agreed Idin's communication was not open and his conduct was not dependable and, therefore, he was a danger. They discussed the situation with Šamaš. He did not understand—didn't the ceremony control the masmas? Yes, but not entirely, they confessed. Šamaš told them warriors would beat a distrusted person. In extreme cases they would kill him. Marat looked to Gibil. He nodded. She was surprised by a sudden warmth filling her. Was it that Gibil agreed to punishment, she asked herself. No. Clarity came to her: Gibil was granting her redress of grievances. Her hand stroked her thigh. She would kill Idin. She would have justice.

***

On the third attack of the battle, Marat waited for the effects of the uzudirig. They were west of the city. Mundu's warriors had marched past Nam Eluti's former estate and others where the field slaves were sowing barley and wheat and the smell of the broken earth filled the air, to the open uncultivated plains where they stopped on a rise before the land became flowering desert. To the south, Marat saw Idin tied to the masmas chair.

"Be calm," she told herself. She relaxed against the restraints that held her in her chair, inhaled deeply, and let the air out slowly. The uzudirig circled through her. The world before her sharpened, and she was awed once again at the detail of the world the Gods had created for them. "Be careful," she reminded herself. Gibil was spinning a fleece of An-mašĝik into a fine thread. A flicker in the riot of color before her announced an attacker's spear.

Nubanda Nanar moved to her side. "We begin," he said.

She nodded.

The sun cleared away the rain. The attackers came. Nubanda Nanar gave his orders. Marat obeyed. The priest exulted the destruction to Inanna. More enemies, more orders, more exultations. Marat signaled for more uzudirig. The priest pushed a date roughly to her mouth, bruising her lip. Nubanda Nanar gave her a few moments, then continued. His orders were strategic. First he would have them destroy enemies in chariots and the advance foot warriors, but not harm the chariots themselves or the onagers for they would become Lugal Daudu's property. Second, he would order the destruction of the enemy's priests and nubandas. If the attackers did not surrender, he would then start killing the remaining warriors, and lastly the pack animals, armorers, and servants that traveled with an army, until they surrendered. If the attackers were mountain men, often every person would be killed. If the attackers were civilized, many lived to become slaves.

There was a lull in action. Marat toyed with a scrap while she waited. Gibil found a scrap and made it dart towards hers. It was a game they played, this chase. Marat's scrap came close to the sand, then dipped into it. She realized she could just see it if it did not go deep. She pulled it along, just under the surface, and surprised Gibil. His eyebrows shot up. She moved her thread to him, dipping it in and out of the sand, as a snake would swim in the water. He blinked his eyes twice, their sign for understanding. He raised his chin towards Dakum and Idin. A question. She understood. Yes, she flared her nostrils.

Gibil split a thread of An-mašĝik in two: one he swirled in front of Marat for use, and the other he held just to her left. Nubanda Nanar ordered her to strike a knot of men, she did, and as En Pakum gave praise, Marat drove the second thread to ground, pushed it hard to Idin, brought it up and around his feet and thighs, and brought it into their world.

Idin screamed. His body slumped.

All eyes jerked to Idin, now silent. And then they went to Dakum and Marat.

"What happened!" Nubanda Nanar demanded of Gibil.

Marat could hear Nubanda Warad yelling at Dakum but could not make out the words. Bile rose up in her throat. Gasping and gulping, she forced it down.

Gibil shook his head. "I do not know. I was watching Marat."

Nubanda Nanar came to Marat, stood in front of her, and leaned down into her face. "What happened?"

Marat stared at him blankly. It was difficult to order her thoughts with the uzudirig altering the world, her mind trying to hide her actions, her heart racing, her stomach roiling. "Idin?" She could not control so many things at once. The uzudirig took advantage and enveloped her in a world of sharp sound and fantastical colors. It was so much better than her own thoughts, waiting to torture her with images of her brother's blood staining her hands. She looked down and the sand spoke to her, some grains telling her they had blown to her feet from the great waters to the south, a darker clump told her it had come from far east in the folds of a camel's saddle, and then all the sand began to chatter at once.

✷✷✷

The attack from Kissura was repelled, but Mundu was not happy. Idin was dead. Marat was in a stupor. Neither Dakum nor Gibil could tell him what happened. Mundu's doctors examined Idin's body—it had marks like many they had seen on bodies struck by An-mašĝik.

Mundu was no fool. He locked Marat in a room beneath the ground with only a thin blanket. Water and old bread were slipped under the door each day. When Mundu felt the rage of Idin's death no longer consumed him, he opened her door and sat outside, dressed in fine blue cloth with a plate of roasted duck, figs, and wheat bread on a table at his side. He filled two cups with grape wine and sipped from one. "Why did you kill Idin?" he asked.

"I did n…," Marat started and stopped.

"Only you and Idin had taken the uzudirig. His body was blackened like the warriors you kill for me. No one except you four—in the entire world—can use An-mašĝik."

"He has long wished to join Ereshkigal. Perhaps she called him home."

"I thought Gibil had convinced him the goddess would be more pleased the more he killed." Mundu stared at her.

"Perhaps he…"

"This is not a game, Marat." His voice was low and even. "I will learn the truth even if I have to kill a hundred men to find it."

Her head dropped. "Yes. I killed Idin." Tears rolled down her cheeks.

He set his wine down. "Why?"

"He liked killing too much." Marat brushed her face. "He was a danger."

Mundu didn't see the sense in her answer. "But you all kill men for me. You are all a danger—but only to the enemies of Adab."

She shook her head. "Idin worshipped Ereshkigal. He killed men for her, not for you." Her hand touched the fern scar on her thigh.

The scar, Mundu thought. An old grudge. He jutted his chin at her scar. "You feared Idin."

Marat nodded. "I feared him. The others were wary but gave trust as it was earned. Dakum insisted." She smoothed the sand on the floor with her hand. "Idin refused to learn from me, a woman—even though Dakum and Gibil told him I have the greatest understanding. So we taught him together, the three of us. During our training, Idin embraced the killing and became distant and defiant. Gibil finally convinced him that following orders would enable him to kill the most men, and he would be welcomed when he went to the underworld and met his goddess Ereshkigal."

Mundu thought that was good thinking by Gibil. The man was sharper than he had given him credit for. He took a bite of the duck and another sip of wine. When he looked back at Marat, he noticed her clothes were stained and her hair unkempt. "Continue."

"When the mountain men attacked us before the rains, Idin pulled fleeces of An-mašĝik from the sky to kill the enemy at Ursag Hammi's outpost. He did this so he could kill more men for Ereshkigal. He disobeyed Nubanda Warad's order to use threads and scraps, to be discreet." Again, her hand brushed the floor. "I went to Dakum because of this breach. He told me Idin could not be controlled. Then he stopped talking, just stopped. I asked him to continue and he told me he would not even discuss Idin with me for fear of repercussion." Marat looked up at Mundu and held his gaze. "Dakum has always spoken openly. This was bad that he guarded his words. That is why I spoke to Gibil. We agreed Idin was a danger."

"Why did you not bring these concerns to Nanar or to me?"

Marat met his gaze. "You could not understand how truly dangerous he was. You would think he was like a berserk fighter—a weapon that can be pointed in a useful direction. He nearly killed me. He often held a knife to Dakum. As I killed him he could have killed the nubanda, you, or the lugal."

Mundu pondered her words. He did not like that they had acted on their own, but he understood the logic of it. Even more he liked that she had acted in part to protect him. "You have been honest with me. I will be honest with you: I will punish you for what you have done, even though you acted to protect others. Warriors must follow the orders of their leaders. If I do not punish you, I will be seen as weak, and others will disobey."

"Šamaš will swim for me."

Mundu frowned. "This is not a matter for the temple. We will not go to the river." He thought a moment. "Your honesty pleases me, Marat. We will not have lies and half-truths between us," he said, knowing it was a lie. "To show you my sincerity, I will tell you a story you might include in the tablets of An-mašĝik's beginning."

Mundu told her of Eluti's childhood. How he had always talked of colors. How he had an investigative mind. And how he doggedly kept after something until he had his answer. Mundu told her their family was from Uruk where the great temples were for An, Enlil, and Enki, and that was why Eluti gave devotions to those gods instead of Inanna. Mundu told Marat how Eluti had found her in the market, how he had enticed her father with a high offer—but would have gone to other means, kidnapping or even marriage, to acquire her. Her father's business had flourished with the influx of Eluti's minas, and he had tried to buy her back just before the war with Umma, but Eluti had refused. Eluti had told his brother there was no amount of shekels or minas he would accept for Marat.

"I agree with my brother's assessment of your value, Marat. I own you. That will never change."

No tears ran down Marat's face.

"I will leave you here a few more days. Gibil will be the masmas and Dakum the ennug and you will do other things until I change my mind."

"Yes, Ursag Mundu," Marat said.

"You understand and agree to bring all issues to your nubanda? And to follow the decisions of your superiors?" He wanted to make sure she understood her place.

"Yes, Ursag Mundu."

"I like you, Marat. You are a good warrior." He stood. "I will tell your servant to come and clean you." He gave her the plate of food and wine, locked her in the room, and left.

***

En Pakum came to En Siduri, bowed, approached at her signal, and whispered in her ear, "We have Idin's body."

En Siduri took her leave of the merchants and followed Pakum to the room where they prepared bodies for sacrifice. The temple doctors standing at the table parted to give her entry. Idin's body, a patchwork of light brown and blackened skin, was laid out.

"Examine him," Siduri said. "He had the gift of sight. See if there is anything in this body that is different from a body without sight."

The doctors found a young man recently deceased and compared the bodies. After several days dissecting and comparing, they reported there was no difference.

En Siduri was not pleased. Mundu's sighted people had said none of the priests had the sight. She did not trust Mundu's people—he was a lying grasping killer.

She had paid heavily for Idin's body and it told her nothing. She motioned Pakum to her side. "Have we any new information on Mundu's house?"

"No, En Siduri."

"Do we know more of his network of infiltrators?"

"It has grown, En Siduri. There is one in our temple, and one in the lugal's house. This is in addition to the ones in the ursag and merchant homes." He whispered their names.

En Siduri stroked her lapis lazuli amulet of Inanna. "Isolate the temple one by giving him orders to learn the sacred marriage rituals. His words back to Mundu will be that he is rising in the order. For the one in the lugal's house…," she smoothed her brow, "let him die a quick, unfortunate death."

"Yes, En Siduri. As Inanna wishes."

* * *

Mundu's counselors brought him the information that Ursag Bulalum was the lugal's son by a servant. Ursag Bulalum went to the temple regularly, and often a high-level priest took him to a private room for prayer. So, it was the temple that was manipulating him to denigrate Mundu. And it was the temple that caused the death of his informant in the lugal's stables

He sent for Marat. "Can you kill a man without leaving the dark marks of An-mašĝik?" he asked her.

"I have not done so, but that does not mean it is not possible," she responded. She turned to Nubanda Nanar and asked, "When you trained me to use the spear, I learned to strike at the groin, stomach, or throat. Are there other weak areas on a man?"

"The nose and eyes are sensitive. A solid blow to the head is disorienting."

Marat turned back to Mundu. "Ursag Mundu, a few thieves or deserters would help my research."

Mundu nodded. "Nubanda Nanar will procure some for you."

* * *

In her boredom, Marat baked bricks. The cook had learned of this and made her special meals in exchange for bricks she used to make a fireplace in her own room. From the kitchen, word spread and soon many servants had little fireplaces. The master house servant learned of the brick trade and after his fireplace was finished, told Mundu. Mundu allowed Marat to trade bricks, but only after she baked thirty bricks for him each day. He ordered several of his older servants to bring three baskets of clay to Marat's rooms where Tuda formed bricks and Marat baked them. Tuda piled the warm bricks in a corner for Ursag Mundu, gave the old servants half of any remaining bricks, and bartered for goods for Marat with the rest.

Mundu gave Tuda uzudirig for Marat's work. Tuda told him it was more than needed and of Marat's secret store just as she had told him of the baking of the bricks from the beginning. He also gave uzudirig to Dakum, whom he had brought back into his household for the sighted to research together. He knew Dakum secreted away a portion. He knew through Gibil's woman that he, too, had secret stores. A small hoard was normal. He allowed it.

Marat had Tuda sew a little pouch to hold uzudirig into her clothing. She stuffed the core of her kisib with uzudirig and plugged the ends with wax. She did not wish to ever be held in a room against her will again.

She bought simple black onyx kisibs for Gibil and Dakum as gifts to show their stature and hide their uzudirig. She had Tuda make little pouches for them as well. She took special pains to be nice to Dakum, who had not yet forgiven her for killing Idin.

In their common room, she discussed how to kill a man and not leave marks with Gibil. When she had begun to tell them of insights learned while imprisoned, he shook his head to silence her. "Let us take a walk," he had said.

They walked through the streets of Adab and stopped to watch men building a house. The warriors guarding them stood back watching the street. Gibil sent their women to the market to get them beer and sweets. "Now we may talk."

"Out here, in the open?" Marat asked.

"Here in the noise with no servants to tell our master what they hear," he replied.

"You do not trust your woman?"

"No. And you should not trust yours."

She looked at him, surprised.

"Do not be foolish Marat. Mundu does not give without reason. But let us talk of your insights. Quickly while the women are away."

Marat told him that in her boredom in the cell, she had played with An-mašĝik fleeces and threads and scraps. He nodded. This was expected: they all wiled away time playing with it.

She continued. Did he remember the other An-mašĝik, the large slabs that move slowly but they have never been able move? Gibil nodded yes. She made it change! His eyebrows arched and he leaned in closer. She explained, "These other… pieces…. are difficult to work with. They are so large. I carved off a piece with a thread—like cutting cheese with a knife."

"Will this An-mašĝik behave like the other?" Gibil asked.

"We must research it," Marat shrugged.

"I will ask Ursag Mundu to send us to the outpost again," Gibil said. "We will determine how to kill a man without leaving marks and investigate this other An-mašĝik. Dakum will come with us, and we will be a family again."

Marat agreed. The women came back. Gibil announced his woman was pregnant with his child. They had a small celebration, and everyone wished the mother health and Gibil a strong son.

***

Traders from the far west came in barges down the river. They brought timber and granite, copper and flint. Several days after they left, the people who had traded with them began getting fevers, coughs, and runny noses. When red rashes appeared on their skin, they were immediately quarantined, and the city closed its gates. The ašipus and azus watched the affected closely: if white bumps formed, it was a deadly outbreak; if white bumps didn't form, only a few would die. After five days no bumps had formed. It would not be a debilitating outbreak.

The priests made sacrifices to the gods. En Siduri complained to the lugal that Inanna was not pleased with the use of the An-mašĝik. Her demons were making the city sick as punishment. The sighted ones should be in the temple.

Mundu kept the sighted ones at the outpost. He kept his house closed. He consulted his ašipu and azu and made the sacrifices they suggested.

***

The slabs of An-mašĝik were not plentiful; however, they moved so slowly that they were within sight for days. Marat, Gibil, and Dakum had been carving off pieces—boulders—of the one that was moving south of them. Each time they let the boulder go, it drifted back into the slab. And they could not move it. They could slice it from the main slab with a thread of the faster moving An-mašĝik, but the cut would heal as the piece rejoined the greater whole.

The slice was so far away that they could not bring anything into its path. Marat took uzudirig to try to bring the slab, or a boulder from it, into this world. It seemed to come, but there was no lightning to indicate she was successful.

They began trying anything and everything. It was Dakum who found that using a fleece, he could push a boulder. They weren't sure what help that was, but they began manipulating the slab with fleeces that were readily available.

Marat tried uzudirig again, and this time Dakum and Gibil helped her maneuver a boulder towards a shrub. Marat brought the boulder into the world, and it crushed the plant. It did not burn it. The three looked at each other.

"Crush something else!" Gibil pointed at some rocks.

The boulder pushed the rocks into the sand.

"Crush the sand!" Dakum said.

The boulder pushed against the earth and the sand shifted lower.

Dakum yelled for a warrior to bring them one of the small animals. He brought a snake in a basket. Marat applied the boulder against it slowly. The reeds of the basket bent, the snake found an opening and started out, but stopped, its tail stuck. Slowly the reeds flattened against the sand. The snake disappeared into the sand.

"Put it between two boulders."

"Cut the boulder in two! Use the boulder with another one!"

"Let's go north where the ground is harder."

Marat stopped manipulating the boulder and looked at them.

"You stopped." Gibil noticed and turned to her.

"Too many orders." The uzudirig slurred her words.

He nodded. "Dakum, chisel off two boulders. Yes, like that." He turned to Marat. "We will help bring them to the other shrub, then you will move the boulders to press the shrub between them."

She nodded. The shrub splintered into tiny pieces, much like herbs broken with a pestle and mortar. She rubbed the boulders together and the shrub pieces became powder, like barley turned into flour for bread.

Dakum cried and pointed. As the boulders moved, they shifted the sand.

Marat tilted the boulder and when she pushed the sand with the boulder and threads, it was like a hand clearing sand to the side.

The men had her push patterns in the sand. They found the buried rocks and she was able to push them up and out of the sand—and then she was able to push the rocks, and finally she crushed them between the boulders of An-mašĝik. She wished Nam Eluti could see this new day of wonders. She thought no, then, and turned and spat. He had been weak. Even if he had survived the river ordeal, he would not have been the warrior she and Gibil and even Dakum had become. She had killed hundreds—men, women, children, babies—it did not matter whether she could see the fear in their eyes or only their backs as they ran to escape. She did as commanded to protect Adab. She was strong.

"Let's return to the tents and celebrate," she said as she turned away from the deserted plains. "I know where Gibil has hidden some fine grape wine."

"You unclean thief!" Gibil shouted. "Leave my wine be! It is my only comfort, here in the sand, having to live with you beggars."

"You horrid child!" Dakum yelled at Gibil and pushed him. "I have given you everything—and you refuse me wine?"

"Old man…" Gibil cocked his arm.

Marat threw her body at them, and they fell, laughing and cussing.

***

The sighted ones demonstrated their discoveries to Ursag Mundu, Nubanda Nanar, and Nubanda Warad in the plains beyond the sentry post. Afterwards, Mundu sent everyone to feast while he conferred with Nanar.

"This other An-mašĝik …," Mundu started and stopped. "Is this possible? Is it demons tricking us?"

"If it were Gibil alone, I might think so," said Nanar. "But Marat, too, insists. She is too faithful to the gods to consort with demons."

Mundu nodded. He scratched his jaw. "Still…."

Nanar rubbed his face. "Yes, it is difficult to believe. With the fleece—and its strands and threads and scraps as they call it—we saw the lightning, large or small. But with this…."

"Nothing."

"Nothing," Nanar agreed. They both stared out across the plains. The Zagros Mountains were too distant to be seen. "Still, it is a tool we have now. We need determine how to use it."

"Crushing," Mundu said. They laughed.

"Grinding, too," Nanar added.

Mundu snorted and laughed again. "Eluti would have been happy to have these herbalist tools available to him for his research."

"I will think on ways this new 'slab' as they call it can be used. Already I have some ideas," Nanar said. "It is fortunate it does not leave marks like the fleece; we might be able to use it against our detractors in Adab without immediate recognition and condemnation."

Mundu wiped tears from his eyes.

"I see no reason to share this new discovery with Lugal Daudu or En Siduri."

"No," Mundu agreed.

"If… When we use it, it will be a modified ceremony."

Mundu nodded.

"We may need to take precautions in giving commands to kill notable people to the sighted ones," Nanar thought aloud.

"Why?" Mundu asked. "They are proven in the battlefield.

"They are proven against obvious enemies of Adab."

Mundu turned to Nanar. "You mean Marat, because of her childish adoration of the high priestess and lugal?"

"Each comes with his own difficulties. Marat has the most skill. She is also the most pliable."

"I am confident you can devise a convincing story to support whatever must be done."

* * *

A sickness passed through the city quickly, infecting nearly everyone, blinding a few, and sending a handful to the underworld. The warriors in the outposts were infected—either from messengers sent to give word of the sickness, or when they returned. There was no second wave. Nobody who had it once got it again. Lugal Daudu sent word to Girsu and Lagash, in part to help them through the sickness and in part to let them know Adab was strong and should not be attacked.

Girsu sent warriors. Adab defeated them. During the skirmish, Ursag Bulalum was killed by an onager. While onagers did sometimes die suddenly, an animal of that size did not usually crush a man. The ašipu determined a demon had been feasting on Bulalum's strength, making him susceptible to death.

The floods came and overflowed the river and canal system. The waters rose in homes and granaries and temples. There was disease that came with this, as expected.

En Siduri continued her complaints to the lugal. She added her concerns of Mundu's increasing power; his infiltrators were in every major household. He was gaining riches since the sighted ones ensured he was the most victorious warrior and was given the largest rewards. And he controlled a great power: the sighted ones. Surely, he would someday desire to become lugal, if he was not already plotting his rise.

Lugal Daudu agreed to improve his alliance with the temple. Although she had never been a warrior, she was the voice of Inanna, and if she said attacks on Adab could be repelled more quickly and with less death, it was something he should consider seriously. A city needed the defeated armies to work their fields.

Mundu learned of this growing alliance. The lugal agreed with the temple more readily on issues they did not previously. Mundu went to his counselors, and they determined something was needed to distract the lugal. Indirectly he moved. There was a quarrel among ursags the lugal had to arbitrate. The temple lost one of their informants in a merchant's home to a snake bite, another in a farmer's household to a fall from a fig tree, and one placed in the lugal's palace drowned in the river with several other people when their boat sank.

# 33. Namurun [Exaltedness]

*Marat age 17.*

Lugal Daudu, Mundu had observed in a meeting with traders, sneezed incessantly and finally asked them to sit further down the table. Mundu noted a strong scent of juniper, which was common in the perfume of Eastern traders. He wondered if the lugal had a weakness to it. Mundu's infiltrators later confirmed this was true—and furthermore learned that no one in the lugal's household were permitted to wear perfumes or perform rites with juniper.

Nanar had noted the lugal and high priestess were growing closer, while Mundu was being held more distant. Now, several of their informants seemed to have become clumsy and met their deaths in slips and falls downs stairs and over parapets. Mundu's inner counsel advocated a counterattack against the temple, and a contingency to move against the lugal.

Nanar devised the story.

The lugal recently acquired a new wife who was possessed by a demon who now was trying to control the lugal. At the high table of the Gods, Inanna was being distracted by several lesser gods who were jealous of her strength in Adab, and so she did not come to lugal Daudu's aid. The demon was ingenious for he had blinded the doctors in the lugal's household and in the temple to his presence. Ursag Mundu, however, heard him sneezing and consulted with his own doctors. They were sure of the demon possession. Ursag Mundu did not wish to harm his lugal, but if the demon controlled the lugal, that would not be good for Inanna or her city and people. Mundu had tried to talk to the high priestess, but she would not listen to him because of her jealousy over An-maŝĝik. So, the task of saving them from the demon fell to the warrior and his household.

Mundu, Nanar, and Warad set the plan into action.

They sent Gibil to the outpost to help train new warriors.

Mundu arranged for Dakum to witness how the demon, drawn out in defense when a person who knows of its presence is near, unsettles the body with sneezing. Indeed, when Mundu neared the lugal, he began sneezing almost immediately. When Mundu retreated, the sneezing stopped.

Nanar and Warad debated the lugal's demon possession where Marat would overhear them. They coached Tuda on Mundu's love and support of Lugal Daudu and his modest ambitions. Mundu himself, after drinking several cups of wine so he would appear slightly drunk and remorse, told Marat of the terrible situation with Lugal Daudu and the demons and what must be done.

Marat took her misgivings to Dakum, who corroborated the demon possession. She paced in her rooms and was consoled by Tuda that Ursag Mundu was honorable.

***

Marat killed Lugal Daudu at the flax harvest celebration. It was done as ordered by Nubanda Nanar on behalf of Ursag Mundu, of course, but Marat was the one who pushed him down the temple steps with a boulder of An-maŝĝik. She had immediately broken the boulder into pebbles and made them flow with the body, a river of movement below his wheeling feet and hands, until he reached the edge of the first level and the river stopped while the man continued over and hit the ground three stories below. From her vantage across the plaza, she could see his face contort in pain. She rolled some of the pebbles into his mouth so he could neither speak nor breathe. She brought other pebbles onto his back, gradually forcing the air from him but not bruising him. This was fine movement of many pieces only she had mastered.

The orders to kill someone away from battle were different, Marat noted, than when in battle. Instead of having warriors listening in on strategy, flanking them for protection, and cheering their actions, this was done quietly with only Nubanda Nanar, Nubanda Warad, Dakum, and a guard. The reason for the killing was explained, like war strategy was. How, when, and where the event would take place was plotted in advance. The nubandas clearly stated diversions from the orders were allowed only under extenuating circumstances. Another change was that while the masmas needed to clearly see the target and surrounding area, for this work the masmas was not to be seen by anyone other than Mundu's men—for a sighted person obviously in a drugged state would immediately be associated to any exceptional activity such as a person dying.

The lugal died. Marat felt ill but did not show her weakness to her commanders and fellow warriors. Mundu came to her himself and put a necklace of lapis lazuli around her neck and told her she had saved Adab. As soon as dusk settled, Nubanda Warad took Marat and Dakum to the outpost.

The citizens of Adab held a grand celebration officiated by the high priestess En Siduri to send Lugal Daudu and his household to the underworld with enough riches and good deeds that Ereshkigal would welcome a man who spent his life a proud servant of her sister Inanna.

* * *

When word spread that Adab had no leader, Shuruppak's lugal sent warriors to claim the town for their god Ninlil. Adab's ursags were expecting such attacks in their perceived time of weakness. The establishment of the sentry posts against raiders had organized them, and as much as each ursag wanted to become Adab's new lugal, they were able to work together, each defending a section around the town and responding quickly to the call for aid of others. And so, they rebuffed Shuruppak's attack.

Nanar and Mundu agreed their regular forces would suffice in stifling the attack and that it would be too dangerous to draw attention to the sighted warriors at this time. Nanar counseled Mundu to act strongly, as he always did, but not to allow any belligerence into his voice or actions. This was an opportunity to show unifying leadership qualities; power grabbing at this juncture would leave Adab fractured and weak before her enemies. Also, if Mundu was chosen to be lugal, it would make it easier for the other ursags to follow him; if someone else became lugal, there would be no bad blood, and the lugal would accept Mundu as a loyal ursag.

***

Siduri watched from the top of the temple. She knew a new lugal should be seated and his strength established quickly to quell more attacks.

Daudu had many bastard sons and daughters, but only a few legitimate ones. Bulalum had been the best warrior. None of the others were old enough or seasoned enough to take command. So, a regent would have to be chosen until the selected son was old enough.

Siduri sighed. She doubted any of Daudu's prodigy would survive to the throne. All the ursags had spies and had been attacking each other's families in attempts to weaken each other in the eyes of the lugal in hopes of ascending closer to power. Mundu was the strongest, she had to admit. And he had the power of the An-mašĝik. Inanna had chosen him in the rituals the temple had performed. That did not mean, however, that Siduri should not extract controls over him. She would need assurances if there was to be peace within Adab's walls.

She called Mundu's informant among her ranks who she had assigned to study the sacred marriage rituals. He came, eager for a private meeting with the high priestess of Inanna, and knelt before her.

"I will be at the temple granary as night falls, making personal devotions to our most just goddess Inanna. I will have an entourage of four priests. There are words I wish to exchange with Ursag Mundu." She paused, noticing the man tremble. "This evening would be a beneficial time for the ursag to personally tithe dogs to help keep the rodent population down in the building." She took a silver mina from her necklace and held it out to the man. "Your position here is compromised; you cannot return. I will not shun you from the order. If a household in Adab takes you on as their priest, I will not inform them of your duplicitous nature. For this, I ask you leave now and convey to Ursag Mundu what I have told you."

The man took the mina from her hand, praised Inanna, and left.

That evening, En Siduri and Ursag Mundu found common ground for agreement and set their quarrels aside.

Pakum, standing witness to the agreement with Nanar, wondered how much faith was built on commerce. Nanar winked at him. He returned the signal: they would meet tomorrow as arranged.

***

The sighted ones were at the outpost when they heard Ursag Mundu had become the lugal of Adab. They marched to town to celebrate with their comrades. Marat was happy to be back in the city with both Dakum and Gibil.

In their rooms, Gibil's son walked to them! He had grown so much and called out "Aya" when his father approached. Gibil lifted him up and gave him a clay dog figurine to play with.

They quickly settled into their old rooms and their old ways. Except Dakum. The stubble on his scalp was white now. When he talked, his speech was slightly slurred. He was more uncoordinated and carried bruises from things he bumped into. He slept more. And he avoided Marat. She noted this and wondered if it was age or something else. She perceived some of these things in herself when she had used uzudirig to perform many tasks over many days. Sometimes the effects lingered. Were they lingering in Dakum—or was it merely old age? She took Gibil aside.

"Do you notice Dakum with his slurred words, bumping into furniture, and sleeping more?"

Gibil thought a moment. "He is old."

"Yes," Marat agreed. "But sometimes my body does this as well. Could it be the uzudirig lingering?"

Gibil was quiet a moment.

"Do you notice this in yourself?" Marat asked him.

"As you say, when I have taken the uzudirig in great quantity. Yes, then my body has these tendencies." He pulled up his skirt and showed her bruises on his calves. "What is our research?"

"To determine if it is the uzudirig, we would need to try different doses. Maybe start with none."

"Mundu would not agree to fewer masmas."

"Perhaps we will have some time of peace. We will say Dakum is slowing in his old age."

"It would be better to say you and I are practicing something new and Dakum is observing."

"Yes," she agreed.

Dakum did not like their thinking. He stole from their hidden uzudirig caches the first week. They created new caches and kept them secret from him. Without the mushroom, he became cranky and spoke rudely to them, but his coordination improved, his speaking cleared, and gradually he slept less.

Marat and Gibil instituted a new rule: the sighted would use as little uzudirig as possible.

# 34. Šeg [Brick]

*Marat age 18.*

The first years of Lugal Mundu's reign were marked with wars as the gods assessed the strength of Inanna's new ruler. He proved indomitable. Even when several cities combined their forces in an attack, Lugal Mundu was able to repel them with small losses to his own forces. Inanna had chosen well, and her seat among the gods improved, her city Adab grew, and her devotes flourished.

In part, Lugal Mundu's success was due to improvements. The defensive walls were clad in strong baked brick. A moat was dug. Both these tasks were completed quickly with Inanna's blessing.

Gibil cursed Marat for her early brick making enterprise and the rewards Lugal Mundu showered upon her. Each day they walked behind chanting priests among fields of wet clay forms. The priests prayed to Inanna to bake the clay, while the sighted ones stumbled behind in their drugged stupor baking the clay with An-mašĝik threads. When the outer wall was reinforced with baked brick, Lugal Mundu had the same reinforcements done to the palace and his new home, and En Siduri had the same done to the temple. Then it was necessary to pave the markets and main thoroughfares with baked brick. Everyone—the priests, the slaves, the ennugs, gurums, and masmases—became footsore and suffered burns from the heat of the day combined with the heat of the baking bricks around them. Gibil would have gladly given up his gold arm bands and earrings for a day of quiet rest.

When the brick work ended, the canal work began. The An-mašĝik slab, at first unwieldly, was an effective tool if two sighted ones manipulated it in tandem. It had taken much research and training, but now Gibil and Marat could clear silt from a length of a canal in one day that took twenty slaves six days. The people in the An-mašĝik ceremony worked from a covered pavilion, and the soreness of their skin from brick work soon abated. The slaves helping muck out the canal developed burns and had to be exchanged every few days.

Šamaš and Dakum, with Nubanda Nanar's consent, forced Gibil and Marat to take periods of rest with no uzudirig consumption. It was agonizing for Marat, her bones crying for the drug, her mind screaming for it. When their days of rest were over and the drug came back, like a lost lover, Gibil said, they fell into the daze of work again.

Gibil's woman had two more sons, and he had daughters by different women Mundu rewarded him with. Dakum sired a son and several daughters. Lugal Mundu had their offspring tested for Inanna's gift by Marat with the blue tunic—and by Nanar in darkness, as he had learned this other method from Tuda. But the children were not blessed. They were cursed, actually, as they did not see even the colors an ordinary person saw. Mundu was tempted to have Marat impregnated to see if a sighted mother would produce a sighted child, but he heeded his brother's fear of losing Marat to childbirth and maintained the order that no man should lie with her.

With the canals well maintained, the yearly floods were controlled. Disease that often followed the floods all but disappeared. There was an increase in demon spawned irritations of the skin, previously only seen in those too long in the fields under a harsh sun. Prayers and devotions to An, the sun god, were suggested by the ašipus and azus. Sandstorms still struck with a gritty vengeance. Some fields began to yield less, but a fallow year was introduced to the crop rotation and yields steadied.

***

Mundu walked in the palace garden with Nanar. "Do you have any word from the other cities?" he asked.

"Our neighboring city states are worried about your power. They fear you will expand your territory."

Mundu nodded. "It is what we feared of them when we were weak. Now that we are strong, they fear us."

"Yes, my lugal," Nanar said. "Several are considering an alliance. Their progress in this direction is thwarted by their competing gods and to a lesser extent by our sowing false rumors among their rivals."

"When we attack the first city, the others will gather together quickly," Mundu supposed.

"Almost certainly." Nanar agreed.

Mundu continued, "If we attack a larger city, the smaller ones won't be as much a threat, but there is great risk in attacking a city larger than Adab."

"But if we attack a smaller city first, the larger ones will form an alliance and be even harder to attack," Nanar finished.

They walked past fruit trees. "What does my war council suggest?" Mundu asked.

"That we take Girsu first. Umma will not come to its aid and there are no other cities close by. Then, with Adab strong facing the other cities to the west of us, we continue to the east: Lagash, then Urukag, and Nina. Once we have stabilized our new holdings, we take Umma, then Shuruppak."

***

The ašipus and azus of the temple came to En Siduri. "The demons continue plaguing our people with irritations to the skin."

She motioned for them to rise and approach closer. "Have they increased their devotions to An and Inanna?"

"Yes," the oldest ašipu assured her.

Siduri put a hand to her chest to indicate Inanna was pleased. "Who are they that I might include them in my devotions?" she asked.

Again, the eldest replied. "They are the brick and canal slaves."

"No other populations?" Siduri wondered aloud.

An azu stepped forward. "Some others, but the majority work in the brickyards and clearing canals."

Siduri sipped her wine. "Which brick yards?"

"Lugal Mundu's, where Inanna's priests sanctify the bricks," the young man said.

She set the cup aside. "There only?"

"Yes, En."

"And the canals?"

"Where Inanna's priests work with Lugal Mundu's warriors to clear the silt."

"Again, only those?" she asked.

"Yes, En."

Siduri let the information sink into her mind.

"The people are afraid to work there, En." The old ašipu interrupted her thoughts. "They think demons are there."

"I will pray to Inanna." She turned to En Pakum. "Let us have these families come to the granary, and we will provide them additional provisions." That would take care of their extra stores and help shore up faith in the temple.

After the meeting, she sent word to Lugal Mundu. He undoubtedly already knew of this, but their agreement was for open communication. Perhaps his sighted ones would know something of this. In the meantime, she would consult the goddess and ask forgiveness, again, for the misuse of the An-mašĝik by those who were not her devoted priests.

# 35. Zal [Pass time, come to an end, collapse]

*Marat age 22.*

Marat, waking, watched the dust in the sunlight as it drifted and settled. She heard Eluti's voice, "Clear sky light blue, sun brick brown, baked brick brown." She groaned at the thought of baking more bricks and closed her eyes. She felt the heat of the brick yard on her skin. The dryness was in her mouth. "Something to drink," she murmured. She heard no response. "Beer. Wine. Tuda!" She raised her voice. Her body spoke its longing, "Uzudirig tea." She was quiet then, both body and mind, listening for Tuda to be moving about, getting her tea. There was no movement. "Tuda, tea," she said louder again, and turned her face into the covers. The emptiness of her body woke and gnawed at her. The image of the dying king came to her, stones falling from his mouth as he tried to speak. She pulled up her knees and clasped them, blinked her eyes, shook her head, and the ache abated slightly. She rocked herself, humming the song Gibil sang to his children when they were sick. Life in the mountains where the water is clear. High above the sandy desert where the air is cool. Mother's hand smoothing away your worries. She slept.

Tuda's hand woke her. "Marat, here is your tea and dates."

Marat opened her eyes to darkness. "Is it night?" she asked.

"No, Nin. A demon has kicked up a sandstorm. We have covered the windows." Tuda helped Marat sit up and held the cup to her lips.

Marat tasted the bitter unumun and earthy tinge of uzudirig. "You are good to me, Tuda, to give me uzudirig."

"It is just enough to keep the demons from shaking your body, as Dakum has provided." Tuda handed her a small plate of dates. "You must eat your dates with the unumun."

Marat took the plate. She wondered how many young women she had served their deaths. She shook off a sudden chill.

"I wonder if they dare do this to the High Priestess," Tuda said.

"You wonder if who dares to do what?" Marat asked, sipping her tea.

"The high priestess—she partakes of the uzudirig to speak to our goddess Inanna. You have told me this. I wonder if the demons dare shake her—our representative of the goddess herself."

"I do not know." Marat took a date, studied it, and set it aside. "Perhaps she does not trample through the gods' thoughts so annoyingly as I do making bricks and clearing canals." Or killing, she added to herself.

"You are angry," Tuda admonished her. "I will rub a salve into your limbs and you will feel better." She left the room to get the unguents for the mixture.

Marat sat back and closed her eyes. There would be no work of any kind today. Demon trickery or not, she was thankful for the storm.

Harsh voices woke her out of her doze. Tuda was refusing someone entry. Nubanda Warad's voice rose, the door opened, and warriors came in.

"Come immediately!" Nubanda Warad commanded Marat. Two warriors lifted her from her cot.

"She must dress!" Tuda ran to the shelves and pulled out a linen tunic.

"Throw it on her if you must, we are leaving now," Nubanda Warad thundered as he turned for the door, his men, half dragging Marat, following him.

"Let me get my feet beneath me," Marat mumbled.

Tuda tugged the tunic over Marat's head as the men pulled her out the door.

They took her down hallways dark because the windows were covered. The men stumbled around corners and over themselves, jumbling Marat between them. She let them carry her, it was easier than insisting she could walk at their pace, which she wasn't sure she could do with her skin aching and the uzudirig disseminating her attention to the sheep and antelopes who had given their hides for the men's tunics and belts. She nearly laughed at the animal complaints. Then one pelt told her the high priestess did not suffer demons to shake her body and she asked, "How is this so?" but was suddenly thrust on the ground at Lugal Mundu's feet.

"You will tell me!" Lugal Mundu said, his voice hard.

Marat stared up at him.

Lugal Mundu turned to Nubanda Warad. "Is she drunk?"

"We took her from her bed, my lugal."

"Throw water on her. That should wake her."

A guard threw a bucket of water on her and it did clear her mind. She sputtered and pushed the wet braid from her face. "What is it you wish, my lugal?"

"Where is Gibil?"

Where is Gibil. The words echoed in her head. Not in his rooms? Not in the kitchen flirting with the cook to get more grape wine? Not on the roof looking at the stars or the city below him? Not at the market, haggling over some nonesuch he didn't want as a means to find people from his tribe in the mountains? "I do not know," she said at last.

"You lie!" Lugal Mundu yelled and stormed to her. He kicked her over. "Tell me!" He yelled as he towered over her.

"With a new woman?" Marat suggested.

Lugal Mundu bent over, pulled her to him by her tunic, and slapped her. "Where is he?" His words and breath harsh against her. "My men cannot find him. He must be hiding!"

Her cheek burned. A slap was a small rebuke from commander to warrior, she told herself and tried to clear her thoughts. "The riverbank fishing?" Her mind leaped ahead. "En Siduri. Did the temple take him? He can swim, but not far."

The fist that held her opened, and she dropped to the floor. "Search the river. Find out if he could be at the temple," he commanded his men. "Query the informants." He looked back down at Marat. "I know how to make you talk." He bellowed after his men, "Bring me Dakum!"

Servants and warriors came back in a stream; none had found Gibil. Dakum was brought before Lugal Mundu and was asked where Gibil was the same as Marat had been asked. Dakum said he did not know.

"It is a game you are playing," Lugal Mundu accused. "I will not be tricked!" He grabbed up Marat again and shook her.

"I kn-know n-nothing of Gibil's pl-plans for this d-day," Marat stuttered out.

"But he has plans! What are they?" He brought her close, his hands tightening on her arms.

She shook her head. "I do not know. I do not know, my lugal. He is a restless man, but he was comfortable in this house. He has women, he has children. He should not yearn, lugal. All his needs are provided for."

Lugal Mundu thrust her from him. "Your words do not tell the whole truth." He pulled a knife from the sheath on his belt, walked to Dakum, and knelt beside the old man with the weapon at his throat. "Tell me, Marat, or harm comes to your brother."

Marat shook her head. "I do not know." She did not bow her head. She knew Lugal Mundu meant for her to watch and if she did not, she would be held—fingers on her eyes to keep them open if necessary. She looked to Dakum, and they held each other's gaze.

The tip of the blade cut Dakum's cheek. Dakum flinched and groaned. "Marat?" Lugal Mundu asked. "Shall I continue?"

"I do not know where Gibil is." A strand of An-maŝĝik caught her eye. She pulled as much of it to her as she could.

The blade cut across Dakum's tunic, parting the fabric, and leaving a bloody line across his breast. Dakum cried out. Lugal Mundu held him firm. "Be quiet old man, unless it is to tell me where Gibil is."

"How can you harm him?" Marat cried, her eyes going briefly to Lugal Mundu's before connecting again with Dakum's. "He has the sight." She brought the An-maŝĝik to Lugal Mundu. If she struck his head, it should not harm Dakum.

"He is old and lame and nearly blind. His only value to me is your sentiment for him." Lugal Mundu flicked the knife over Dakum. "If you do not tell me what I wish to know, I will cause him great suffering."

Several warriors came in with intelligence that Gibil was not in the temple or held by any ursag, merchant, or nin.

The knife blade bit deeper into Dakum's chest.

Marat's hold on the An-maŝĝik slipped. The uzudirig was diminishing.

Dakum cried out, "The storm!"

Marat hesitated—did Dakum know where Gibil was? The thread started to resume its normal course.

Lugal Mundu asked, "What do you mean, old man?" He twisted the blade.

Tears ran down her cheeks. She tried to gather the thread again.

Dakum's howl of pain filled the room.

Lugal Mundu stopped twisting. "Tell me!"

"He… Gibil… storm. He walks away in the storm."

Marat froze. Gibil, after all these years of talk, was escaping. She caught Dakum's eyes and squinted, questioning. He shook his head. He would not answer.

Lugal Mundu yelled at Marat, "What does he mean? Do you create storms with An-maš̂gik and have not told me?"

Her gaze was pulled to Lugal Mundu. "No. I do not know how to do that." Marat whispered. Would Gibil have learned something and not told her? She thought of the boulders pushing the silt from the canals when they were learning to maneuver the boulders with threads. Sometimes they pushed too hard and the boulder tilted and the sand was flung up into the air. She rubbed her nose. Would that appear to be a sand storm? Suddenly she got up and ran to the window and cast aside the hide covering.

"What are you doing!?"

"I must see this storm." She said and ran to a doorway and slipped through the covering to the terrace. Lugal Mundu was quickly at her side. "Is this what a sandstorm is like?" she asked him. "I have never been out unprotected in one."

He turned slowly. "The wind… it is there, but it is not enough."

"I cannot move the wind," Marat said, turning as she studied the storm around her. She saw a break in the sand and choked. He was there. Leaving her. Going home. She could not join him; he was too far away. Cold ran through her, fear and anger, she realized. She hated him for leaving her behind. If she told Lugal Mundu, they would bring him back. And then he would hate her. She shook her head. She could not be disloyal to her brother. Tears threatened but she forced them back. She would not betray him. Tears flooded her vision.

Lugal Mundu searched the dark sky in the direction she was looking. There was a break in the storm. "Is this Gibil's doing?"

Marat wiped her eyes and looked at the sky to the south and then the west, turning away from Gibil. There, a fleece of An-maš̂gik, moved steadily past, untouched by the winds. "If Gibil has done this, you should fear all storms for hiding an attacking army." She said this as if she were discussing battle tactics with Nubanda Nanar. Gibil, her brother, was fleeing, and she was protecting him. She nearly stumbled at the sense of loss.

They watched the storm a little longer, then returned inside. Dakum lay still on the floor in a pool of blood, his hands grasped on the dagger deep in his chest.

"You killed him!" Marat screamed at Lugal Mundu as she ran to the body. She looked wildly around for An-mašĝik, found a thread, and pulled it to Lugal Mundu, and tried to bring it into shared space… but the uzudirig had ebbed and she could not. She cried out in rage.

"No, of course I did not kill him!" Lugal Mundu ran up to the body. "He has killed himself, the fool."

Marat rocked back and forth before the body. "Why would he do that?" Tears now freely ran down her cheeks.

"Because he did not want to betray Gibil under duress."

"Your hand forced this blade," she yelled.

"Do not anger me, Marat. I have suffered greatly today." He called for a guard to take Marat back to her rooms and confine her there.

Marat, in her room, sank back onto her cot. Gibil had fled. Dakum was dead. She was alone. They had lied to her, not shared their knowledge and intentions—why? She wiped the tears from her face. Since they had met, Gibil accused her of childlike naiveté. She accused him of paranoia. Dakum brought them together. Always cautious. Were Gibil's worries right? Could she trust no-one but her family? But now her family was gone. Šamaš! She moved to rise, to find him. Tuda came and helped her up.

"Where would you go?" Tuda asked.

Marat looked at her. Gibil had said Tuda was not trustworthy, that anything from Lugal Mundu or his people was tainted. Marat wished to talk to Šamaš, to have him explain what had happened so suddenly to their family, but she hesitated. If she went, the servants would tell Nubanda Nanar and Nubanda Warad who would tell Lugal Mundu, and Šamaš would be in danger. She looked at Tuda. Studied her face.

Tuda dropped her gaze to the floor. "What does my nin wish?" she asked.

"I wish…" Marat hesitated. She heard movement in the hallway beyond her door and quiet voices. Was there a guard at her door? Was Lugal Mundu confining her again? She looked back at Tuda, whose hands were grasping the hem of her shawl tightly. "I wish some porridge with dates."

"Nothing more?" Tuda seemed to be asking to help.

"No." Marat shook her head. She was not sure of anything.

Tuda left to get the meal from the kitchens. Marat began searching for her caches of uzudirig. None behind the loose brick in the wall, or in the jar low on the shelf, or in the hem of her tunic. Or in her kisib. Gibil and Dakum had known of these hiding places and could have taken her stores. She felt for the glob of wax holding a pinch of uzudirig on the underside of the table and found it had been scraped off. She quietly approached the door and looked for the wax by the hinge. It, too, was gone. Only Tuda had known of those.

Marat went to the table and sat. She was a prisoner once more.

***

En Siduri reiterated to her most knowledgeable azu the need to find what was different in Dakum's body from everyone else—everyone who didn't have the sight. The azu nodded and returned to the body. He had not found anything and was not likely to find anything. Siduri wondered if it was something that went to the underworld—perhaps back to the Goddess Inanna, the rightful owner.

She turned back to the azu. "Did you inspect the bodies of the workers in the brick yard and canal?"

"Yes, En."

"What did you observe?"

"The complaints varied, En. Some lost hair off their bodies, others had irritated eyes or nostrils or teeth and lips. However, they also had some shared complaints. The servants in the brickyard said their feet burned and many had lesions on their feet and legs.

The servants at the canals had similar complaints, but for all of their body except the head." He bowed.

"Did our treatments heal their complaints?" she asked.

"The salves cooled the irritations. Some healed more quickly than others, three died. The duration of the ailments varied, but most improved in one or two months."

Siduri thought on this. For most disease and demon tricks, people suffered similarly. "What is your opinion?"

"I believe it is plague of demons, En Siduri, driven from the body by increased devotions and the benevolence of our Goddess Inanna." He bowed again.

She nodded. "Please have the scribes document your findings. Provide the findings to Lugal Mundu and to Masmas Marat."

"Yes, En. As you wish."

✷✷✷

Mundu commanded Nanar and Warad to test every person in Adab for the sight, including caravans and messengers from other cities. And to be wary of attacks disguised as sandstorms. And to determine how they might create a sandstorm so they might attack under its guise.

Two were found who might have the sight: an old crippled woman who had been thought to be crazy with her wild talk of colors, and the vibrant five-year-old daughter of a boat maker. Families were compensated and the potential sighted ones were taken to the palace.

The old woman proved to be truly mad and was quietly killed and the body returned to her family with twenty shekels. The girl, Aea, became Marat's apprentice. Nubanda Warad became their overseer, ensuring progress was made and no harm came to Aea.

Tuda's reports on Marat became worthless. Tuda was crucial to controlling Marat. Mundu conferred with Nanar and Warad. It was agreed Marat no longer trusted her handmaid, and the best course of action was to make it appear Tuda was loyal to Marat but was forced to give Mundu information for he would—indeed had—harmed her. To prepare Tuda, Mundu sent her to the temple of Ninlil to learn of female passion from the sacred prostitute, and then starved and beat her. Nanar instructed Tuda on her new duties, and she was returned to Marat.

* * *

Marat held no ill will towards the girl Aea but understood in warrior thinking that one would naturally want to destroy one's nearest competitor—and any harm that befell Aea would be assumed to be at the hand of Marat. So, she worked hard to shield the girl in addition to teaching her. Protecting her even from Lugal Mundu, who expected progress far quicker than was wise from one so young. Aea would not be pushed down the same path as Idin.

Marat also took in and protected Tuda, who suffered Lugal Mundu's temper. The handmaid confessed her betrayal of Marat. Together they determined what Tuda could tell Mundu to appease him, and what she could tell Marat—and not tell Mundu—to keep Marat's faith.

The young woman, weeping and hurt in Marat's arms, brought out protective feelings toward her and anger at Lugal Mundu. Marat bathed her and put balm on her wounds. Tuda slept. She woke untroubled and soothed Marat's anger and showed her a physical intimacy that brought great joy. Together, Tuda promised, they could find a path amongst the connivers and plotters to a peaceful existence. In her embrace, Marat believed it possible.

Šamaš was not so trusting. He warned Marat that Lugal Mundu's deceitfulness was multifold; no one could be trusted save himself, his wife Zimu, and Marat. She disagreed, telling him of the secrets Tuda had brought her, but abided his wish to keep the depth of their familial relationship secret.

Marat grieved the loss of her brothers. Their wives and children were sold. Their rooms in the palace were given to other servants. The only family left to her were Tuda and Aea. Aea, with her constant chatter, exuberance at being in a palace and wearing fine clothes, and throwing tantrums when she was thwarted, filled the voids.

Marat immersed herself in teaching Aea and learning more of An-mašĝik herself. The dust storm turned out to be a simple thing: moving a boulder round and round to stir up the wind while adding sand with another boulder much like sifting barley flour into a bread mix. Gibil had probably thought of it while talking to the cooks as they prepared meals.

Nubanda Nanar determined the An-mašĝik boulders were not useful in battle as they killed onagers and damaged chariots. They were useful, it was found, in pushing boats up river or against the wind.

Marat puzzled over the temple's clay tablet describing the illnesses of the brick yard and canal workers. She arranged for several workers to be brought to her. She inspected their bodies for An-mašĝik but found none. Neither did their ailments resemble any wounds she had seen on bodies struck by An-mašĝik. Marat returned to the brickyard and canals looking for An-mašĝik or even a new color but found nothing. The burning of her own feet had abated after a month. Gibil had similar complaints but had healed more quickly. They had not told anyone they had been affected. She read the tablet again. "Demons. Cure by devotions to Inanna." Gibil did not pray to Inanna, so why would the goddess cleanse him of demon trickery? Did Inanna approve of his intention to return to his people and their gods? Or perhaps it was not demon trickery. She had no love of brick baking but wished to return to it just to watch the An-mašĝik closely.

Marat went with the army to claim another city for Lugal Mundu. The attacks did not take much effort: Nubanda Nanar usually asked her to swath the city in a sandstorm until the warriors were in place, crush the city's wall, and strike at the enemy with large threads briefly. When the warriors were ready, Nubanda Nanar told her to rest. Usually the city's lugal came forward begging their mercy. Sometimes it was the en of the local deity acquiescing to the power of Inanna. Less and less they fought. In any case, Marat was away only a handful of days before she returned to her studies, her teaching, and Tuda.

## 36. Halam [Be bad, evil; forsake, forget; destroy]

*Marat age 23.*

Aea touched Marat's clay kisib indifferently. "What did you do to receive this gift, Nin?"

Marat looked over to the shelf where Tuda kept her jewelry. Aea was fascinated with it. She knew the stories of all the lapis lazuli and gold gifts Lugal Mundu had given Marat for their victories. Marat went over to Aea and touched the kisib. "This is my most treasured piece."

"This?" Aea turned it in her hand. Her gaze swept over the necklaces and arm bands, earrings, bracelets, and pins. "The artwork is intricate, but it isn't made of carnelian or even onyx."

Marat took it gently from Aea. "My father and I created it together in his shop. He gave it to me the day he sold me to Lugal Mundu's brother, Nam Eluti." A heaviness entered Marat's heart. "It was the last time I saw him."

"But then you learned to be a masmas! And you have all these beautiful pieces now!"

Marat smiled at Aea's positive thought process. "It is a good life," she agreed. Tears pricked her eyes as an image of her father and mother entered her thoughts. She wondered if Aea missed her family, and if Marat and Tuda could provide her as good a replacement as Dakum and Gibil had been for her. That reminded her Nubanda Warad had several people for her to test for the sight. She wiped her eyes clear. "Let us drink our tea and see if any of this new lot can distinguish dry sand from wet."

Aea laughed sweetly. "Or at least water from blood."

Later, after testing people for sight, Aea's lessons, and a demonstration of An-mašĝik's destructive power to visiting dignitaries from a city Lugal Mundu wished to peacefully acquire, Marat made her devotions to An, Enki, and Enlil, and worked on her tunic. Tuda had brought skeins of all the different shades of blue threads she could find at the weavers for Marat to choose from. She had been searching for just the right variant to embroider a tunic that would replace Eluti's, which had been cut into pieces so Lugal Mundu's men could each question people for the sight. On the remnant she kept, a dark blue gazelle jumped over a canal. For the second time that day she wiped tears from her eyes. The tunic had been too large for her to wear anyway.

In the night, Marat woke from a nightmare of a war against children. She slipped away from the warmth of Tuda. As she pulled a chair to the terrace, it scraped the floor and Tuda stirred. Marat took a pinch of uzudirig from the pot on the table. She found a heavy tunic and wrapped herself in it as she waited for Tuda to settle. She stared at the chair. It told her it was sturdy and she was not. She acknowledged she was not strong in the way other warriors were strong. The chair scoffed at her. She went outside, found a fleece and slab of An-mašĝik, cut off a rock, and pushed it back into the room. Marat looked over to the bed—Tuda stirred. Marat thought a moment, flattened the rock, and moved the chair onto it, and pushed the rock with a scrap. The chair glided quietly towards the middle of the room. She stood, held back the hide covering the doorway, and floated the chair through to the terrace.

***

Mundu bathed in scented water in preparation for the sacred marriage ritual. The servants polished his gold helmet, lapis lazuli necklace, gold arm band, and lapis lazuli and carnelian wrist bands. His lion pelt sash and long sheepskin skirt were combed out. His blue linen belt with fringes lay across the table next to his burnished gold ceremonial axe.

While he stood for the women to oil his body and dress him, he thought of Siduri. They still clashed regularly, and he found her voice grating; however, taking her in front of his subjects was very rewarding. There were several offspring of their uniting. He felt himself stir. There would be more. He smiled.

Later, surrounded by his men and the chants of the crowd, Mundu ascended the black base of the temple. Pakum greeted and accompanied him, as tradition dictated, up the stairs of the red level. Between shouted verses of prayer, Pakum told him, "En Siduri is displeased with you. Beware." Mundu nodded. They came to the blue level. His men and the temple priests knelt as he continued to Siduri, who stood above him at the top of the steps next to the goddess' divine temple. When he reached her, he knelt and presented his gifts. She spoke the blessing of the goddess Inanna and bade him rise. Two temple maids in hooded tunics fanned the incense burners. They came forward and untied Siduri's tunic and removed it from her shoulders. Mundu thought he smelled something, but then Siduri's hand was on his chest, removing the lion sash, untying the blue belt, and pushing his skirt down. She saw his erect member and smiled up to him. The crowds below them roared. Siduri took his arms and pulled him to her, giving him approval to take her.

He pulled her into a kiss and was assaulted by the rancid smell of death. His member quivered. He straightened. "What is this trickery?"

Siduri rubbed against him. "I do not know of what you speak. Take me, most powerful lugal, protector of Adab."

He felt himself firm again and bent to kiss her but was again assaulted by the foul odor. He nearly wretched. He brought his hands to his face to clear his nose and smelled the foulness on them. He looked down his body, at his weakening member, and Siduri's oils upon him. Siduri beckoned the handmaids closer. "The lugal is in need of help."

The women pushed their hoods back to reveal misshapen faces as they knelt before him. Mundu stepped back.

"They will help you rise, Mundu," Siduri explained.

The women moved to him, reaching for his decreasing member. "Stay!" He ordered them.

The crowd below them had stopped chanting. There was a yell and then another.

Mundu whispered fiercely to Siduri, "What is this trickery?"

"What trickery was it that made you lugal? What trickery is it that En Pakum tells you temple secrets?"

Mundu smirked. "What of it? So you have been bested in battle. Do your part as Inanna and let us be done with these games."

Siduri shook her head. "No, Mundu. Inanna wishes you shamed. Here your people see your weakness." She pointed to his now flaccid member. "Only a servant of Inanna may lead the people of Adab."

Laughter reached his ears from below. He grabbed his skirt and tied it tight with the sash as he descended to his warriors who escorted him through the heckling crowds.

***

Marat had never seen the sacred marriage rite end as it had. Instead of the joyful consummation and cheering, there were grumblings and jeering. She herself felt unsettled. The lugal coupled with the high priestess, and from that the barley would grow, its heavy ripe grain bending the stem. The dates would cascade down from the crown of the tree. The goats would graze in the field, fatten, mate, and drop their young. But the ceremony had not completed. The devotions were not said. The people did not rejoice in the goddess Inanna, instead they feared her dissatisfaction.

Often when Marat took the uzudirig, she felt the presence of the gods. In fear of them—and of the ennug—she performed her tasks swiftly and left the realm of the gods quietly. If they were angered, would they still allow her into their realm? The possible loss frightened her. She went to temple in Lugal Mundu's house and gave devotions.

This day she included Inanna. It had been many years, yet she remembered the words. A calm descended upon her as Inanna accepted the tribute. She wondered if the sacred rite had failed because Lugal Mundu gave devotions to other gods. She knew the gods had their jealousies. An idea came to mind: if they donated more to the temple and placed more statues in the temple, Inanna would be appeased. A statue of Marat giving her undivided devotion to Inanna for all time. The thought warmed her. She went to Lugal Mundu.

***

Mundu was furious. It took several washings to remove the stench from his body. The clothes, he cast off to be burned. He called his council. They were discussing responses when Marat asked to see him. The council had no good ideas, perhaps Marat would, Mundu thought and gave her admittance. She came with a request for statues in Inanna's temple.

He laughed harshly. "En Siduri does not wish my statue in her temple."

The coarseness of warriors was not new to Marat. She did not blush. "A statue in my likeness, my lugal," she clarified. "I was born in Adab and have sung Inanna's praises since my father taught me the words."

Mundu rose. His anger rose with him. "You wish a statue in your likeness in a temple?" he asked. "You are a servant! There is no place in a temple for your likeness."

"I am a warrior. A masmas. I would give my bracelets and necklace to the temple for the statue to be made," she said with great sincerity.

She was so naïf, Mundu thought. He would crush that faith. "You are such a child! Do you not know we battle the temple for existence just as we battle other cities?" The confusion on Marat's face urged him on. "Siduri—not Inanna—controls the temple just as I command my warriors. There is no communing with Inanna—Siduri does as she wishes in the name of the goddess, but not by the wishes of the goddess. She killed my brother out of jealousy. She forced her priests into the An-maŝĝik ceremony to usurp control of it… of you!" Mundu ranted through the list of slights he had suffered at Siduri's hand. "It was her servant who pushed the knife into Dakum," he lied. "Today in the sacred marriage ritual, she came to me bathed in the scent of dead fish to kill my passion. She has thrown the heads of five priests over the wall into my courtyard."

Marat startled. "E-Ereshkigal," she stammered.

"What do you say?" Mundu demanded.

"Ereshkigal," Marat repeated. She fell to her knees. "She has trapped Inanna again in the underworld and takes her place in the temple."

Mundu stared at Marat, who trembled before him in fear of Inanna's sister. A chair scraped. He turned. Nanar had risen. He came around the table to Marat and lifted her.

"Marat, I remember you have been to the underworld and met Ereshkigal. Eluti saved you." Nanar beckoned to a counselor. "This is indeed grave! Ereshkigal has tricked Inanna and En Siduri. Let the counsel ponder this. Rest. There will be work for you to do." He released her into the councilor's arms and held the door for him to take Marat to her rooms. Nanar turned back to everyone staring at him. "This is perfect! Siduri has poisoned her own cup!"

"Do we spread this word? I'm not sure how many people will believe it," Mundu said.

"Your clothing—it will be proof!"

"You must rub yourself with rotted fish, put on the fetid clothes, and speak to the people of Adab."

Everyone in the council took up the idea. Mundu held up his hand and they quieted. "Nanar?" he asked.

"Siduri is a dangerous enemy," he responded.

Everyone nodded.

Nanar continued. "The temple is not a city to be taken and its people to be enslaved. It is a city to be destroyed, its people crushed beneath the rubble of its walls."

Someone wailed. "But this is a temple!"

Mundu nodded. "We will build a new temple to Inanna once we have rid our city of her sister."

"Siduri has many faithful. She will tell them it is the lugal who is false," Warad said.

Nanar nodded. "We must act quickly to remove her ability to counterattack. Speak today to the crowds, Lugal Mundu. Plead for help of An to right this wrong done by his progeny—and…" he looked to the others to help with ideas.

"And if he helps, we will build a build a temple for him."

Nanar nodded. "And we destroy Siduri's temple. Today."

Mundu nodded. "Yes."

* * *

The crowds in the city for the festival were rallied to hear Lugal Mundu speak. He told them of Ereshkigal's treachery and how he had narrowly escaped. He walked among them in the same clothes they had seen him wear to the temple and they shrank at the smell of the underworld.

Nubanda Nanar took Marat and a contingent of warriors to a roof top near the temple. He explained to her how she must crush the entrances to the temple first, then the entire structure. This would trap Ereshkigal's servants inside so they could no longer subvert Inanna's followers.

Marat used An-mašĝik boulders against the entrances. She brought a large slab down on the top of the structure. Tears stained her face as Inanna's personal blue temple collapsed. She had helped clad the temple in baked clay. It did not give easily. She pounded down the slab. Again. And again. And again. Nubanda Nanar touched her arm and she stopped.

Dust swirled and gradually settled to reveal a hill of rubble.

People ran and cried out in the streets. Mundu's warriors spread the story of Ereshkigal and the lugal's promise to build an even greater temple.

***

Marat wept. She feared sleep, for it was like the underworld, populated with the warriors and innocent women and children she had killed. And now also priests. Ereshkigal beckoned her warmly. Inanna, bound at her sister's feet, stared at her with the eyes of one who will have revenge.

Mundu hired workers to build a temple to An on the ruin of Inanna's temple. He sent Marat and Aea to the brickyard to bake bricks for An. Each day Marat went, more and more often supported by warriors as she had no energy to walk without stumbling. She became ill as before. When Aea showed signs of illness, Marat refused to work.

She was brought before Lugal Mundu.

"You refuse your lugal. You refuse your god," he said.

"I cannot work." She shook her head, thinking of the lesions on her legs and arms—of the redness around Aea's mouth and eyes.

"You will work," Lugal Mundu said simply.

"I am sick." She lifted her skirt, showing him the lesions on her legs.

"The azu and ašipu will see you." He waved his hand dismissively at her legs. "Their salves and devotions will help you."

"It is more than that," Marat insisted. "I cannot sleep. Ghosts torment me."

"You are weak! Do you not think every warrior is followed by the ones he's killed?"

Marat felt her eyes blink and breath stop—Lugal Mundu suffered? She shook her head. "The gods are displeased with me. When I take the uzudirig, they no longer give me free passage in their realm. They send demons to torment me."

Lugal Mundu stilled. He sat a moment in thought. "Increase your devotions. I will have our priest join you. I will ask him to hold a festival and we will sacrifice lions and aurochs. The gods will allow you passage."

Marat's shoulders slumped. "I do not think so, my lugal. Inanna is displeased. She has turned them against me."

"You do not know this. The ašipu has read nothing of this in the entrails of the sacrifices he makes each day."

"Please let me break from this work. Let me fulfill my duties to the gods another way. Perhaps as a scribe…" Her voice was barely audible.

"No!" Lugal Mundu rose above her. "You must go back to the brickyard and make my bricks! You must go with Nubanda Nanar on the next attack!"

"I cannot, my lugal," Marat whimpered.

Lugal Mundu paced in front of her. "I have your father. If you do not do as I command, I will kill him."

"Then he will go to the underworld, my lugal," she said with equanimity.

Lugal Mundu stared at her. He swore at her, but she did not move or acquiesce. "Take her to her rooms," he ordered the guards.

They drug her to her rooms, shut the door, and latched it on the outside. Marat sat. Tuda came to her but she motioned her away. They sat quietly.

"Where is Aea?" Marat finally said.

"Nubanda Warad teaches her sword play."

"She is too small for a sword."

"Daggers, then."

There was a shout outside their door, and Tuda went to it to listen. There were more shouts and scuffling. Tuda whispered "It's other ursags trying to take you, but the lugal's men have beaten them and saved us."

Marat did not care. "Let them take me," she said.

Tuda frowned and took her seat next to Marat.

The days continued. Warriors carried Marat to the brickyard where she hid from the gods as she fired the bricks. It was a relief when they went to war because her legs began to heal and the pain faded—but the people she killed in the war swelled the ranks of the ghosts who haunted her. Victory came and she was returned to the brickyard where she entered the haze of uzudirig and the lesions returned. Finally, she became lost in the god's world and did not respond to anyone's pleading or shaking.

The doctors visited Marat each day, rubbing salves onto her reddened skin, mixing cures for her to drink, and leading her in devotions that would drive the demons away.

Šamaš' daughter, Hedu, came to Marat with sweets from the kitchen when Tuda and the doctors were away. "Your family worries about your heath, aunt," she said. "We pray to the gods to spare you."

"The gods loathe me. Do not let them know we are family—they will send demons to torture you."

"Here, take a sweet," Hedu lifted it to Marat's mouth. "It is a date stuffed with honey and almonds. I remember you enjoyed them when we lived with Nam Eluti."

Tears welled in Marat's eyes and spilled down her cheeks as she took the sweet. "Those were good days."

"My father says we can have good days again. He sends counsel: allow these ministrations to heal you, but do not show your improvement. When you are restored, we will leave this evil place."

Marat sank back. "How?" Her voice was full of despair.

"Trust my father, aunt. Do as he suggests. Šamaš is wise in these ways." Hedu wiped the tears from Marat's face. "I must leave now. But know you are cherished." Hedu rose and turned to leave. She knelt back down and placed the last date in Marat's hand and took the plate. "Do not tell anyone, aunt. Not Tuda, not Aea. We can take them with us, but they cannot know until we cross the threshold. Promise me, aunt, you won't speak of this." She grasped Marat's hand. "All our lives are forfeit."

"I promise, Hedu. I don't think this will come to pass… I cannot imagine a day away from this pain… but I promise to do as Šamaš counsels."

It did not seem possible, but Marat gradually improved. She fabricated headaches as her skin healed and insisted she was still too weak to walk. The doctors made her drink vile tasting remedies. She showed minor improvements.

Tuda served her abulillum and unumun each day with Aea but ceased providing uzudirig. Lugal Mundu was wary, Marat knew, for Tuda had removed all the uzudirig from their rooms. He was worried she would strike against him or harm herself. She struggled against the deprivation of uzudirig. In her anger and pain, she began to watch Tuda more closely.

Tuda was helpful and kind. She fretted that Marat was too weak for intimacy, so they shared only a brief kiss each evening before they slept. Tuda cared for Marat's body, bathing it, rubbing the salves into it, braiding her shank of hair. Tuda was exceptionally caring with Aea—but also firm. She admonished the girl if she did not take care of her things, was lazy, or complained. Marat began to wonder about the quality of her relationship with Tuda. Did Tuda love her—or was she a practical servant making the best of a situation? Marat thought back to Nam Eluti and his wives and servants. Nam Eluti had cared most for Nin Aruru. And she was the one with whom he quarreled the most. All of his wives felt free to complain to him. His servants, on the other hand, never quarreled with him.

"You never disagree with me," she said to Tuda one afternoon.

Tuda looked up from her sewing. "You wish to argue?" she asked.

"Wish to?" Marat repeated. "No." She shook her head. "But most people have their differences."

Tuda shrugged. "We have no differences." She bent her head to her work.

Marat tried to think of a difference. She rose from the pallet she was resting on. "I wish to practice. I will need uzudirig."

"Lugal Mundu forbids it." Tuda did not even look up.

Marat studied Tuda. Her dark hair included strands that were lighter black—Marat had named several blacks on the tablets "black as Tuda's hair, black like the new hair behind Tuda's ear, black as it turns to brown in Tuda's hair." She thought of sifting that hair through her fingers and a warmth spread through her. She turned away and took a deep breath. "I am bored and wish to research technique," she said. "We have hidden uzudirig in the room. Can I not have it now?" she asked calmly.

"There is none. Lugal Mundu's men have removed it." Tuda spoke behind her. "You are weak, Marat. Lie back down. Rest."

Marat leaned against the table. She turned and watched Tuda again. "I am tired of resting."

Tuda stopped working the thread. "Shall I call for entertainment? Musicians?" She looked up at Marat inquiringly.

"There will be uzudirig for Aea's training. Nubanda Warad will give you some if you tell him it is for her to improve her technique."

"Nubanda Warad will say she is only to train in the yard under his supervision."

"Tell him I am having convulsions, as I often do, when it is withdrawn."

"But you are not having convulsions, Marat."

"So small a thing, you will not do for me Tuda?" Marat bent her head to appear disheartened but watched Tuda through her lashes.

Fear skittered across her lover's face. "It is no small thing you ask for."

Marat sniffed as though she was crying and pinched her leg through her tunic hard to make tears well in her eyes. "An-mašĝik is all I have, all I am," she said, watching Tuda closely.

Thoughts flicked across Tuda's face. She put the sewing down, rose, pulled her tunic off one of her shoulders, crossed the room to Marat, and embraced her. "You have me, Marat," Tuda said and nuzzled Marat's neck. "Perhaps you have healed enough for this." Her hand pulled Marat closer.

Marat allowed the caresses. She let Tuda take her to the pallet where she removed their clothes and continued her caresses. Marat felt her body quicken, but her mind, for the first time, held back, watching.

Tuda's practiced touch faltered. "Do I not please you?" she asked.

Marat took her hand and clasped it to her side. "Perhaps I am still weak," she apologized.

Tuda stayed with her a moment, then returned to her sewing.

"I will need the uzudirig, Tuda," Marat said quietly. The sound of thread pulling though hide stilled. "Please bring it to me tomorrow." Marat feigned sleep.

The thread pulled through the hide again. The skirt was set down. Light footsteps crossed the room. There was a scratch at the door and a whisper. The door creaked slightly. Tuda was gone.

Marat waited a moment, then sat up. Was Tuda going to get uzudirig? If yes, Marat wanted to know where it was kept. She pulled on her tunic and went to the door. She tried it. Locked. She knocked and a warrior opened the door. "I need to offer devotions to An. Could you bring me pigeons, dates, and flax seed?"

He nodded and motioned for her to return to the room. He barred the door. There was a command, then a long wait for a servant to bring her offerings. The warrior opened the door and gave her the items.

"I am going to Lugal Mundu's temple. I should be safe there," she informed him.

"I will take you there."

She followed him, surreptitiously watching for Tuda. In the temple, it seemed she would not be allowed solitude or freedom of movement. She told her guard she was hungry and asked him for date sweets from the kitchen with almonds and honey. Hedu brought her a plate.

"Please find out where Tuda has gone just now. I have asked for uzudirig. I wish a secret store," she whispered. In a normal voice, she said, "Thank you for these sweets, girl. You may go."

"As it pleases you, Nin." Hedu nodded and left.

The next day Marat antagonized Tuda again. Again, Tuda left their rooms. Marat requested porridge. Hedu brought it. Marat requested the servant stay to help her bathe. The guard politely left the room.

"Tuda goes to Lugal Mundu," Hedu said.

"Did he give her uzudirig?" Marat walked to the pitcher of water. She offered a rag cloth to Hedu.

"No." Hedu took the cloth and dipped it in the pitcher.

Marat thought a moment. "She tells him of my actions." She removed her tunic.

"Yes." Hedu wrung out the cloth.

Marat looked at Hedu. Hedu dropped her gaze to the floor. "There is something else?"

"Yes." Hedu looked directly at Marat, then away again. "It is not good, aunt."

"I will hear it." She took the cloth from Hedu and washed her arm.

"They talk. She tells him of your health, your stubbornness. He counsels her. She pleasures him."

"She pleasures him?" Marat was struck at the thought. "Yesterday?" She gave the cloth back to Hedu.

Hedu rinsed and wrung out the cloth. "All days," she answered.

Marat's brows furrowed. "All days? What do you mean?"

Hedu gave Marat the cloth. "When Tuda leaves your rooms, always she goes to Lugal Mundu. Always they talk. Always she pleasures him in some way."

Marat felt a coldness enter her. Her fingers tightened on the cloth. "Why? Why do you tell me this now? Why does she do this?"

Hedu took the cloth from Marat and washed her other arm. "There are rumors, stories, bragging among the servants. It is not easy to know the truth in a house so full of deception. Šamaš believes Tuda is faithful only to Lugal Mundu." She rinsed the cloth and began washing Marat's face and neck. She whispered, "When you were punished after Dakum's death, Lugal Mundu sent Tuda to the temple of Ninlil. That is the temple where men go to ask the gods for female companionship."

"Yes, I know that." Marat's jaw tightened.

"The temple also teaches men and women the trade of pleasure. Tuda returned and became your companion."

Marat was silent.

Hedu dipped the cloth into the pitcher again, turned Marat, and bathed her back. "It is said that Lugal Mundu enjoys Tuda more because she is with you, and less for her skills."

There was a knock and the door opened. The guard looked in, his gaze caught by Marat's bare back. He nodded and shut the door.

Anger welled in Marat. Her face heated. "I am an animal kept in a cage," she seethed.

Hedu raised the tunic over Marat. "Šamaš says we are ready."

"I need uzudirig. I cannot leave without a supply."

"We have enough," she whispered. "I have not washed your legs."

Marat sat. "How do we leave?"

"You will ask to give devotions to An in the temple, as before. It must be in the evening. After a festival when the guards drink is the best time. You will ask the guard to bring you fish—two simma—and a bowl of sesame oil," Hedu said as she washed Marat's legs. "That is all you need to know." She finished and put the cloth down. "If you wish to bring someone, they must be in the temple praying with you."

Marat nodded. "Thank you, Hedu."

Hedu clasped Marat's hand, transferring a small packet. "Be well, aunt," she said and left.

Marat unfolded the fabric enough to verify it was uzudirig. She quickly hid it under her pallet and lit incense to mask any odor.

When Tuda returned, she asked about the incense and the bath. Marat replied she had felt the need to cleanse, but was tired now, and would rest. Marat asked after Aea.

"She has been training with Nubanda Warad's men."

Fear ran cold down Marat's back. In her refusal to be masmas, had they decided to push Aea's training along faster? It made sense. She calmed herself and said, "I wish to see her. Please bring her here, Tuda. She must improve her work with An-maŝĝik slabs if she is to be truly useful."

Aea came full of excitement. "We are soon going to the outpost to learn war strategies! I will soon be a great masmas like you, Marat, and people will give me beautiful gifts," she gushed.

Marat sent Tuda for sweets and made accommodating responses to Aea. Internally, she translated Aea's words: they were going to begin training her to kill and increase her uzudirig consumption. She was seven years old—the same age Idin had been when he was trained. "I have been in the city too long. I will enjoy the stale bread and rain dripping in the tent."

Aea's face fell. "You are too weak to come, Nubanda Warad has said."

Marat forced a smile. "I am recovering. I will let them know I am able to help with your education again."

"Do not tell them!" Aea put her hand to her mouth, as if to capture the words already said.

Marat tilted her head. "Why not?"

"I am sorry. That was wrong of me," Aea apologized.

Marat studied her. "We are masmas, Aea. There are only two of us. We must work together."

"You have worked alone."

"At great cost, Aea."

"And great gain, Marat," The girl's eyes darted to the jewelry on the table.

"I would give up all my riches to have Dakum or Gibil back at my side," Marat said truthfully. Aea hesitated and Marat realized the girl had changed while Marat was ill. "The truth, Aea. We are family in a house of many deceivers. We must help each other, or we are lost." She reached out and drew the girl into a hug.

Aea put her arms around Marat. "They say you are the deceiver. Nubanda Warad says I learn quickly and Lugal Mundu is pleased with me. I want to learn and do more, Marat. They tell me my training will be completed when we go this time to the outpost."

Tears welled in Marat's eyes. She affected joy. "Yes, it will be the end of the warrior training." She wiped her eyes. The door opened: Tuda returned with a tray of sweets. Marat beckoned her to join their embrace, "Tuda, Aea is about to complete her training—the gods are smiling upon us!"

They had a small fete of dancing and singing, eating and drinking. The guards hushed them several times until, finally, the women fell into a laughing heap on the pallet and slept.

The next day Marat announced she and Aea must pray to An to ensure his benevolence towards her. She asked for two simma and a bowl of sesame oil for their devotions. Tuda asked if she should accompany them. Marat stared at her a moment, touched her face. Tuda looked at her inquiringly. "You would be bored. You do so much, Tuda. Why don't you stay here and rest?"

Tuda agreed readily. She mentioned she had personal tasks to complete.

Marat felt her anger rise, knowing those tasks were for Lugal Mundu, and turned quickly away. Tuda helped them bathe and dress. She left on her errands when Marat began questioning Aea about colors. Marat decided they should wear plain sheep skin skirts and shawls, to show their humbleness before An. While Aea changed, Marat put the uzudirig, her kisib, a handful of minas, several pieces of jewelry, and a medicine packet the doctors gave her to induce sleep into a satchel. She looked at the clay tablets on her table. There were too many to take. She stared, then roused herself. What she needed she would remember. She added a blanket to her satchel. At the door, she turned back to the tablets. She told Tuda she had forgotten something and would catch up. When she was alone, she took a pinch of uzudirig, found a boulder and scraps of An-mašĝik, and scrubbed the writing off the tablets. Marat smiled. Of course, Mundu had other copies, but these latest insights he would not get.

A kitchen servant awaited them in the temple. She indicated the fish and oil and asked if anything else was needed. Marat asked for wine. The wine came, Aea lit the oil lamps, and Marat began their devotions. Aea's voice joined in sweetly.

After An had feasted on their offering, Marat shared it with Aea. Hedu came and cleared the platters. She gave Marat a fresh carafe of wine. "Valerian root was steeped in this," she whispered. As she was leaving, Marat asked her to return and straighten the temple when they returned to their rooms.

Marat poured a cup of wine cup for Aea and took some uzudirig. She offered the remaining wine to their guard. After another prayer, Aea slumped into sleep. The guard's cup rolled across the floor.

Hedu returned with Dadiya, her husband, who gathered the sleeping Aea into his arms as Marat gathered her things.

They met Šamaš and Zimu in the halls. Šamaš led them through the gardens to a side door, past the fishpond, through another door, past the waste pile, through a gate, and finally, the musty smell of the river reached them. Dadiya handed Aea to Šamaš and ran ahead.

"There is a boat hidden in the reeds," Šamaš whispered to Marat. "I know you do not like travel by water, but it is fastest."

Marat nodded. She looked up at the castle. "Did Tuda go to Lugal Mundu?"

"Yes. She told him you were improving and that you expressed excitement upon learning of Aea's training."

Marat felt the anger rising in her again. She heard a frog's croak as Šamaš herded them to the boat. When Dadiya began to row, Marat stayed his hand. She took another pinch of uzudirig, brought threads forth, and sliced a boulder from a slab high above them. "Downstream?" she asked Šamaš.

"Upstream until we are past the city, then across the desert to the Idiglat River where it is at least a day to Larak." Šamaš sat with Aea on some bundles.

Marat nodded. She cut a wedge in the boulder, brought it behind the boat, and pushed it with the threads. The boat jolted forward and everyone grabbed at the sides. The boat steadied, and they passed by Adab. The loud bickering of men full of drink, soothing voices of singers, dogs barking, and onagers braying gradually faded.

"They will follow," Šamaš said at her side. "We will shave our heads completely and say it is lice, then grow it out without the slave's mark. We will change our names. We will start new in Larak. Perhaps we can buy land and be farmers."

Marat's heart stopped when Šamaš had said "they will follow." Of course, they would follow. Lugal Mundu would not let his masmas go. His anger would be prodigious. He would punish her, maybe even kill her for taking Aea. And then he would have Aea. Marat looked at the child asleep at her feet. She could not let him ruin her. She looked ahead at the river; the moon flickered on the water. She would not let him imprison her again. "Šamaš, I must make sure we are not followed." He nodded.

They came to where the Buranum River passed a hill. Marat pushed the boat to the bank and climbed, Šamaš following. She searched the night for An-mašĝik, found it, and instructed Šamaš to give her four dozes of uzudirig at reduced intervals. When she felt the stars looking upon her, she turned to Adab and draped an entire fleece about the castle and brought the ends together. A streak of light burst open the dark sky. The ground trembled. The castle crumbled. She smiled. Lugal Mundu was gone.

But what of Nanar and Warad and the council? the dust rolling past them asked.

Marat's smile hardened. She quickly found another fleece and a slab and pushed in the walls of the city, crushed the roofs of the buildings, and pushed the river out of its bank to wash over the ruins.

Weight left her body. She was free of them. The sand beneath her feet rejoiced. The wind swirled around her in joy. She embraced Šamaš. "It is done."

They returned to the boat and continued upstream until she was exhausted. Dadiya and Šamaš poled against the current while she slept.

# 37. Zagmuk [New year; beginning of a cycle]

*Marat age 24.*

They called Marat "Malag"—second wife, because her own name was known as the weapon of Lugal Mundu. No one in Larak doubted their story of leaving Adab because of a family dispute, or of shaving their heads because of camping in a nest of fleas along the Buranum River on their journey. They were welcomed in the temple of Ninhursag, the mother goddess.

When word reached Larak of the gods' destruction of Adab, Šamaš' family portrayed surprise. It was an easy task, for although Marat had told them she ensured Lugal Mundu would not follow, she had not told them she had crushed the castle to rubble, pushed the city wall inwards, flattening buildings and homes along its entire length, and changed the course of the Buranum River so it no longer flowed by the once great seat of power, but over it. Ninhursag's priests said it was divine retribution for demolishing Inanna's temple.

Šamaš' family mourned their dead friends, they told embellished stories of Adab's beauty, professed an adequate dislike for the now dead Lugal Mundu, and shared their shocked disbelief at the ruination of Inanna's temple and priests. A few refugee families from Adab migrated to Larak. Audiences hungry for information and entertainment left Šamaš' family in peace, finally, and flocked to those with first-hand experience of the fright of the walls grinding in, homes collapsing one after another, people crying out, and animals shrieking in the night.

Marat gave Šamaš a necklace to sell. The proceeds were enough for him to purchase a date palm orchard, acquire servants and goats, renovate the abandoned house on the land, and build servant quarters. Zimu gave Marat the uzudirig plants taken from Lugal Mundu's garden. She told her everything she had learned from the woman who tended them, and together they planted and harvested uzudirig. Aea habituated herself to the new environment, though she refused to forgive Marat for taking away her life of ease and fortune. Hedu bore a son, Ishkur, for Dadiya.

The ghosts of the dead did not leave Marat; she learned to go about her life with them sometimes arguing and glaring at her. She thought perhaps if she told their story, they would leave her alone. She requested clay tablets and with Aea began documenting An-mašĝik again, adding how it was used for evil and how to grow uzudirig. When it was discovered the new owners of the date farm could read and write, people approached them to document their transactions and teach their children to be scribes. It was a good opportunity for additional income and a way for Marat to busy herself. It would be good for Aea to continue her lessons and perhaps become a teacher herself.

Many a young man showed interest in Aea. Fortunately, Aea was not impressed with any of them. It was not necessary for Šamaš to refuse a match for suitability, for a new family member would need to be trusted with the family's secrets—an ability Šamaš did not see in any of the young men. It was fortunate for Marat as well: she did not need to decide yet if she would control the path of Aea's love life as Nam Eluti and Lugal Mundu had hers.

Soon enough, the cities Lugal Mundu had controlled became free again and began warring with each other for power. Marat held her tongue and kept Aea away from warriors. If either of them said anything of fighting and dying, a warrior would quickly be able to determine who they were and the power to be gained by controlling them.

Before their second year in Larak had passed, they came to realize how they had gotten an established orchard with large gardens for so few minas: mountain men attacked Larak regularly and their farm was in the raiders' path. Marat was tempted to instruct the lugal how to defend his people's land. She thought of Gibil and almost cursed his starving people. She missed him, her brother. They had endured the warrior life together—Gibil better than any of them—and had helped each other through joy, grief, and horror. Her hand went to the kisib at her throat and thought of the one she had crafted for him. Did he still wear it? An idea came to her and she discussed it with Šamaš: if they painted the foreign markings from Gibil's kisib across the outward side of the garden wall facing the mountains, surely the mountain men would think one of their own lived here and at least hesitate to attack? Šamaš thought it could do no harm.

One night after date harvest and before the fall rains came, a brown-haired man came to the gate and asked to speak to the head of the household. Šamaš met with the visitor briefly before calling for Marat. The young man asked if she understood the writing on the wall. She explained it was on a gift she had given a dear friend, Gibil from the Zagros Mountains, years ago. "It is a blessing, in his language, from a song you sing to children who cannot sleep," Marat told him. She began to sing the song, and the young man joined her, nodding. He wished them well and left. The attacks on their farm stopped, but they did not stop on the rest of Larak. To minimize suspicion, the family spread rumors that they were such poor farmers that not even the raiders would take their harvest.

Šamaš suffered in trading, but it was a much more acceptable loss than being attacked by raiders or being killed by their neighbors suspecting them of colluding with the enemy.

* * *

In their fourth year in Larak, the floods damaged their buildings. Marat surreptitiously helped the bricks bake with An-mašĝik. One evening she watched Aea run threads across the bricks and noted a flicker of dust.

"Aea," she called, "did you see that? A sparkling dusting like the stars, there, where the thread touched the corner of the brick." She pointed.

Aea turned. "No, Malag." She stared at the spot. "I don't see anything."

"Warm the brick again. Touch the thread to it."

Aea huffed but did as she was told. There was no flicker. She looked to Marat for direction, for Marat was never satisfied with something happening once but not again.

"Warm clay that has not been touched." Marat spun around. "There." She pointed.

Aea brought the thread close to the misshapen bricks—not nearly as neat or decorative as the ones she had baked for Lugal Mundu—and skimmed it along the sides of several, creating a small eruption of faint sparks.

"Ah!" Marat exclaimed. "It is so faint—no wonder we did not discover this earlier." She moved to the warm clay. There was a barely perceptible glow that faded. She bade Aea perform the task again, this time watching closely both the sparks and the glow.

"Yes, I see it," she said dully.

A slight frown came to Marat's face. For all Aea's knowing An-mašĝik, she had no caring, no wonder of it. "Have you seen these colors before?" she asked.

Aea cocked her head and thought a moment. "No, Marat."

"No, Malag," Marat corrected her.

"I have not seen those colors before." Aea stubbornly refused the lesson.

"Would you like to name them?" Marat offered the prize.

Aea looked up. "It would be written on the tablets?"

"Yes."

Aea contemplated the bricks. "Yellow like the sparks An-mašĝik leaves on the baking brick."

Marat nodded. "Very good."

"Red like a baking brick."

Marat hesitated. "I have seen many variations of bricks baking. Can you make it more specific?"

Aea closed her eyes to concentrate. "Red like the glow in the brick warmed by An-mašĝik."

Marat nodded. "I agree. I will add these colors to the list."

Aea smiled.

Marat brought home an old beggar and gave him the job to guard the bricks. She fed him well and provided him plenty of the diluted beer he was fond of. While he slept in a drunken stupor, she grazed the clay around him with An-mašĝik, the haze of sparks cascading over him and the red in the clay glowing like fire embers. In not so many days his eyes and lips developed sores. Marat provided salves and more beer and continued her research. Soon lesions appeared on his exposed arms, legs, and scalp. She changed his sentry point to just outside the brickyard and he gradually healed. She changed his location back to the interior but did no work with An-mašĝik and he remained healthy. She killed and buried him according to custom, then she found another brick guard.

This one she had stay with the bricks that had been baked and with the clay before baking: he maintained his health. She demanded he sleep covered except his feet, and she baked the bricks around him while he slept until lesions appeared on his feet. Marat changed his location and gave him healing salves, then she moved him back with instructions to sleep covered except his arms. He nearly protested such odd requests, but in the end merely ate his food, drank his beer, and did as she asked.

It was the An-mašĝik that caused the illness, Marat determined. She thought back to walking through Lugal Mundu's brickyard, day after day, pulling the An-mašĝik thread along beside her—and not seeing the showers of sparks or the faint red glowing in the light of day.

Marat continued the experiments. If the guard was placed near the bricks several hours after the heating of them, the illness took longer to appear. If he was not placed there for several days, it would be months before the lesions developed. Marat killed her second guard and acquired a third. She repeated her experiments and was delighted when the results were similar.

On the fourth guard, she experimented exposing him to the sparks. The results, confirmed by the fifth guard, were lesions. Exposure to the red glow produced the sores around the eyes and mouth, confirmed by the sixth and seventh guards.

Šamaš stopped her experiments. "You are killing too many men," he said.

"But they are street beggars!" She responded. "Their families have abandoned them, the temple does not care for them, and I treat them well."

"Still, I have heard whisperings of demons luring beggars from the market and leading them to grisly deaths."

Marat looked down at the tablet with documentation of her latest findings and sighed. "I do not wish to be discovered—as either the missing masmas or as a demon-possessed woman."

"I know your work is important to you, Marat." He put a hand on her shoulder and gently squeezed.

"I understand the conditions well enough. I will stop."

They cleared the bricks from the yard and covered it with soil. When they found nothing would grow there, they constructed a small temple for Ninhursag.

***

To keep herself occupied, Marat celebrated the harvests; tutored students on writing; taught Šamaš and Dadiya what she knew from her days with Nam Eluti of managing servants, optimizing harvests, and bartering with merchants; made and mended garments with the women; and took her turn caring for the children.

Aea found a man, Ududu, who she felt deeply for and who Šamaš felt could be discreet. Marat did not have the heart to forbid the marriage. They married. Their first child was born misshapen, which Aea attributed to the unumun, abulillum, and uzudirig. She stopped all An-mašĝik work—and why not since there was no benefit of shekels or jewels, she challenged Marat. Marat remained silent—how could she explain the horrors she had saved Aea from that were the price of such riches?

Aea's second child, a girl, was healthy. The third, a boy, lived also; but Aea did not. Ududu left with the children. Dadiya saw him in the markets and reported Ududu had married again, and his wife treated Aea's children well, as was the law.

Marat had wanted to keep the children, but she was not a blood relation with a claim, and Ududu had not wished or needed to sell them. She did not insist. She had begun to realize the best course of action often could not be followed—in war, in business, or in family matters. Logic was superseded by custom, posturing, and feelings. One moved obliquely in the desired direction, hopeful the desired outcome could be reached before another obstacle emerged to be navigated around.

***

The weather turned warmer as the snow melt from the mountains poured vigor into the lackluster Idiglat River. The flax had been harvested and the wheat sown. The men were in the orchard trimming the dead fronds from the date palms when a sandstorm came across the plains from the north. Everyone went to the buildings and shut the doors and secured hides over the openings.

It was not the time of year for dust storms; they usually came in the heat of summer. Marat went to the roof and looked across the plains. As it came closer she could see, finally, how Gibil had created his escape. Her guess had been fairly accurate, but more complicated than was practically necessary. Gibil. Her chest pounded and she could not be still. She sent word to Šamaš that they would be hosting travelers soon: build up the fires, slaughter a calf, and bring out the grape wine.

She sent acknowledgement to Gibil: strands of An-mašĝik breaking like lightning to lend credence to his storm. She trailed a few more in an abating path to herself. The storm continued its path to the south and east of them, and a small group of men separated from it whose path led directly to Marat. As she ran to the gate, Šamaš met her and insisted they meet the mountain men together.

The men rode onagers and wore scarves wrapped around their faces to protect them from the storm's flying grit. As they approached, one broke ranks and rushed forward, dismounting just in front of Marat and Šamaš. Gibil drew the scarf from his head. "Marat!" He was bearded and his hair was thick and long. His skin was darker and weathered. His eyes glistened in the late afternoon sun as he opened his arms in welcome.

Marat ran to him and embraced him fiercely. Gibil's arms tightened around her. Šamaš embraced them both.

Šamaš broke apart first. "Come, come to our home," he said, motioning to the men. "We have food and drink. You may rest safely here with us."

Marat pulled Gibil in closer yet, he laughed, and she released him all but his hand. He said something in his language and walked with Marat, hands entwined. The men followed them through the gates where the onagers were taken away and fed, and the men were given a place to store their equipment. Everyone gathered under the shade of palms.

"Gibil." Marat shook her head in wonder. She touched his cheek. "Brother. I have missed you so much!" She hugged him again.

He laughed. "I am relieved to see you well, sister." He touched her hair. "A free woman!" Gibil wiped his eyes. "I worried Mundu would work you to death, but I had to leave, Marat. My people needed me, and I needed them."

Tears ran down her cheeks. She had not cried in many years. "I know you had to leave. Of course, I do not forgive you! So do not ask for it," she admonished him playfully.

Šamaš called them to the terrace where tables laden with food waited. Gibil took up the cup Marat offered him and smiled. "I have missed grape wine," he said, then drained the cup. His men cheered. Šamaš had the servants play music and dance for their guests. At the head of the table, Marat and Gibil were deep in conversation.

"How fine a woman you have become!" Gibil complimented her aging gently. "How is Dakum?"

"He was killed soon after you left."

"Killed? Not died of old age?"

"No. It was either Mundu or Siduri. The hate between them caused much destruction." She told him of their spies, antagonisms perpetrated, and final escalation.

"You destroyed Inanna's temple? You were devoted to her!" He said in amazement.

"I was led to believe her sister Ereshkigal had usurped her place." Tears ran down Marat's cheeks.

Gibil reached over and carefully wiped them away. "I am sorry, truly, for leaving you with that demon of a man. Mundu was truly wicked."

"I missed you so much." Marat wiped her face. "But come now let us rejoice for we have both escaped!" She signaled for their cups to be refilled and they drank to each other's survival. "Tell me of your people and how they cherish you more than I do—and how your attentions improve their lives so much more than they improved mine!"

Gibil told her his people celebrated maŝĝik—he had dropped the "An" because his people did not believe in that god. He had strengthened their defenses and implemented new tactics in their raids, which led to fewer deaths and increased stores in their warehouses. The changes had made their lives more secure. And, with security had come other problems—squabbles over sheep and land and pretty daughters—but those were trifling and easily resolved. He told her of finding his sister's family and settling himself with a lovely woman who had born him two sons and a daughter. He did not ask after his wives and children in Adab; she did not tell him she had probably killed them when Adab fell.

Marat did tell him of Tuda and Aea. How she missed Tuda even though she knew her affection was false. How Aea had been gifted, but not driven.

Gibil shared that he had two apprentices with the sight. He agreed training was difficult—he had thought so in Adab with Idin, and realized nurturing the skills, awareness, and sense of responsibility was difficult regardless the student. Gibil confided in Marat that their raids, while they appeared to be for food, were really aimed at getting more uzudirig and other rare goods.

Marat nodded. She saw their dead in the shadows growing as the sun descended. Killing did not appear to disturb Gibil. His people celebrated the sight—they looked for more with the ability and nurtured them.

He shared with her how to make a simple storm. She told him how to move boats against the wind or river current. They discussed the sickness of maŝĝik on the brick workers and how it undoubtedly worked similarly on the canal workers.

In the dark of the night, Gibil took her hand and asked: "Come with me and live in the mountains, Marat. You will be revered."

Marat looked into his earnest eyes. She turned away "I cannot continue killing, Gibil. I have never taught successfully. I would be of no use to you."

"You need not come on raids!" He exclaimed. "You could share your knowledge with the apprentices. You could find new uses, like moving the boats. You could continue researching the illness."

She shook her head. Despair filled her. Any new use would be used to improve raids. Any apprentice would join the raids. "I cannot contribute to the underworld. I have too many ghosts haunting me now."

"You could come just to live peacefully. My people are not afraid of the sight—they cherish it. They would cherish you. You would find companionship—a man or a woman, however you wish it." Gibil tried again to convince her.

She hugged him and cried on his shoulder. "I cannot."

He squeezed her gently. "You are still so stubborn!"

She pulled back and saw tears on his face.

"I cannot protect you here," he said.

"Don't raid this city and that will be half of it," she said, laughing.

He took her hands. "It is your people I fear more."

"You forget Šamaš can swim."

Gibil did not mention Šamaš was an old man now who had troubles walking. "I wish the best for you, Marat."

She gave him most of her uzudirig supply. She did not tell him how to grow it, for even if they would no longer need to raid to acquire uzudirig, eventually they would raid to increase their territory. By morning, the mountain men were gone.

Marat watched the desert for days. She worried Gibil would come back and force her to go to the mountains. She worried she would never see him again. She knew his fear for her—that her own people would kill her—was well founded. She worried her knowledge of mašĝik would be lost—or worse yet that it would be used in war. Marat shared her fears with Šamaš. The family painted a devotion to Ninhursag over the mountain blessing on the wall, they sold the land and servants, and bought passage on a barge to Lagash, two days downriver.

## 38. Ni [Fear]

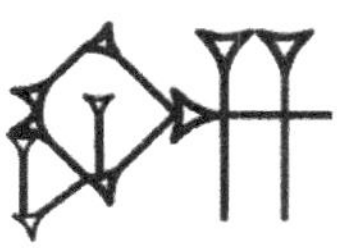

*Marat age 32.*

Lagash was a growing city on the Idiglat River under the rule of Lugal Nanshe, a proud man who put his likeness on each building he constructed. The temples he built were to Inanna.

After discussion, Marat decided they would live in the city. Šamaš sold another of Marat's necklaces and purchased a large brick home. They converted the front room into a school for scribes, the middle rooms to an inn, and kept the back kitchen and former servant rooms for the family home. Marat, "Malag" outside the family, began teaching Hedu's children the scribe's trade and soon had other students. Dadiya managed the inn with the help of Hedu and Zimu. Šamaš lent his wisdom, but more importantly meandered through the markets and drank beer with their neighbors and brought word home of local events and grumblings.

Marat watched and listened closely also. It was possible Inanna's priests in Lagash had traveled to the temple in Adab—or lived there. Marat's devotions to Inanna were scrupulous, and she took care the family's gifts to the temple did not bring attention to them.

It was possible that warriors from the outposts of Adab had migrated to Lagash to work for the benevolent lugal rising in power. Marat wore her hair long, unadorned. She attached no jewelry to her arms or ears or fingers—indeed, she had Šamaš trade her last rings and necklaces in Larak for silver minas. She wore a plain linen tunic similar to the fashion of official scribes.

One day scribes from the temple came to Marat's school. They wished to challenge her ability to teach. Marat instructed her students to work on their lessons while she spoke to the temple scribes, who, she told the students, the scribes might ask them to work at the temple someday should they ever be able to do something more meaningful than make marks in clay a bird might make with its beak.

The scribes asked Marat to write a standard student lesson: the sale of land with a house. She called for Dadiya and asked that the scribes be served wine and dates. While they inspected her school and drank her wine and ate her sweets, Marat took a clean tablet and pressed in the marks.

A built-up house plot of half a garden with a second floor and a wooden roof; the door is there; its exit is on the market lane, next to the house of Lugirgilu—the house of Amarabzu son of Lugalezen from Amarabzu Dingirdanumea bought; its full price, one mina silver, he paid him. In the future Amarabzu and his heirs, as many as there will be, will not raise a claim to this house; thus he swore in the name of Lugal Nanshe.

She handed the finished piece to them. They passed it around among themselves, whispering, then asked her for a land transaction between a father and his soon-to-be-wed daughter. Again, she pressed in the marks and gave the result to them to review.

They pointed to a few words, asking for explanation. She begged their correction, for her teacher had been taught in Uruk and possibly used different phrasing than the scribes in Lagash.

Lastly they asked her to write the first lines of a hymn to Inanna. Marat wrote the section of the prayer she had said every day with her father.

Great light, heavenly lioness, always speaking words of assent! Inanna, great light, lioness of heaven, who always speaks words of assent! Ninegala! As you rise in the morning sky like a flame visible from afar, and at your bright appearance in the evening sky, the shepherd entrusts the flocks of Kiengir to you. Celestial sign, glory of heaven! All the countries are building a house for you as for the risen sun; a shining torch is assigned to you, the light of the Land.

They indicated they would review her work with the other scribes at the temple and return in a few days with corrections. It would not be good for her to teach the children of Lagash incorrectly. She agreed with them wholeheartedly and sent them on their way with several shekels each for their learned instruction and a small gift for the most insightful goddess Inanna.

* * *

In her own rooms, Marat etched kisibs from green serpentine and chlorite, red carnelian and jasper, black obsidian, and the most desirable blue lapis lazuli. The work was relaxing for it reminded her of her time with her father, whom she hoped still lived and had not died by Mundu's orders or her destruction of Adab.

In the quiet of her rooms, she could be angry and swear at the dead for what they had done to her, or weep for wanting them back from the underworld, without having to explain her moods to this family that didn't know death. Or killing.

She slept as little as possible to avoid the dead in her dreams. Awake, a memory sometimes surfaced, and she found herself trembling uncontrollably. Strong beer was a good medicine, as was making fine cuts across her thigh—hidden, so she would not have to explain them either.

***

Lagash was not immune to attacks from other cities and the mountain men. Lugal Nanshe was a not a warrior, but commanded his men well for they defeated their enemies and suffered few losses. Still, Marat worried for her life and knowledge. She did not wish to flee and have to write the knowledge of mašĝik again on tablets. Her fingers ached now more than before, and while she had learned to use mašĝik to write, she tired more quickly of tedious work. She much preferred to spend her evenings drinking grape wine with Šamaš and Zimu and listening to the buzz of their children.

***

The temple scribes returned with a thin young man, Nergal, who reminded Marat of Eluti. They wished her to take him on as a student. Of course, she professed honor that they should trust her to instruct one of their young men. Secretly, she was suspicious. The family discussed the development and agreed to watch him closely.

Nergal was a diligent student. Marat thought the work came too easily to him for he didn't struggle as other students—even the bright ones—with the complexities of the language. Dadiya found him sometimes talking to a man who had become a regular visitor to their inn. Šamaš followed Nergal on his days off and discovered he went to the palace—not the temple or a home. He was an infiltrator. Marat reviewed their actions but could not find anything suspicious. Perhaps the scribes were mistrustful. The family discussed their situation. They agreed with Marat that she would go to Girsu with Hedu, Dadiya, and their youngest son, Šulgi. Šamaš and Zimu and the other children would stay in Lagash and run the inn. The school would be converted to a sitting area for the inn guests.

Marat and Hedu's family took passage down river to Nina on the pretext of seeing one of the great temples there. When they arrived, they found a way out of the city at dusk, and once they were sure they were not being followed, Marat floated them across the sands to Girsu on a thin maŝĝik rock.

# 39. Pag [Leave, leave behind]

*Marat age 36.*

Dadiya bought a small brickyard just south of Girsu with the family's minas. Marat had decided living outside the city provided more anonymity, and brick making was easier than farming. The people here had temples for An's children: Ninhursag, Enlil, Ninlil, and Enki. It was good fortune: many temples meant a greater need for bricks.

Marat resumed the habit of walking among the bricks at night. She found a way to pull the glowing red mašĝik from the brick and push it, along with many of the small stars, to the Idiglat River where it flowed away. Dadiya made sure the bricks were given a day to rest after baking, which reduced exposure to any residuals not swept away. None of their workers got lesions or became ill from working in the brickyard.

Marat cultivated and consumed uzudirig sparingly, which improved the gods' disposition towards her. Without the weight of their anger, she began to explore ways to keep mašĝik at hand instead of having to search for it. Forming a circle of intertwined threads and rocks, like a dog chasing its tail, kept both types close by, although untangling it lead to the pieces immediately resuming their natural courses across the landscape. If she made a series of smaller circles, she could use one and let the unused pieces go, or combine them to make a smaller circle. It was comforting to have them float above her, like coracles in a river, readily accessible should a need arise.

Marat etched her discoveries into tablets. She shared her knowledge with Šulgi, who would sit with her in the evening and sip beer, but she missed being able to show someone how she manipulated the threads and rocks, and she missed having others bring their discoveries to her to examine and improve upon.

* * *

Girsu did not suffer attacks from mountain men. Instead, it was prey to expanding cities: Umma to the west, Uruk to the south and west, Larsa and Ur to the south, Nina and Lagash to the east, and the former powerful Adab in ruins to the north.

The city was ruled by the priests of the temples, representing the council of gods. They staved off disaster through treaties and free passage of armies through their lands on the way to subjugate more recalcitrant neighbors.

Lugal Nanshe's warriors came from Lagash. Marat worried they had followed her, but they were only in Girsu to create an agreement. Still, she stayed hidden in her rooms until they left the city.

After the fall harvest festivals, Lagash's warriors returned in great numbers. Girsu's priests gave them the land north of the city for an encampment. More warriors arrived and the encampment became its own small city. Merchants set up a market there, and the priests made a small temple to Inanna and held daily devotions for the army. Still more men arrived—and chariots and onagers and the men and women who cared for the warriors and their needs. Finally the army moved on—to Umma, it was said. But a good number of warriors remained. Their ranks swelled, then reduced as Lagash attacked Uruk, and then Larsa further south.

The hiding became insufferable for Marat. The warriors were now a constant presence that impeded her movements every day. More temples were being built to Inanna, which was good for making bricks, but she could see the signs that soon Girsu would be under Lugal Nanshe's complete control.

The family met once again to discuss their livelihood. Dadiya travelled to Lagash to talk to the rest of the family. He returned a few months later and reported Zimu had died. Šamaš grieved the loss of his wife. He wished to travel to Dilmun to see if he could find peace in the mythical paradise. Dadiya and Hedu wished to be reunited with their children, and the children wished to be with their parents. The inn at Lagash was the logical choice as the city was stable, being the seat of Lugal Nanshe's power and requiring fewer servants and less work.

Marat had to decide her direction. She went to the river and drank wine while she watched workers building a bridge.

She was tired. She did not care about pleasing the gods of Girsu; she was tired of running in shame from Inanna, whom she truly revered; and she did not wish to send any more people to the underworld for Ereshkigal. There was no spiritual peace, no way for her to perform her work for the gods she was devoted to.

She did not wish to serve the lugals and priests who represented the gods. The priests would drown her; the lugals would force her to kill for their personal glory.

There was Gibil, if he still lived. He was one who understood death and killing and ghosts. But like the lugals, he continued to use mašĝik for destruction. She thought of the tablets in her room. Perhaps it would be better to destroy them and go with Šamaš to Dilmun. Marat stumbled home. After dinner, she tried to pull Šamaš into debate on what she should do, but he refused, saying only she understood enough to decide.

In the end, she agreed to their wishes. They sold the brickyard and divided their shekels and minas, the majority going to Hedu and Dadiya for the family. Šulgi was given enough to travel with Šamaš and Marat to Dilmun, situate them comfortably, and return home. Marat destroyed the tablets.

# 40. Inimdug [Peace, reconciliation with the gods]

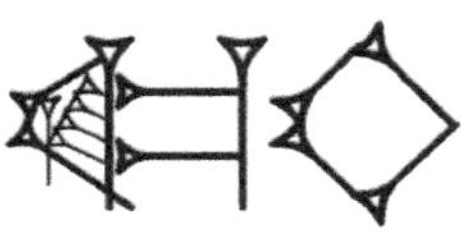

*Marat age 39.*

They had crossed the desert to the Buranum River and gone as far as Ur. Already Marat regretted her decision. She could not abandon Šamaš on his journey, for he had stood by her side through so many years and uprooted his family to do so. Yet... Yet the thought of the crumbled tablets brought tears to her eyes. She felt she had failed Eluti, and Dakum, and her father, and maybe her mother also. And all the gods, too, somehow.

They boarded the large boat, and it took them out on the great sea so far that land was only a thick ribbon on the horizon. They were served food they had never heard of: fish as large as a person and shelled animals with many legs.

In the night, Šamaš took sick. Marat and Šulgi stayed at his side and prayed to Inanna, reminding her of the work her devoted Šamaš had done and was still capable of doing. After two days he died and they put his body overboard. Marat thought perhaps Inanna was angry they were leaving Kiengir and had sent a demon to stop them in any way possible. She feared she or Šulgi would die next. She asked the boat's owner to turn back. He would not. When Marat explained how Inanna had sent a demon, he laughed at her. "Enki rules the waters, and only for him would I turn this boat around. I have goods that must be brought to Dilmun, and goods that must be brought back to Kiengir."

Marat helped the boat move through the water faster than the slight breeze filling the sail was able to do. The boat's owner commented that they were making good time. When they reached Dilmun, Marat was relieved that Šamaš had died, for it was not paradise but a city like most others, albeit lush with vegetation and peoples of different colors speaking in unintelligible ways, and animals that were familiar yet strange, and astonishing quantities of goods—cloth in all the colors, lapis lazuli rocks the size of your fist, copper in sheets and coils, timber, carnelian, steatite, turquoise, tin—but a city nonetheless where there was pain and disease and old age.

The people of Dilmun prayed to unfamiliar gods. Marat and Šulgi made an offering to their Inzak on behalf of Šamaš and held a private ceremony on the shore to Enki.

Marat thought to stay, trades were documented in her language and she could work as a scribe, but every time she saw a fleece or slab of mašĝik pass, she was reminded of her power and responsibility to it. Eluti had done so much! He had trusted her with his knowledge. In her dreams he cried at the loss or berated her selfishness.

One morning when the city was still quiet, she turned a thread of mašĝik round in a circle while she waited for the servant to bring her morning meal. She played absentmindedly with the thread: thinning and fattening it, slowing it down and speeding it up. There was a soft "clack" and it was gone—in its place a pebble. Transformation! She stood and paced, could not eat the meal when it arrived, and finally woke Šulgi and told him about transformation even though he did not understand it.

Marat made Šulgi rent a small house outside the city where she manipulated threads to pebbles and rocks to scraps. She recounted her findings to Šulgi each day. At the quarter moon he went to the market and did not return. She found him drunk in a tavern.

"Šulgi," she shook him. "Come home!"

"No." He moaned, head in hands. "I will not return to that hut and listen to you rant all day and wake screaming each night."

She hushed him and pulled at his sleeve.

"No," he refused again. "I will not go."

Marat ordered food for them, and beer. "I am sorry, Šulgi, for how you have had to care for me. You should return home to your family, as we had planned."

"I cannot return," he moaned. "I have promised to see you settled." He drank from his freshly filled cup. "You will never be settled, aunt."

Marat drank. They ate the roasted mutton, spelt bread, and honied dates the server brought. "We will return to the family in Lagash," she finally said.

"Who is this man, Gibil, who you speak to in your sleep?"

Marat turned the cup in her hand. "He is my brother," she said and told Šulgi of her father and being sold to Eluti and finding her second family in Dakum and Gibil. She was quiet a long time, remembering. Eluti's passion for understanding mašĝik . The day of wonders. The day he showed her how to cut a river reed into a stylus for writing. His warm embrace when she had done something well. She set the cup down. She would not let her work with Eluti become dust in the desert.

In the morning, Marat had Šulgi buy them passage on a boat that would take them to Elam, Kiengir's neighbor to the east, where he would continue to Lagash, and she would start her search for Gibil and his Guti people in the city of Awan. Marat looked across the waters and smiled. She would teach Gibil to ride a thin rock slice across his mountains. He would bring her into his family. They would drink and argue and laugh about the past.

Thank you for reading my novel. I hope 2500 BC Sumer came alive for you. Magic shows up in many speculative and fantasy works. I thought it would be fun to show how it could have been discovered in our world. After reading Jared Diamond's *Guns, Germs, and Steel*, I decided the fertile crescent was the place to set my story. My research uncovered a much more advanced society than I had expected.

Please leave a review on Amazon for me to read your thoughts and for others to determine if this story is for them

# Pronunciation Guide

Using what is known of the Akkadian language, scholars have determined approximately how Cuneiform was pronounced. Below is a simplified pronunciation guide.

A as in pass.
B as in bad.
D as in day.
E as in yet.
G as in get.
Ĝ as "ng" in Ingrid.
H as in hope.
I as "ee" in seen.
K as in keep.
L as in left.
M as in map.
N as in nap.
P as in peel.
R rolled slightly.
S as in see.
Š as "sh" in shell.
T as in toy.
U as "oo" in moon.
Z as in zero.

Pronunciations of the main character names are below.

**Aea** – (ah-eh-ah) Young female who can see an mašĝik.
**Aruru** – (ah-rroo-rroo) Wife to Eluti.
**Dakum** – (dah-koom) Older male who can see an mašĝik.
**Daudu** – (dow-doo) King of Adab.
**Eluti** – (eh-loo-tee) First person who can see an mašĝik.
**Gibil** – (gee-beel) Male from the mountains who can see an mašĝik.

**Idin** – (ee-deen) Young male who can see an mašĝik.
**Marat** – (mah-rrat) female who can see an mašĝik.
**Mundu** – (moon-doo) male warrior.
**Nanar** – (nah-narr) male warrior.
**Pakum** – (pah-koom) priest.
**Šamaš** – (shah-mash) male slave.
**Siduri** – (see-doo-rree) high priestess.
**Tuda** – (too-dah) female servant.
**Warad** – (wah-rrahd) male warrior.

# Glossary

**Abulillum** – Boxthorn (plant and berry), similar to the wolfberry and goji berry.

**Adab** – A city on the Euphrates River, prosperous around 2,000 BC.

**An** – Supreme God and "prime mover in creation", embodied by the sky. All the deities were believed to be the offspring of An and his consort Ki. Associated colors: red, white, black.

**An-mašĝik** – Heavenly (from heaven) + sight (special). A term created from existing words for this story.

**Ašipu** – Spiritual doctor. Specialty is with demons' trickery, Gods' punishments, and mental issues.

**Auroch** – Ancestor of cattle. Aurochs had large front-facing horns. The bull was darker in color and grew up to 6 foot high at the shoulder; the cow was lighter in color and about a foot shorter.

**Azu** – Medical doctor. Specialty is with diseases, common ailments, and broken bones.

**Buranum River** – Euphrates River.

**Enki** – God of the subterranean freshwater ocean, who is also closely associated with wisdom, magic, incantations, arts, and crafts. The son of An, he is theologically conceived as the "immanent" facet of An. Enki is the divine benefactor of humanity, who helped humans survive the Great Flood. Associated color: green.

**Enlil** – God of wind, air, earth, and storms and the chief of all the gods. He is theologically conceived as the "transcendent" facet of An. The Sumerians envisioned Enlil as a benevolent, fatherly deity, who watches over humanity and cares for their well-being. Associated color: blue.

**Ennug** – Watch guard.

**Ereshkigal** – Queen of the underworld.

**Gurum** – Watch over, restrain.

**Idiglat River** – Tigris River.

**Inanna** – Goddess of love, sexuality, and war. She is the divine personification of the planet Venus, the morning and evening star. Associated color: copper, blue.

**Kiengir** – Name of Sumer (Sumeria) as called by the people at that time.

**Kisib** –Small cylinder with a design etched into it that was used to roll one's signature (or seal) on a clay document. Kisibs were made of clay, lapis lazuli, and other precious stones. A hole ran through the kisib so users could insert a rod for easier rolling, or a string to wear it about the neck.

**Lugal** – King.

**Masmas** – Sorcerer, incantation priest

**Mina** – Early form of money (see also Shekel). One silver mina is worth about sixty shekels.

**Nam** – Sir, lord.

**Nin** – Ma'am, lady.

**Nubanda** – captain; overseer.

**Onager** – The most horse-like of wild asses. Onagers are short legged and large bellied. Their coat is a reddish-brown with white muzzle and belly; a black stripe runs down the back. The species is not easily tamed.

**Shaduf** – Bucket tied to a rod, suspended and counterbalanced on two uprights and used to move water from a stream to a canal.

**Shekel** – Early form of money. With one shekel you could get six days work for a common laborer, 1.5 bushels of barley, 75 bricks (unbaked), a jar of date wine, or rent a small home for six months.

**Triad of Heaven** – The gods An, Enlil, and Enki.

**Unumun** – Saffron.

**Ursag** – Hero, warrior of great distinction.

**Uzudirig** – Mushroom.

**Zeh** – Piglet.

# References

Ager, Simon. The Epic of Gilgamesh in Sumerian, sung by Peter Pringle in the original Sumerian language and played on the Sumerian long-neck gishgudi (guitar). https://www.omniglot.com/writing/sumerian.htm

Barrett-Morison, James. Sumerian Language; a blog of conversational Sumerian. https://sumerianlanguage.tumblr.com/about

Bertman, Stephen. Handbook to Life in Ancient Mesopotamia. Oxford University Press. 2003.

Black, J.A., Cunningham, G., Fluckiger-Hawker, E, Robson, E., and Zólyomi, G. Sumerian Proverbs from The Electronic Text Corpus of Sumerian Literature. Oxford 1998-2003. Provided by Kinnes, Tormod, at http://oaks.nvg.org/sumer-proverbs.html

Bottero, Jean. Everyday Life in Ancient Mesopotamia. John Hopkins University Press. 2001.

Brooks, Beatrice. "Marking slaves." Journal of the American Oriental Society, Vol. 42 (1922) pp 80-90. https://www.jstor.org/stable/593615?seq=1#metadata_info_tab_contents

Bunker, Michael. "Harvesting Wheat by Hand." June 29, 2015. Blog. https://discovery.ucl.ac.uk/id/eprint/1349279/1/454702_vol1.pdf

Chiera, E. "Legal and Administrative Documents from Nippur; Chiefly from the Dynasties of Isin and Larsa." University of Pennsylvania. The University Museum. Publications of the Babylonian Section. Vol VIII. 1914. No. 1. http://etana.org/sites/default/files/coretexts/14901.pdf

Civil, Miguel. "Sumerian Harvest Time" Expedition Magazine 5.4 (1963): Expedition Magazine. Penn Museum, 1963 Web.

25 Feb 2020
http://www.penn.museum/sites/expedition/?p=652
Coleman, M, and J. Scurlock. "Viral Haemorrhagic fevers in ancient Mesopotamia." Tropical Medicine and International Health. Volume 2. No 6. Pp 603-606. June 1997.
https://onlinelibrary.wiley.com/doi/pdf/10.1046/j.1365-3156.1997.d01-329.x
Cook, Mike. Shaving with obsidian blades.
https://www.youtube.com/watch?v=QWSTE6WLB0Y
Copper Development Association Inc. The Sumerians and Chaldeans.
https://www.copper.org/education/history/60centuries/ancient/thesumerians.html
Eckholm, Erik. "Mesopotamia: Cradle of Haute Cuisine?" The New York Times. May 15, 1985.
https://www.nytimes.com/1985/05/15/garden/mesopotamia-cradle-of-haute-cuisine.html
Ellison, Elizabeth Rosemary. "A Study of Diet in Mesopotamia (c 3000 – 600 BC) and Associated Agricultural Techniques and Methods of Food Preparation. Institute of Archaeology. Thesis submitted to the University of London in the Faculty of Arts for the degree of Doctor of Philosophy. May 1978.
https://discovery.ucl.ac.uk/id/eprint/1349279/1/454702_vol1.pdf
ETCSL (Electronic Text Corpus of Sumerian Literature) Translation: t.4.07.4, A hymn to Inanna as Ninegala.
http://etcsl.orinst.ox.ac.uk/cgi-bin/etcsl.cgi?text=t.4.07.4&charenc=j#
ETCSL (Electronic Text Corpus of Sumerian Literature) Translation: tr.563, The farmer's instructions.
https://etcsl.orinst.ox.ac.uk/section5/tr563.htm
Gordon, Edmund I. "Sumerian Animal Proverbs and Fables: 'Collection Five.'" University Museum, University of

Pennsylvania, Philadelphia, PA, USA. [AUTHOR: May be from the Journal of Cuneiform Studies, 1958, The University of Chicago Press.] https://www.jstor.org/stable/1359157?seq=1

Hays, Jeff. "Mesopotamian Cooking." September 2018. Blog. http://factsanddetails.com/world/cat56/sub363/entry-6401.html

Hays, Jeff. Mesopotamian customs, life, homes. Clothes, drugs and recreation. http://factsanddetails.com/world/cat56/sub363/item1522.html

Higgins, Chris (and Irving Finkel). "Learn How to Write (Very Basic) Cuneiform via YouTube. Mental Floss. July 30, 2017. https://www.mentalfloss.com/article/503174/learn-how-write-very-basic-cuneiform-youtube

Jameson, K.A., Winkler, A.D., and Goldfarb, K. (2016). Art, interpersonal comparisons of color experience, and potential tetrachromacy. Invited Proceedings paper for the 2016 IS&T International Symposium on Electronic Imaging (E1 2016). Technical Session on Human Vision and Electronic Imaging. http://static.concettaantico.com/email/new-science/uc-irvine-study-on-tetrachromacy.pdf

Jones, Josh. "Listen to the Oldest Song in the World: A Sumerian Hymn Written 3,400 Years Ago." History, Music. July 8, 2014. http://www.openculture.com/2014/07/the-oldest-song-in-the-world.html

Mark, Joshua. "Health Care in Ancient Mesopotamia." Ancient History Encyclopedia. May 21, 2014. https://www.ancient.eu/article/687/health-care-in-ancient-mesopotamia/

Mark, Joshua. "The Nimrud Dogs." Ancient History Encyclopedia. January 12, 2017. https://www.ancient.eu/article/1001/the-nimrud-dogs/

The First Dog People. All Mesopotamia. March 21, 2018. https://allmesopotamia.wordpress.com/tag/mesopotamian-dogs/

Middeke-Conlin, Robert. The Scents of Larsa: A study of the Aromatics Industry in an Old Babylonian Kingdom. Middeke-Conlin, Universite Paris Diderot. Published in the Cuneiform Digital Library Journal 2014:1. https://cdli.ucla.edu/files/publications/cdlj2014_001.pdf

Niazi, Amjad Daoud. "Plague Epidemic in Sumerian Empire." The Iraqui Post Graduate Medical Journal. Vol No. https://www.iasj.net/iasj?func=fulltext&aId=92816

Olver, Lynne. "Ancient Mesopotamian Foods." Food Timeline Library. http://www.foodtimeline.org/foodfaq3.html#mesopotamia

Paulette, Tate. Chapter 7: Domination and Resilience in Bronze Age Mesopotamia. (http://faculty.washington.edu/stevehar/Paulette2012.pdf). Full article/book: Surviving Sudden Environmental Change: Answers from Archaeology (Eds. J. Cooper and P. Sheets). University Press of Colorado., 2012.

Penn Museum. About Cuneiform Writing. https://www.penn.museum/games/cuneiform.shtml

Peterson, Jeremiah. "A Study of Sumerian Faunal Conception with a focus on the Terms Pertaining to the Order Testudines." Dissertation in Near Eastern Languages and Civilizations. University of Pennsylvania. 2007. https://www.academia.edu/2286616/A_study_of_Sumerian_faunal_conception_with_a_focus_on_the_terms_pertaining_to_the_order_Testudines

Pruessner, A.H. Dates in Mesopotamia. January 28, 2018. Blog. https://allmesopotamia.wordpress.com/2018/01/28/dates-in-mesopotamia/

Rohrlich, Ruby. "State Formation in Sumer and the subjugation of Women." Feminist Studies, Inc. DOI: 10.2307/3177651. https://www.jstor.org/stable/3177651

Scurlock, JoAnn. "The Techniques of the Sacrifice of Animals in Ancient Israel and Ancient Mesopotamia: New Insights Through Comparison, Part 1." Andrews University seminary Studies, Vol. 44, No. 1, 13-49. 2006. Andrews University Press. https://www.andrews.edu/library/car/cardigital/Periodicals/AUSS/2006-1/2006-1-02.pdf

Teall, Emily K. "Medicine and Doctoring in Ancient Mesopotamia." Grand valley Journal of History. Volume 3. Issue 1. Article 2. October 2014. https://scholarworks.gvsu.edu/cgi/viewcontent.cgi?article=1056&context=gvjh

Tomczak, Matthias. The Sumerian number system; Absolute and place-value number systems. Lecture 4. Flinders University of South Australia. May 4, 2016. https://www.mt-oceanography.info/science+society/lecture4.html

University of Oxford, Oriental Studies. The Electronic Text Corpus of Sumerian Literature. http://etcsl.orinst.ox.ac.uk/#

University of Pennsylvania Museum of Anthropology and Archaeology. ePSD (electronic Pennsylvania Sumerian Dictionary. http://psd.museum.upenn.edu/nepsd-frame.html

Wikipedia. Law of Ur-Nammu (Sumer, 2100-2050 BC). https://en.wikipedia.org/wiki/Code_of_Ur-Nammu

Yale Law School, Lillian Goldman Law Library. The Code of Hammurabi. http://avalon.law.yale.edu/ancient/hamframe.asp

# About the Author

Paula Schumacher has been writing since she was first taught to hold a crayon. First she learned how to write her name (which is how her father knew who was writing on the walls in the closet upstairs), then poems and stories.

Paula grew up in the Upper Penninsula of Michigan and has settled in the Midwest. Today, when not at work or writing, she is tinkering about the house, working on some crafty project, or hanging out with friends and family (eating, drinking, playing dominoes, listening to music, watching sports, etc.).

# Books By This Author

### The Glass Road: A Marie Gardner Murder Mystery

Marie Gardner, reclusive forensic accountant, finds herself dealing with a new type of puzzle: the murder of a wealthy art-collecting professor. To find answers, she'll have to step away from her files and ledgers and focus on people--the professor's estranged family, tormented graduate students, and his old disobliging friends.

Forced to work with a team, Marie is challenged by an unwanted office crush, training a new hire, and proving to her boss that she's capable of more than paperwork—all while hiding a secret behind her high fashion looks that if discovered, it could end her career.

### Beginner's Guide to Office Boxing: The How-To's of Workplace Self-Defense

Does dealing with the people at work wear you out and beat you down? Have you ever thought you might be in the wrong job? Do you think that maybe the problem is you? Odds are you're beating yourself up when you should be defending yourself. This guide to dealing with difficult people at work will help you understand your Office Boxing antagonists and provide you with options for success.

Made in the USA
Monee, IL
02 May 2023

32756967R00163